4 Days in Paris

4 Days in Paris

Lexi Haddock

Chrysalis Press

Cover design by Stephanie Anderson, Alt 19 Designs

Edited by Jen Milius and Dakota Nyght

Published by Chrysalis Press, an imprint of Kat Biggie Press

Columbia, SC

Publisher's Cataloging-in-Publication Data

Names: Haddock, Lexi. | Bigwarfe, Alexa, 1976- .

Title: 4 days in Paris / Lexi Haddock.

Other titles: Four days in Paris.

Description: Columbia, SC : Chrysalis Press, 2022. | Series: Sparks in Paris ; book 1. | Summary: Callie came to Paris to be with the love of her life, only to be dumped. Now it's New Year's Eve 1999 and she's returning to the U.S. in four days, ready to start the next chapter of her life... until she meets her best friend's brother and sparks fly.

Identifiers: LCCN 2021914000 | ISBN 9781955119184 (paperback) | ISBN 9781955119191 (ebook)

Subjects: LCSH: Friendship—Fiction. | Man-woman relationships— Fiction. | New Year—Fiction. | Paris (France)—Fiction. | BISAC: FICTION / Romance / Holiday. | FICTION / Romance / Romantic Comedy. | FICTION / Women. Classification: LCC PS3608.A33 2022 | DDC 813 H33--dc22 LC record available at https://lccn.loc.gov/2021914000

For Kerry, Lisa, Tia, Charlotte, Smail, and Ludo. My favorite souvenirs from my time in France.

1

I GLARED at the Eiffel Tower as if it was her fault. Although her soaring presence generally filled me with awe at the way she'd transformed from a world's fair exhibit into a global symbol of love, today, as the frigid wind whipped my clothes and the dreary sky dampened my spirits, her enormous metal frame seemed to mock me. The enormous digital display mounted on the side of the tower—J-1—glowed brightly, a visible countdown to the end of the century, the end of the millennium.

Ticktock, the tower seemed to whisper.

"Yes, I know," I responded quietly. "One day left of 1999. Almost time to go home."

A sudden gust of wind caught the ends of my short brown hair, and I reached up to tuck it behind my ears before jamming my frozen hands back into the pockets of my black pea coat.

"Now what am I going to do?" I chuckled and glanced around to ensure no one noticed I was literally talking to the Eiffel Tower.

Kicking at the ground with my Doc Marten boots to get the

blood flowing to my legs, I pulled my hands out of my pockets again to tug my scarf tighter around my neck and up over my nose. Painful memories surfaced, erasing months of closing the door, little by little, on the plans I'd made for my life with Vic. I'd moved across the ocean to be with *him*, yet my hopes, the proposal I'd expected, the life I'd been planning... everything had changed drastically with four little words.

It's not working out. I fought back a twinge of anger.

In my journey toward healing, I had formed a relationship with this gorgeous pile of metal. She was breathtaking. The wide base narrowed and climbed magnificently into the sky, a sight visible from all around the city. Usually, as I stared at her from my apartment, morning coffee in hand, she felt comforting, inspiring me to think about what might come next after the colossal failure of my Plan A. Today though, the countdown mounted on the side of the tower was a visible, condescending reminder of my botched happily ever after plot.

Aren't you past all of this, Callie?

Until today, I'd sure thought so. But as my time in Paris ticked away, my thoughts were drifting all over the place. Emotions and memories locked up and hidden away now burst into my consciousness, reminding me of how painful those first few days here on my own were.

It didn't help that I was surrounded by images of love. An older couple strolled slowly past with their small dog leading the way, demonstrating who was clearly in charge. Although the couple appeared to be at least in their seventies, the man's arm was still wrapped lovingly around her shoulders. It was sweet, even if it reminded me of what was missing in my life.

To my left, a young couple stopped to stare at the Eiffel Tower and the man bent in to sweetly kiss the woman's forehead. It wasn't too uncommon to see these scenes when standing before the world's greatest symbol of love, but my stomach churned at the visible reminder that I was alone.

If my life were a musical, this was the part where I'd burst into a haunting rendition of Celine Dion's epic masterpiece. "All by myself. Don't wanna be..." But my life was *not* a musical. Instead, I glared at the metal masterpiece and hissed, "I blame you."

She brought the lovers. The lovers reminded me of the gaping hole in my life. Clearly, it was her fault.

No, this is not the way this is going to go. He does not get to ruin my last few days. Sucking in a deep breath and exhaling slowly, I pushed Vic out of my mind and checked my watch.

Where was Lila? My best friend in Paris, another American I'd met a few weeks after arriving, was rarely late for anything. But with a few extra million people in Paris for the New Year's festivities, public transportation had to be pretty jammed up. Sighing, I kicked my feet again, trying to put some feeling back into my toes. My heart laden with emotion as I prepared to return home, I couldn't help but think of all that had happened in the last six months in this magical city.

Close to where I stood, people poured out of the Musée de l'Homme into Trocadero Square, ready to find food and escape the cold of the early afternoon. Some stopped to take in the beauty of the Eiffel Tower, lit up by lights as the daylight faded, while others rushed to the nearest metro stop.

I will miss this.

Despite being dumped immediately after arriving, I had never regretted my decision to remain in Paris and find my own way. Truthfully, staying was easier than tucking my tail and running home to face an inquisition about my early return from my mother, sister, and friends. There would be so many questions. Had Vic cheated? Had I cheated? Was it just too difficult to be so far away from home? Had the snobby Parisians forced me away?

No. Returning home to all the questions was not an option at that point. So, I had stayed, in part hoping Vic would change his mind and beg me to take him back. But days and weeks had passed. Vic had never called and slowly I rebuilt myself. A fresh start! A new apartment, even if it was barely larger than a shoebox. New and some old friends. I had even landed a great job. And I had done it all without Vic. But not in solitude.

Lila and Emilie were the best things to come out of the last six months. Lila, a true kindred spirit, had fallen into my life serendipitously. She and Emilie, a close French friend I'd met while studying in France two years earlier, had both helped me tackle one of my biggest fears—being alone. Perhaps it's melodramatic to worry about being alone at twenty-three, but that's practically old maid territory in the south. Most of my friends at home were engaged or already married. Even Lila, who was also returning to the US in a couple of days, was practically engaged to her boyfriend, Matt. Meanwhile, I was in a relationship with the strong, *very* silent type. I glowered at the tower.

"I thought we were friends. Why are you reminding me of all of this?"

Jumping as arms wrapped around me, I spun around to see Lila laughing at me. Her long, silky black hair whipped wildly in the wind as she clung to the—oh my God, was that a raspberry-colored beret?—on her head. I was stunned that Lila, who hated berets as much as I did and had spent her fair share of time mocking women who wore them, had mastered this look.

"Who were you talking to?" Lila asked.

I tried to play it off. "What do you mean?"

"I heard you say something. Were you talking to her again?" She tilted her head toward the Eiffel Tower. It had become a long-standing joke between us, my love-hate relationship with the tower.

"I was," I admitted sheepishly.

Lila laughed. "Has she answered yet?"

"Nope, still radio silent. I continue to berate her for tormenting me anyway."

Lila shook her head, smiling. "I thought you two were on good terms. What did she do to deserve that?"

"Well, it's the stupid countdown timer. One day left of this year, then you leave in two days. And then I'm going home. I'm sad." Sticking out my bottom lip in a pouty face, I leaned into her.

"Don't remind me!" she said. Her face contorted as she blinked back tears.

I hugged Lila tightly, willing her to feel all my love for her and how much I cherished our friendship. After releasing her, I cocked my head to the side and pointed to her head. "What exactly do we have going on here? You channeling Prince now?"

Lila giggled. "Oh this? You know, I thought it would make a great souvenir." Lila had her own sense of style, and the French beret was not it. Dressed in her work clothes this evening—all black—she looked amazing, even with a beret on her head. But I doubted it would pair well with her usual attire of long, flowy shirts and loose pants that told the world she was peace, love, and sunshine, not a stuffy professional.

"Don't hate me, but you look kinda amazing."

Lila nodded eagerly, her eyes sparkling with mischief. "I'm glad you think so, 'cause I got one for you too!"

"Oh no, say you didn't!"

But she had. She pulled a black beret from her bag and positioned it on my head, gently adjusting my hair around the hat as though she were completing a masterpiece. "Gorgeous!"

I placed my hand on my hip and playfully struck a pose.

"Perfection. Now you really look French, Callie!"

My hands dropped to my sides, and I reached up, pulling the beret from my head, running my fingers through my hair.

"What is it?" Lila asked.

"I guess I failed at that."

"What have you possibly failed at?" Lila asked.

She knew the entire story, but I never shared my full investment in Vic. "You know... the French transition."

Lila tilted her head, furrowing her brow.

"I had it all mapped out. Arrive in France to be with Vic, have an insanely romantic proposal here, with the tower as our witness. A brief engagement and a simple wedding. Begin our days with *pain au chocolat* and coffee and end every day with wonderful food and red wine and be deliriously happy." I stared off into the distance, wistful for that fairy tale ending.

Lila placed her hand on my arm. "You really put some thought into this, huh?"

"Oh yes," I continued more playfully. "And after a couple years of marriage we'd have two perfect, bilingual kids, a nanny, and a dog, because that's what French people do, a large apartment in Paris, and we'd vacation for a month each year on the coast. Perfection." I smiled at Lila.

"Are you having regrets about Vic? I mean, let's not forget just how terrible he was to you."

"Oh, it's not forgotten." No, I had absolutely *not* forgotten how devastated I was when Vic unexpectedly ended things. I had believed, with all my heart, that Vic was everything I had ever wanted. When I'd met him halfway through my study abroad program in my junior year of college, he'd seemed gorgeous, witty, and exciting—all the qualities I was looking for. It was love at first sight.

From the moment our eyes locked across the dance floor,

lasers bouncing all around the otherwise dimly lit nightclub, he had me. Our bodies moved in sync to the music, pulled together like magnets. After a few songs, he grabbed my hand and led me to the bar, ordering us drinks. We tucked ourselves away in a booth on the edge of the dance floor and spent hours lost in conversation, talking about everything imaginable until his buddies forced him away.

"I'll call you," he'd promised, as we stood in the foyer saying our goodbyes. Smiling, he exited the club without kissing me. I stood there, flushed with disappointment, embarrassed by the strong feelings I'd developed that he clearly didn't share. Then, the door opened and Vic reentered. Mouth agape, I held my breath as he marched right over to me, grabbed me in his arms, and kissed me briefly but passionately, leaving me stunned.

That's all it took. He stole my heart. We spent every possible moment together after that, making lifelong plans and promises, despite the date of my return to the States looming in front of us. We knew a long-distance relationship while I finished my last year of school would be a challenge, but we pledged to make it work. And we had. After graduation, I packed up my life to move to France with a vision of becoming an expat, married to Vic.

I had believed Vic and I were happy. Right up until the moment he dumped me, less than six hours after I got off the plane.

No, I absolutely had *not* forgotten that pain and humiliation. How could I?

"No regrets about Vic allowed," Lila commanded, with her hands on her hips. "Put this," she grabbed the second beret and placed it on my head, once again tucking my hair in place, "back on and embrace your inner Frenchie. And screw Vic. He obviously was not the *one*."

I smirked, arranging the beret on my head. "Don't worry,

I'm not planning on drunk dialing him or anything. I'm just struggling now because..." I didn't really know how to explain to her what I was feeling. A tremendous sense of loss, but not because I wasn't with Vic anymore.

"Because you thought you had your life figured out, and then you didn't," she finished for me, gently.

I nodded emphatically.

Lila placed her hand gently on my arm. "And then you made a new life for yourself, with no help from a dude, by the way, and now everything you've worked for here is ending, too. It's hard, I get it."

I blinked back tears. Lila's perceptive comments nailed my exact sentiments. We'd shared so much in our five short months of friendship—travel adventures, drunken shenanigans, late nights sharing our wildest secrets and dreams. Lila knew me better than I knew myself at times.

"Somewhere deep inside, I think I believed either Vic would come back to me, or I would meet someone else and stay here. I don't think I ever believed I'd actually be going home in January. This wasn't the way I thought this chapter of my life would end."

Lila laughed. "Well, you've still got four days left to change your fate."

I raised my eyebrows in disbelief. "You think I'm going to meet and fall in love with someone in the next four days?"

"Probably not, but we can at least have fun living to the fullest?" Lila shrugged her shoulders, eyes twinkling.

She was right. I had no intention of trying to find the man of my dreams these last few days. Sighing deeply, I turned back to face the tower and whispered, "I'm mostly ready to go home, but I just feel like something is not done."

"Well for starters, you haven't packed your bags yet," Lila quipped.

"I'm not talking about my bags!" I laughed.

Lila nodded, leaning in close as if she had a big secret to share. "Well, I too feel incomplete. I feel incomplete without another one of those crêpes." She nodded in the stand's direction, just off to our left.

She steered us in the direction of the crêpe stand on the edge of the square, both of us giggling like little girls. Lila was not wrong. There was something magical about these delicate pastries, best enjoyed warm, filled with cheese and ham, or, as I preferred, something sweet. Sadly, there would be no more crêpe stands once I was home.

We took our place in the line and I turned to Lila. "This nagging feeling is driving me nuts."

"You're probably just scared about screwing up Emilie's demands for our amazing New Year's Eve party!" She dug in her pocket and produced a piece of paper. "As a reminder of this daunting task, I remind you about the *list*," she said, waving it in my face. The meticulously written list included specific instructions on what Emilie needed from the store.

"No substitutions!" Emilie had warned us. When we had planned our party, Emilie volunteered to prepare most of the food, since, as she pointed out, she was the French one and Lila and I lacked creativity in the kitchen. A baguette and a round of Camembert cheese fit my appetite and budget just fine, but Emilie had insisted an end-of-the-millennium party needed extra flair. Lila and I agreed. Emilie would prepare the food, and Lila and I had volunteered to do the shopping.

I laughed. "Yes, the party shopping! Ugh."

"Two capable American girls shopping for French cheese and delicacies? Nothing to worry about." Lila shoved the list back in her pocket, winking at me.

Maybe Lila was right, and this feeling in my stomach was just anxiety. Not about Emilie's list, necessarily, but about the long list of things I needed to do in the next few days to wrap up my life here in France.

We inched slowly forward in the line, my tummy growling as the smell of crêpes drifted our way. When we finally arrived at the front, my mouth watered as the vendor slathered Nutella on our order. The francs had hardly left our hands before we were cramming the crêpes into our mouths, warm chocolate oozing from the triangular sides as we moved out of the way of the others patiently waiting.

"Mmmm, I am going to miss these," Lila sighed, shoving the last bite in her mouth before wiping her mouth with a napkin.

"We're forever ruined by French delicacies," I said. My waistline was proof. I don't know why they say the way to a *man's* heart is through his stomach and leave the women out, because France had me at buttery-crusted croissants. From the moment I'd arrived, *pain au chocolat* and *chausson aux pommes*, a delicious concoction of cinnamon-spiced apples nestled in a buttery, flaky puff pastry, similar to but so much better than an apple turnover, called to me like sirens, crushing all my willpower.

Polishing off my crêpe, I paused. "I forgot to tell you! Emilie's inviting her brother and two of his friends to the party."

"Wait, Emilie has a brother?" Lila stared back at me, her eyebrows raised high.

"I know. I had completely forgotten about him. She has only mentioned him to me once or twice. He's actually her half brother, and I'm not sure what the full story is there. She just refers to him as the 'computer geek.'"

During my exchange year, I hadn't just met Vic, I'd also met Emilie, a quiet French girl who had become one of my closest friends. We'd stayed in contact when I returned to the States, and coincidentally, she had accepted a placement in a

Master of English program at the Sorbonne at the same time I returned to Paris. She'd been a rock in the aftermath of everything happening with Vic. However, I'd never once crossed paths with her brother.

"Hmm, well maybe there's potential for a fun fling with one of those guys?" Lila wiggled her eyebrows, already planning a love match. "Just stay away from the brother. That's always sticky."

"Yeah, let's hope one of his friends is hot." Privately, I told myself that the last thing I needed was anything complicating my return home. It was time to just go home, regroup, and figure out the rest of my life.

"We better get going. Time is a-ticking!" Lila tugged me toward the street. I nodded but took a moment to glance back and admire the beautiful tower, realizing just how much I would miss my strolls and private conversations about life with this enormous structure that never talked back.

"Hang on a minute," I said. I needed to do one last thing. I pulled my backpack off my shoulders, retrieved my camera, and asked a woman standing nearby to take our picture. Lila and I rearranged our berets to sit at a cocky angle and posed perfectly with full, toothy American smiles, my tower friend in the background.

"Hope it turns out well!" the woman said as she handed back the camera. I wasn't worried. I had the perfect frame in mind for the picture when it was printed, and already knew I'd place it front and center on my dresser when I found a new apartment at home. Of all the things that had transpired in Paris, one of the greatest gifts was my friendship with Lila.

Lila looped her arm through mine and we left the square. The Christmas lights and decorations glimmered in the shop windows and adorned the streetlamps, which already aglow in the gray afternoon. Paris was always beautiful, but the magical effect of garland hanging everywhere, trees shimmering with white lights lining the streets, and the smiles on the faces of the usually stoic Parisians, made everything seem happier.

A sense of calm settled over me, an acceptance of my current situation.

Lila was right. It was time to leave the past in the past, focus on the next few days, and prepare for whatever would come next.

2

WARM AIR BLASTED us as we entered a store, and Lila and I each grabbed a basket before making our way into the produce section. Lila pulled out the list and began to read off the items we needed, and I moved from display to display to make our selections. As I squeezed tomatoes to find just the right ones, a couple nearby caught my attention.

Why? Why am I seeing all these cute couples today? I watched as he showed her some pears. She smiled up at him and stroked his arm, nodding her approval. Jealousy ripped through me.

Lila snuck up beside me. "You ready to head to the cheese?"

Yes, please.

"My favorite part of the store!" I said. I turned around quickly, nearly knocking over a big display of oranges in my haste.

After ensuring the stability of the oranges, I followed Lila to the back of the store. A plethora of tantalizing cheeses and meats decorated one wall. Lila and I stood side by side, perusing the nearly endless options in the cheese case. Picking up a block of bleu cheese, I flashed back to the last time I'd eaten it and my stomach roiled.

After I'd arrived back in Paris, Vic and I had made our way to the hotel room I'd booked for our first night back together. I was eager to make up for lost time, but Vic had brushed me off, declaring he needed food. We chattered politely through our appetizer and the main course, right up until the traditional after-dinner cheese course.

Right as I shoved a healthy bite of bread and Roquefort bleu cheese into my mouth, Vic quietly said, "It's not because I don't love you, Callie. It's just not working out."

One Heimlich maneuver later, after I'd choked on said bread and cheese, Vic walked out and left me alone in the hotel room. I never saw him again.

Now staring at the Roquefort with so much intensity it should have burst into flames, I realized I'd never gotten closure. Perhaps it was because I hadn't seen the end coming, whereas he'd obviously been planning it. Or perhaps it was because he'd left so rapidly. Or because he'd never called to see if I was okay. It felt unfair. Bleu cheese would forever remind me of that day.

I squeezed the Roquefort tightly, punishing it for its role in my sadness. The strangest growl came from deep within. "Aaarrggh!"

Lila's head swiveled toward me. "Callie?"

"It's the stupid bleu cheese!" I yelled, wiping tears from my cheeks.

"What? Are you feeling okay?" She put her hand on my forehead.

I pointed at the cheese case. "Most of these cheeses didn't even exist until Vic insisted I try them." One particularly nauseating cheese sat on the end of a row of stinky cheeses. I pointed at it and gagged. "For the record, that one was disgusting."

"Kind of like him." Lila had never met Vic, but she'd heard enough to form her opinion.

I shoved the cheese in my hand toward her. "This is what I was eating when he dumped me."

"This one?" She grabbed the Roquefort from my hand, checked to see if anyone was watching us, and then dropped it unceremoniously on the ground and stomped on it. "Whoops." Her dark eyes sparkled with mischief. "Take that, Vic."

I burst out laughing. "Lila!"

Kicking the Roquefort under the display, she set down her basket and calmly dug in the pocket of her black pea coat, handed me a tissue. As I wiped the tears from my face, she continued to read off items from her list.

"Emilie wants Camembert, and can you grab the Comté from over there?"

It didn't have the same effect as, I don't know, punching Vic in the face might have, but as I picked up the cheeses Lila had pointed to, squeezing and smelling until I found the best one, the self-pity faded a bit. Lila had my back. And she would love me forever.

Finally satisfied with our selections, we locked arms and wove through the other people in the store to the escalator, riding it up to the second level where the wines were.

The wine selection aisles went on for days in this store, larger than all the snack aisles combined. I loved French priorities. However, it did make finding the exact brands Emilie requested slightly challenging. Still irritated, I turned to Lila, throwing my hands up in frustration. "But seriously. How could he do that to me Lila?"

"Okay, so the cheese stomping wasn't the end of this." Lila

set her basket down on the floor and faced me, waiting for me to continue.

"I'm sorry. I know you've heard this all before. Until today, I really believed I had completely moved beyond all of this. But..." I waved my arms in annoyance.

"It's okay, Callie. You need to get this shit out. I'm here for you, honey." She waved her arms about. "And so is the wine and the cheese."

I snickered. "It's just so darn frustrating. I sacrificed everything for him, and he just walked away. Without any reason or real explanation. I never even got the chance to yell at him. I want to yell at him!"

With each word my voice ratcheted up in pitch. A man shot me a dirty look, so we shifted a few feet to the left to get out of his way.

Lila waited patiently for me to continue, her eyebrows arched. I stood there for a second, considering my next words. Raising my arms again in surrender, I said, "Why didn't he tell me before I came over? Or even give it a chance to work out before ending it?"

Lila pursed her lips in thought. "Would it have been better for him to allow you to settle into a life with him if he was already having these doubts?"

I shook my head back and forth. "I don't know. Probably not."

Impatient shoppers shoved their way around us. Yet neither of us moved or said anything. Lila intuited my need for space to process this, rather than jumping in with advice.

"I didn't realize I still held on to this much anger."

Lila placed her hand on my arm and looked me directly in the eyes. "Of course you do, honey. It's only been a few months. The heart takes time to fully heal. Even when we know it's the best thing for us. Even when we're broken by a jackass."

"It's not even that I'm heartbroken anymore. I'm just mad." I grabbed a bottle of wine off the shelf next to us, and Lila swept it out of my hand.

"No bottles of wine need to be injured in this!" She placed it safely in the basket.

I laughed. "You're the one destroying things tonight."

"Listen, Callie," she said. "You didn't deserve what happened to you. But it doesn't have to be the end of your story. He doesn't get to have that much power over your happiness. He doesn't get to ruin your last few days. I won't allow it." She flashed the list at me, reminding me to stay on our mission. The store would be closing soon.

Naturally, she was right. I needed to get past this. To close this chapter of my life and open the door to my next adventure. And more than anything, I wanted to just enjoy the last few days I had left with my friends before we were all separated by thousands of miles.

After we finished our shopping, we made our way back out into the busy street, arms loaded down with our loot. I stopped to admire some of the lights and decorations and sighed. It was all so sickeningly romantic.

Lila turned toward me, her eyes very soft, and placed a hand gently on my arm. "Don't give up on it, Callie."

"On what?"

"Love, romance, all the things you want. You are the most romantic person I've ever met, and I know someone perfect is waiting for you. It might even happen before we leave."

I snorted and rolled my eyes. "Unlikely."

"I know I said earlier that you should just focus on fun and going home, but you deserve something epic to happen. You've got your short bucket list to do before leaving. Why not add 'fall in love' to it?"

"You're crazy!"

"Romeo and Juliet fell in love in what? Like three days?"

"And look how that ended? Six people died!" I chuckled. "And look what happened to me the *last* time I fell in love too fast."

"Well, we just have to make sure we don't set you up with the son of your family's sworn enemies, and you should be fine." She winked.

"I think we're safe." I said. I readjusted the bags on my arms, and we started walking toward the metro. I took a deep breath and silently committed to letting all this go and enjoying my last few days in Paris, *sans amour*.

AFTER CLIMBING four flights of stairs with all our heavy shopping bags, plus my backpack stuffed with items for the party, my arms and legs burned as we finally burst into Lila's apartment.

"I will not miss life without elevators!" Lila said, huffing.

"You'd think we'd be more in shape by now," I replied.

"Especially you, with the eight flights you climb every day."

Setting down my bags on the table, I opened the window in Lila's spacious studio room and lit a cigarette, staring out into the courtyard as I puffed away. My thoughts returned to our earlier conversation. Lila joined me and handed me a drink. We clinked glasses.

"Whatcha thinking about?"

"Our conversation earlier."

"Oh." Lila lit a cigarette and took a long drag. "Which part?" were the words that came out, but what her tone said was, "Are we doing this again?"

"What if I can't fall in love again and trust that I'll be loved back?"

Lila turned to me. She looked at me for a long moment before replying. "I think it's normal to have these fears, Callie. Obviously, I never saw you and Vic together, but from what you've told me, it feels like you might have stayed in the relationship even if you knew deep down it wasn't right."

I considered her words, staring out into the courtyard. "Maybe. I truly believed I was in love with him."

"And he obviously was not." She shrugged her shoulders.

That stung. But they were truthful words. I crushed my cigarette butt in the ashtray.

"I don't mean to hurt you," Lila replied, put her cigarette out, then reached out and put an arm around my shoulder. "But if he loved you as much as you loved him, he wouldn't have treated you like that."

"And that's what I'm most scared of. Giving myself fully to another person who's not in it with me fully."

"There's always a risk with love. But if you're not willing to take a leap at some point, you'll never know." She set her drink down on the table and sat down to take off her shoes, glancing in my direction. Lila said, "What I know about you is that you're fun, you're generous and kind. You're smart. And when the right guy finds you, there will be nothing that will keep him from you."

My lips curved into a half-smile. I hoped she was right, but I didn't quite believe it yet.

The door to the bathroom opened and Matt popped around the corner, surprising both of us. Smiling, he gave me a big squeeze on my shoulders.

"Ditto what she said." He looked at Lila and grinned. "I came all the way to Europe to stay close to this one."

His nose wrinkled, as though he had followed Lila into the bowels of hell, rather than Europe. His hair, curly and a bit long, flopped around on his head. He reminded me of a mountain man with his full beard and flannel shirt. Lila and Matt had met during Matt's freshman year in college, when Lila was a sophomore. When she decided to work in Paris after graduation, he'd found a study abroad program in the Netherlands for the first half of his senior year.

I shrugged my shoulders. Obviously it was possible, but was it possible for me?

"And if nothing else, you live in Paris and it's almost the end of the millennium!" Matt's pearly whites shone from beneath the beard.

"If we don't all die tomorrow night," I joked. When both of them gave me questioning looks, I continued. "Haven't you been watching the news? They haven't stopped talking about the possibility of a terrorist attack in major cities, or if that doesn't get us, Y2K is going to shut us down."

"This is why I don't listen to the news!" Lila piped up. None of us were really that scared about either of those two events, but we were certainly aware of the possibility of trouble.

"You know," I said, "I touched something wet on the subway railing yesterday, and nearly convinced myself I was going to die a brutal death from a chemical weapon."

Matt chuckled. "I give you credit for that imagination of yours, Callie. And might I give you some advice? If you meet a guy tomorrow night, I wouldn't suggest you lead with these topics." He winked.

"Noted. Sorry, when I talked to my parents earlier, my mom went on and on about the increased threat of terrorism in all major cities on New Year's Eve. She really filled my brain with stuff I'm just going to drink out of my mind tomorrow night!"

"Pfft," Matt waved his hand to dismiss the thought. "Terrorism is so 1980s."

"On the plus side, if terrorists get me, I don't have to pack all of my stuff," I said.

Lila laughed, surveying her large, furnished studio apartment—easily four times the size of my place—which prominently featured a king-sized bed. Despite countless hours spent hanging out at Lila's apartment, we'd never used the fireplace that took up a large chunk of the wall directly in front of the bed, it added a lovely ambiance, nestled in between built-in wooden bookshelves, crammed to the hilt with older, leather-bound books. The shelves, made from knotty pine, added a sense of rustic charm to the cozy atmosphere. A leather-covered reading chair and a small table sat close to the fireplace. To the right of the bed the room was open, and this is where we sat around a small round table with four chairs, next to the large window that opened into the courtyard.

Lila sighed. "Now the question is, how long is it going to take us to get this place ready for the party?"

I stood. "Let's get to it. But first, we might need this." I grabbed my backpack and pulled out a bottle of vodka.

"You read my mind," she said, taking the vodka and pulling me in for a big hug. "It's New Year's Eve 1999, Callie girl!"

"We finally get to party like it's 1999!" It was a tired joke by now, but that hadn't stopped us from saying it over and over.

3

WE CLEANED and organized Lila's apartment for about three hours, sipping on our preparty beverages and rehashing our favorite memories from our time together in Paris. I'd brought all my party gear with me and excused myself to the bathroom to shower quickly. Matt ran to the store for some last-minute items we'd asked for and Lila showered after me. As I finished the last touch-ups to my makeup, Emilie banged on the door.

"It's pissing down dogs out there!" she exclaimed, pulling off her wet jacket as she came in. Lila and I looked at each other and burst into laughter.

"I think you mean it's raining cats and dogs?" Lila suggested.

Emilie raised her arms and smiled. "Same difference!" While her English was nearly perfect, sometimes the phrases she concocted were hilarious.

"Hope this stops soon, or our plans are toast," I said. I didn't want to think about it. We'd followed the news about the grand spectacle Paris had planned for this night for months.

After kissing each of us on the cheeks, Emilie dug into the

groceries we'd bought and began organizing them for her food-prep marathon. She staged vegetables and fruits in one area to be chopped, meats, cheeses and breads on the opposite counter, and dessert items next to the fridge. With the final ingredients in place, Emilie put her hands on her hips and nodded in approval. Lila playfully wiped her hand across her brow and I smirked. We'd succeeded in our shopping task.

Our other friends would arrive at 8 p.m., giving us just enough time to prep the food for the party and finish setting up for guests. Lila and I moved into the living room to move furniture around and set up the food table.

"I'll check on Emilie," I said when we'd finished.

Lila nodded and returned to putting away all the bras and undies hanging on the clothesline strung across her living room, her final preparty task. Neither of our apartments had laundry machines, so we'd grown accustomed to hand-washing our delicates and lugging the larger items to the laundromat when we had no clean clothes left. Oh, the cherished washing machine and dryer.

Back in the kitchen, I observed Emilie as she threw a pile of freshly cut mushrooms into a pan with onions sautéed in butter.

"Smells good. Whatcha making?" I asked.

She smiled. "Quiche."

I nodded my approval as she turned back to chopping. "What can I do to help?"

She stopped chopping the mushrooms, wiped her hands on a tea towel, and scanned the counter. She picked up a platter of strawberries, blackberries, and raspberries. "Will you wash these and cut them up?"

"How do you want them cut?"

"Medium-sized pieces, please. Not too big. They are for the top of the cake."

"Mmmm. You speak my love language."

Emilie's lips curled up into a half smile. I settled into my station in front of the sink, moving from time to time so she could reach around me for items in the cupboard. Lila's kitchen was the right size for about one and a half people to be in there, but Emilie was so petite, she was practically half of a person.

Lila turned on the music in the living room and appeared in the kitchen doorway with three glasses of vodka and cranberry juice.

"Cheers!" she said, handing them over to Emilie and me. We clinked our glasses together.

"To the best friends ever. Thanks for making my time in France an exceptional experience," I said. My voice wavered slightly, and we clinked glasses again and sipped our drinks in silence for a moment.

"So, Lila, how was your last day of work?" Emilie asked.

Lila rolled her eyes, grabbed a strawberry from the tray, and popped it into her mouth. She chewed for a moment and then smirked.

"Well, I guess it was par for the course with *Madame la Witch*. It's over now, that's all that matters. She didn't succeed at chasing me out early and I stayed the course!" she exclaimed, raising her arms in victory. Lila had endured a horrific boss for the last three months. *Le Witch,* as we called her, found fault with everything Lila did at work. We found tremendous satisfaction in bashing her at every opportunity and we'd drunk many bottles of wine while swapping stories of misery. Lila and her terrible boss, me and my broken heart, and Emilie's annoying professors at the Sorbonne.

"What about at your office?" Lila asked me. "I'm sure they were amazing."

"Yes, what did Gerard do to see you off?" Emilie seconded, wiping her hands on the tea towel again and turning to me.

Emilie was directly responsible for my job. She had invited me to lunch one day with her father, and his friend Gerard was there. As luck would have it, Gerard was in need of a bilingual secretary and I fit the bill.

"He was awesome. We had a nice lunch party, and then he gave the whole staff the afternoon off." I immediately regretted the admission, which I hoped Lila wouldn't perceive as gloating.

"I'm glad one of us had an awesome experience," Lila said, wrinkling her nose at me.

I patted her on the back. "You have love, I had a better work situation. We can't all have it all."

"Touché," she chuckled.

My whole job experience had been exceptional. Gerard was the director of an architectural firm, located in a very posh area of Paris near les Pyramides. The other employees had treated me like one of the team from day one, despite my terrible French accent. Today, they'd surprised me with cake, champagne, and gifts. Gerard had given me a nice little cash bonus and a special gift.

"I brought the gift they gave me, to share." I opened the fridge door and retrieved the bottle I had wedged in earlier between the bottles of beer on the top shelf. "They gave me this bottle of champagne. Perfect for New Year's Eve!"

Emilie took it from me and her eyebrows nearly shot off her face as she looked at the label. "Callie! This is at least a $500 bottle of champagne!"

Lila snatched it from her and read the label. Whistling, she said, "I heard 1990 was an excellent year for Dom Pérignon. This is *nice.*"

"Are you sure you don't want to take that one home and save it for a special moment?"

"What's more special than the last evening that all three of us will be together?" I asked, saddened at the thought. "Besides, I already have no idea how I'm going to get everything home!"

"I'll take anything you don't need." Emilie had come to Paris with very little beyond a few pieces of furniture for her flat.

"Don't worry, I already have two boxes for you, and there will likely be more," I reassured her. I reached around her into the cupboard, grabbed three champagne flutes, set them carefully in the tiny amount of space on the counter, and popped the cork. We all squealed at the pop.

"To love!" Lila cheered.

"To love!" Emilie repeated.

"To not being so drunk by the time our guests arrive, I don't pass out and miss the fireworks," I chimed in.

They both laughed and raised their glasses once more.

"To love," I said, under my breath. With my focus on my friends, my job, and healing the last few months, I'd pushed aside the idea that I'd meet someone and fall in love until the Eiffel Tower had cruelly reminded me of that hope today.

"Welp, this champagne is divine, but I'd better go put the rest of my undies away before the rest of our guests show up," Lila said, standing up and stretching.

"Yes, we definitely don't want our guests seeing all your lacy bits," Emilie teased, before turning to me. "I need you to slather those pieces of toast with this salmon paste." She grabbed a platter out of her bag. "You can fill up this plate."

The "toast" was actually small crackers, similar to dried bagel bites.

"So, tell me about your brother's friends. Are they cute?" I asked Emilie, while I spooned generous dollops of salmon spread on the toast, maybe taste testing a few along the way.

She swatted my arm playfully. "Save it for the guests!" Her

lips pursed in thought. "I don't know much. He just told me he's bringing two friends from Uni. Why do you ask?"

"Oh, I don't know. I wouldn't mind a fun fling right before going home," I said casually.

"Mm-hmm, that might be fun," Emilie said. "Do you think you're capable of a fling?"

"Have a fling? Pretty sure I'm up to the task." I shimmied over to her and gyrated my hips in exaggerated circles, flipping my hair back to demonstrate my obvious sex appeal. She giggled, shoving me away.

"I meant, do you think you're able to do a no-strings-attached situation?" Emilie knew I didn't really do flings.

"I don't know. I've only got a few days left, and with it being such a big, romantic night, I am not opposed to the idea."

I shoved down the tiny mental voice that insisted Emilie was right. I'd never been the fling type. I was an all-in kind of gal. As much as I thought I'd escaped the southern lady's indoctrination, when I'd fallen in love with Vic, I'd found myself quickly on board with the idea of love, marriage, and kids. I'd been robbed of that future when he dumped me. But it was probably silly to think a prince would come riding in on a horse, kiss me at midnight, and save me from being an old maid.

"What about you, Em?"

"Nah. I'll stay away from drunken snogs and regrettable morning afters."

I snorted. "When you put it that way..."

Emilie was many things, but a hopeless romantic was not one of them. I'd never seen her pine over anyone. She'd dated some guys on and off, but had never seemed to care if they stuck around or not.

"If you want my honest opinion, I think you'd do well to avoid the bros tonight too," Emily said, brows furrowed in concentration. Her knife snicked as it cut through a cucumber with just a bit more force than was called for. "And, if you want to know why I say that, let's just reminisce about Gavin, Olivier, and Loïc for a minute."

My face immediately went red.

Lila appeared in the kitchen, suddenly very interested in our conversation. "Who are Gavin, Olivier, and Loïc?" she asked. She snagged a salmon toast, popping it in her mouth as she leaned back against the door frame of the entry to the kitchen.

"Do we have to?" I whined.

"Fraid so, sister!" Lila piped in.

"Shall I do the honors, or do you want to?" Emilie asked me as she wiped her hands, picked up her glass, and leaned back on the counter.

"Gavin, Olivier, and Loïc were supposed to be rebounds," I said, and sighed deeply, reluctant to share this embarrassing history. "I met all three of these guys in the month before we met, Lila, when it was just me and Emilie out on the town."

"Why have you never told me this part?" Lila asked, refilling her champagne glass and topping off ours.

"It's not the stuff dreams are made of."

"Ooh, continue," Lila encouraged.

"I'll spare Callie the pain," Emilie said, winking at me. "Callie went on a wild dating spree that first month. We went out drinking every night. Dancing every Saturday. She'd meet a guy, have a great evening with him, and then, well... let's just say none of them were long-term material, but Callie sure tried." Emilie giggled. "I'm sorry, I'm not trying to mock your pain, but you have to admit, it was pretty funny."

I hung my head. "Absolutely *hilarious*," I replied, sarcastically. "It's true though. I thought I'd found Mr. Right three times that month. I was a little intense."

"Poor guys had no idea what they were in for." Emilie

shook her head back and forth, giggling. "Gavin was the best though. He's here at the Sorbonne from Ireland. We saw him about a month after Callie lost it on him, and he actually *ran* from us. Like we were going to harm him." By this point Emilie was bent over, laughing so hard her breath was labored and tears streamed down her face.

Lila turned to me, her eyes wide. "He ran? Like literally? What on earth did you do to this guy, Callie?"

"I might have found out where he lived from some of Emilie's friends who knew him, and shown up at his place a couple of times," I said, sheepishly.

"Callie!" Lila chuckled.

"Not my finest moment." I was giggling too. It was not funny at the time, but now, remembering the Gavin event, it was both mortifying that I'd behaved this way, and also, terribly amusing.

"What about the other two guys? I still can't believe you never told me about all of this!" Lila grabbed for another salmon toast, and Emilie playfully swatted her hand away, then gave in and handed one to Lila anyway when she pouted.

"Oh Lila, I was so ashamed. So Loic, well, we met in a bar. He was totally attentive. We only saw each other in the bar. He bought me a drink several nights in a row and spent the evening with me. We went back on night four, and there was another girl sitting in his lap."

"No!" Lila turned to Emilie.

"Yep." Emilie, finally regaining her composure, confirmed it.

"And Olivier, well, we also met out dancing," I started.

"I'm seeing a trend here," Lila interjected.

I nodded. "Yes, he was supposed to take me out on a proper date, but he never showed up. I sat waiting by my phone for hours."

"Well, that's not very funny," Lila said, rubbing my arm.

"Now you can understand why, by the time I met you, I had given up on dating."

"I also understand now how we came to meet. You put your stalking skills to use!"

"Hey!" I feigned shock and hip checked her. Lila and I had become friends because we just kept running into each other in places around Paris. One time, it was three times in one day, which was pretty exceptional for a city this size. We were both on the hunt for jobs and apartments and we'd received the same list for leads, so maybe it wasn't all that surprising, but I liked to think it was fate.

"Who knew you were so crazy?" Lila reached for the bottle of champagne, and once again filled our glasses before raising hers in another toast. "To Stalker Callie. May she not terrify any men tonight!"

I smirked and hip checked her again.

"Hear, hear," Emilie said, as she also raised her glass. She glanced at her watch as she did and her eyes widened. "Girls, we've got to get to it! Guests will be here in less than two hours!"

4

"Callie, can you grab the door?" Lila hollered from the kitchen. The music in the studio room, where I was chatting with Matt and a group of Emilie's friends from work, drowned out the sound of the knocking. Scooching around two of Emilie's friends in the tight hallway, who stood waiting for their turn in the bathroom, I made my way down to the door. In the kitchen, Lila balanced a big tray of drinks and Emilie had her hands immersed in whatever she was whipping together. They both looked gorgeous, Lila in a loosely flowing white peasant shirt and khakis, and Emilie in a formfitting silver tank top and tight black pants.

"Smells so good, Em!" I called out in passing. The scents of garlic and *herbs de provence* hit my nose, and my mouth watered.

Emilie brushed her black hair away from her face carefully with her forearm, so as not to ruin her hair or her makeup. "It's gonna be yummy!" Emilie replied.

Lila and I had worried about what the stress of preparing food for fifteen people would do to Emilie, but she was taking it in stride. And, like she'd told us several times, it's not like she was cooking for the queen, but just preparing a ton of appetizers and simple delights. Also, the day-drinking had certainly helped relax her.

I smoothed down my top, patted my hair, and threw open the door.

Blue eyes. Like the ocean. Gazing back into mine.

Unable to move or react, I just stood there, mouth agape. He smiled, a smile that reached his eyes, and I let out a small, but audible, exhale. *Whoa!* As he pulled off his black cap and ran his hands through his shaggy brown hair, I realized there were two other guys standing next to him.

Warmth crept up my neck and tinted my cheeks. Tucking my hair behind my ear, I finally acknowledged them with a quiet, "Um, hi."

"Hi, we're looking for Emilie," the short one said. I assumed he was Emilie's brother, based on height. Thank goodness he'd brought a hot friend.

Flicking my eyes quickly in his direction, I mumbled, "Mm-hmm, this is the right place," and then returned my gaze to Blue Eyes. Hot damn, I was going to have to figure out how to be fling material for this one.

Three steps away, Emilie popped her head out from the kitchen. "Julien! You made it!" She shoved past me and pulled Blue Eyes in for a hug.

Noooo.

This was Julien? This tall, blue-eyed babe with giant dimples was her *computer geek* brother? He smiled at me, and all the blood rushed to my face. Lila's admonition to "Just stay away from the brother" reverberated in my ears. My brain might have been telling me no, but my body was screaming yes.

"Hi Fred!" Emilie leaned in to the shortest of the three, the one I'd incorrectly assumed was her brother, and kissed him on the cheeks. Then she turned to the taller, thin guy with short brown hair and glasses, and kissed him as well. "Philippe, glad you two came!"

Emilie turned to me. "Callie, this is my brother, Julien. And his friends, Philippe and Fred."

Nodding, I tried to swallow, but my tongue had glued itself to the roof of my mouth. No words came. I stood awkwardly, desperately willing my body to work with me. *Oh crap, I've got to kiss them.*

Although I adored most of the French traditions, I felt the kiss-kiss introduction was a pure violation of personal space. Sweat beads formed on my forehead as we began the "Which cheek will we go for first?" dance. Trembling, I leaned in to greet Julien, praying that I didn't fall into him or choose the wrong cheek to kiss first and end up planting a kiss right on the lips of this stranger, as hot as he was. As Julien's lips brushed gently against my cheek, first one side, then the other, I breathed in the dreamy scent of his cologne. Hugo Boss. My favorite. Falling into him might not be so bad.

Sadly, I did not tumble into his arms and the moment ended, with me a bit drunk on his scent. My stupid tongue was still a lead weight.

I turned to Fred. A kiss on the left, a kiss on the right. Two down, but we weren't out of the woods yet. Cautiously moving forward to kiss Philippe, I stretched up, putting too much momentum into it and my face smacked hard against his glasses.

"Oh! Um, I'm sorry!" He smiled shyly and shoved his hands in his pocket, eyes cast downward.

Moving aside as Emilie ushered them inside, I closed the door, leaned back against it, and sucked in a deep breath, surprised by the unexpected and intense reaction I'd had to Julien. My heart hammered against my chest like I had just run a marathon. Problem is, I don't run unless it's to save my life. Clearly, my vascular system needed some extra-strength conditioning. Only slightly more composed but fully curious, I entered the main room just as Julien removed his coat, tossing it onto the pile on Lila's bed. I tried not to drool as his sculpted arms moved to smooth down his shirt. His jeans snugged his bum perfectly—not too tight, not baggy—highlighting his assets nicely.

His *assets*. I giggled, turning away before anyone noticed.

Vile woman, calm yourself. I slid back into the kitchen, fanning my hands to cool my flushed face, and saw Lila busily shifting drinks from the counter onto a tray.

"Did you see him?" I asked. Reaching for one of the pink drinks off her tray, I gulped it back like a shot.

Chuckling, Lila set the tray on the newly cleared counter. "He *is* cute. He's also Em's brother." She paused. "But it's nice to see your eyes light up like that, and well, rules are made to be broken, right? Now replace that drink so we can serve our guests!"

This round of drinks was my drink of choice, a lovely blend of vodka, Sprite, and a splash of cranberry juice. I quickly applied an additional layer of lip gloss, smacked my lips together, and glanced in the mirror over the sink to make sure my hair wasn't behaving badly before following Lila into the main room. *Game on!*

Confidence drained away from me the moment I turned the corner. Sexy Callie would strut right up to Julien and run her hand lightly up and down his arm as she purred something suggestive in his ear, melting him to pieces. A more likely scenario included me tripping, scratching him as I raked my nails down his arm to brace my fall, and hurling curse words on my way down. *Not* sexy.

Time for Plan B. Turning to Lila, I ordered, "Hand me the tray!" Eyebrows raised, she complied.

Careful not to trip and shower our guests with cranberry-colored vodka, I maneuvered my way across the small distance to the other side of the room, where Julien and his friends chatted in front of the fireplace.

"Cocktail anyone?" I offered, beaming. He reached for a glass, face lit up in a smile, causing my innards to fry in heat. *Words, Callie, words!* Nothing came. Frozen in place, a stupid Joker grin stuck on my face, I prayed for anyone else to say something. *Do something, Callie!* Unable to think of a single smart or even cute thing to say, I shoved the tray at Philippe, then Fred, who both smiled, gratefully accepting a beverage.

My legs managed to take command, returning me to the kitchen, my safe hideout.

Emilie, who was back at work piling food on a large plate, looked up. "Drinks all delivered?"

"Mm-hmm. Hope your hot brother likes girly cocktails." Placing the empty tray on the counter, I grabbed the stack of cups to start the process over again.

Emilie stared at me for a second and then continued to arrange the hors d'oeuvres on the platter. "You know, college students. A free drink is a good drink," she said.

Nodding, I turned back to the tray, adding four fresh plastic cups before an idea hit me. While it was a lovely idea to continue making and serving our guests drinks, I wanted to enjoy the evening too, not spend my entire evening tending to everyone else. I opened a cupboard, found a large container to use as a bucket, and filled it with ice. With vodka, cranberry juice, and Sprite in tow, I made my way to the table in the main room and set them out along with the bottles of wine and beer. Angling myself to spy on Julien, I noticed he was still deep in conversation with Fred and Philippe.

In what I hoped was one of my last trips to the kitchen of the evening, I stood in the doorframe of the tiny kitchen, hands on my hips.

"Emilie, why have you never introduced me to him before?"

"Take this one, please, and send Lila back here. I need her help." Stepping back, I swallowed, perplexed about why she ignored my question. *Did I miss something?*

Avoiding any potentially awkward conversation, I dutifully made my way to Lila. I whispered, "Your presence has been demanded in the kitchen."

Lila rolled her eyes. "We have enough food for forty people. What does she want now? I'm ready to party!" Lila popped a slice of brie in her mouth and I gently nudged her toward the kitchen.

Better her than me.

Matt's playlist, a mix of pop and alternative rock, played softly in the background, but not so loudly that our guests had to raise their voices to engage in conversation. Julien, Philippe, and Fred had formed a small circle with a couple of Emilie's friends from work, and Matt, Lila, and another of Emilie's friends stood close to the table, smiling and talking politely. Unsure of where I should stand or who I should talk to, I circled the room, pretending to ensure our guests had beverages and snacks while I worked up the courage to rejoin Julien.

A crude expression about using the pot or getting off of it crossed my mind. We only had another hour before it was time to leave to watch the fireworks. If I wanted to talk to Julien before the evening got crazy, this was my chance. *You look hot, Callie,* I reminded myself. Lila had helped me blow out my hair to give it a lot of volume for the short cut, and my new dark-purple velvet halter top and swanky black pants hugged my body in all the right places. My black boots made me a solid three inches taller, giving my short body a bit more oomph. But the extra height didn't increase my courage to strike up a conversation with Blue Eyes. Every time I thought about moving in his direction, my tongue went numb.

Turning on my heel, I retreated once more to the kitchen, empty tray in hand again, berating myself for being a coward.

Guilt washed over me as I saw Emilie was still working in the kitchen. "Emilie, you've done an amazing job with the food."

"It did turn out well," she said, smiling at me. She turned back to loading some tiny cream puff pastries onto a plate.

Watching her for a moment, a sadness clutched my heart. "I'm going to miss you. I don't know how I would have survived the last few months without you and Lila."

She stopped fiddling with the pastries and turned in my direction.

"You're amazing friends," I added, choking up a little on the words.

Emilie's eyes welled up. "Even though I'm French, I don't think I would have ever had such a great Parisian experience without my two American besties."

I leaned over and kissed her on the cheek, and Emilie squeezed my shoulders in return.

Picking up the tray of pastries and headed back out the kitchen door, I looked back over my shoulder and said, "I'll catch you on the flip side."

This time I immediately made my way to Julien, Fred, and Philippe, and stood there for a moment as they discussed the Rugby World Cup, something the French were especially proud of as the French team had taken second place earlier that year.

"We got to meet the team," I interjected into their conversation.

The three of them looked at me, eyes wide. "Really?" Fred inquired, as he grabbed a handful of pastries and shoved them in his mouth.

"Yes, they came through all the bars in this neighborhood the day after the Cup, and we had some drinks with them."

Julien nodded in appreciation. "What were they like?"

"Some were nice, one was a complete asshole and super rude to me. Clearly, he has a strong dislike of Americans."

"Huh." Philippe seemed as if he wanted to say more, but instead, he popped more pastries in his mouth. "That's unfortunate."

"It happens from time to time." I looked down at the ground, remembering a few incidents in which we'd been treated poorly for being American. "But thankfully, most of the French have been cool."

They nodded their heads, still chewing away.

"I never knew my sister was so talented!" Julien said, grabbing his third pastry.

"She's pretty special," I agreed. My flirting game sucked. After standing there awkwardly for a few moments and coming up with nothing, I smiled at the three of them and turned to the other guests.

"Dessert?" I asked the group of Emilie's coworkers.

"You ladies have put together a truly nice evening," said one of Emilie's friends, Zara. She didn't have very French features. While she was tall and quite lanky, the shape of her eyes and proportions of her face made me think she must have some Eastern European or Russian heritage. Her black dress came down to just above her knees, and her legs were bare. She wore ankle boots, and I wondered how she would stay warm once we left to watch the fireworks.

"I give most of the credit to the chef, Emilie. She did the hardest work."

"Well, there's something to be said for ambiance as well," she replied, graciously. After a pause, she continued. "I don't know many Americans, but you and Lila are unquestionably different from the stereotype."

"Thank you," I giggled. "I guess our job here is done! Changing hearts and minds!" We all laughed. It was no surprise to me that many French thought most Americans were loud, obnoxious, and lazy.

"Emilie said you're leaving soon?" she asked, turning toward me.

My smile disappeared, shoulders slumping a bit. "Yes. After tonight, I have four days left."

Perhaps coincidentally, Julien's head turned swiftly toward me. I thought he'd been wholly engaged in a conversation with his friends—might he have been eavesdropping? Was that disappointment I registered in his eyes?

"Oh, that's not long at all," Zara said.

Julien held my gaze, causing a ripple of heat to pass through my body.

"No, and I have such mixed emotions about it," I said to Zara, but my eyes were still locked with Julien's. As my face flushed, he blinked and then turned back to Philippe, shoving one hand in his pocket, pulling his jeans tighter across his backside and setting off a tiny explosion of warmth that skittered from my fingers down to my toes. A tiny breath escaped me.

"You must miss your family?" Zara's question broke me from my trance.

"Oh, er, yes, I do. I spoke with my parents this afternoon. They are anxious to have me home." I didn't go into the fact that when I'd left home, I wasn't planning on returning for a much longer period of time, and how happy my parents were that I was coming home earlier than expected. My mother had never had a high opinion of Vic anyway, so while she played the role of supportive mother, I think she was also relieved that we were no longer together.

I nodded my head politely as Zara chatted away for a few minutes, racking my brain for a reason to approach Julien again. Food was a good reason, right? Returning to the kitchen, I loaded up another tray and returned, smiling my best toothy smile, which froze on my face as soon as I saw Zara cozied up next to Julien. As he said something that must have been hilarious, she placed her hand on his arm and threw back her head in laughter. *He sure as hell better not be her plan for keeping warm tonight.* No longer just Emilie's pleasant friend from work, Zara advanced to enemy number one.

My jealousy was totally unmerited.

Disgruntled, I leaned against the wall, periodically popping one of the tasty treats on the platter into my mouth. Everyone else seemed to be enjoying themselves. Emilie, Lila, Matt, and two of Emilie's friends were immersed in conversation on the other side of the room across from Julien and the other guys, who were laughing at whatever Zara was telling them.

Matt walked up beside me and offered me one of the two drinks in his hands. I accepted and gave him a quick kiss on the cheek, his beard tickling my lips. Matt threw one arm over my shoulder and leaned in closely.

"What's going on here, Callie?"

I stepped back slightly and rotated in his direction. "Just having some me time," I deadpanned.

He chuckled, his dark eyes lighting up with his smile. Then, turning more serious, he pursed his lips together, narrowed his eyes at Julien and his friends, and asked, "So, which one do you have your eyes on?"

"Am I that obvious?" Turning my face to look at Julien, my cheeks warmed.

"Probably not to anyone who doesn't know you like I do."
He patted my arm.

"Did Lila tell you my plan to make tonight more
interesting?"

He nodded. "A little New Year's Eve fling is never a bad
thing. So, who's the unknowing victim?"

I turned around to face him, my back to the guys. "Don't be
obvious, but the one in the middle."

"Whew. Cause the other two seem a little dorky." His face
lit up at his own joke.

I snickered.

"Definitely the one I would have matched up with you," he
continued, sizing Julien up. "He's cute but not supermodel hot,
seems confident, obviously takes good care of himself, and I'm
pretty sure he's interested in you, too."

"You think?" He read that situation quickly! What kind of
superpowers did Matt have? Some kind of dude radar?

"I chatted with them briefly when you were delivering
snacks, and I've been watching the room, not like it's that hard
in this tiny little space, and he's taken notice of you, for sure."

"No he hasn't!" I squeaked, turning to see if anyone heard
me over the noise of the room. To my relief, no one was paying
attention to us.

"Why would I make that up? Go talk to him."

"Okay, I'm going to do it. Right after I get a little more
liquid courage!"

"That's the spirit!" Matt gave my shoulder a squeeze. "And
not for nothing. Callie, I know I can say this without you taking
it the wrong way, but you look hot."

I blushed, not quite knowing what to say, but nodded my
head at him. I appreciated his encouragement.

"Now give me this," he demanded, trying to pry the tray of
pastries out of my grasp.

"No way, this is my intro prop!" I pulled the tray back. Considering how quickly they'd devoured the first tray, more food should be an easy way in.

Matt just chuckled. "Food is always the best way to a man's heart."

"I don't need his heart tonight, Matty, I just need his..."

Matt covered his ears. "I can't hear you!"

"Who says I was going to say anything dirty? Maybe I just need him as a dance partner for later?" I winked, knowing full well there'd been plenty of innuendo behind the statement. I wasn't the one-night-stand type, but I love a good play on words. I turned to the table on my right, poured another strong beverage and downed it.

"Another one?" Matt teased, eyes, twinkling. "Remember, you want to have a conversation with him, not throw up on his feet."

I winked at him as I set my empty glass on the table. "Now I'm ready!"

I walked over to where Julien, Philippe, Fred, and a couple of the other guests were still deeply engaged in a conversation about sports. Fred's arms flailed wildly as he reenacted the world's greatest moment in soccer. When he'd finished and danger seemed averted, I shoved the tray forward.

"More dessert?" I asked in French. Fred eagerly snatched three more pastries, while Julien and Philippe took one each.

You can do this Callie. You know how to make words. "So, when did you arrive in Paris?" I winced as my voice came out pitched too high.

"Yesterday," Fred said eagerly, mouth full of pastry. I agreed with Matt's assessment that he was positively goofy. He had a military-style haircut, was not much taller than me, and was a little round. But he had kind eyes. He seemed safe.

I turned back toward Julien. "From Strasbourg, right?" He

nodded, flashing a mouth of perfectly white, straight teeth. Thank goodness. And did I say dimples?

"I love Strasbourg. I think it's my favorite city in France," I continued, looking him up and down as subtly as possible. Based on his excellent chiseled but lean physique, my bet was that he played soccer.

"You've been to Strasbourg?" Philippe asked.

"Yes, a few times. It's beautiful."

We discussed Strasbourg for a few more minutes, the conversation going easily with Philippe, while I fought my body's urge to hurl myself into Julien's arms. He smirked in amusement at something Philippe had said, a half smile lifting one side of his lips, and his eyes crinkling. I chewed the inside of my cheek.

"What, huh?" Oh shoot. Julien had asked me a question. I blinked, certain my face was now the shade of dark cherries. Think, quick. What had he just asked?

He chuckled. "I asked if this was Lila or Matt's place?"

"Oh, this is Lila's flat. It's lovely. And in such a great area of town."

Words flowed from Julien's full lips, but I barely heard them over the whooshing in my ears. The palpable energy between us drew me toward him, like a bug to a zapper. I inched closer to him, my eyes held prisoner by his mesmerizing blue eyes. As he told me about their trip from Strasbourg to Paris and the tiny hotel they were staying in on the other side of town, I fought the urge to reach out and touch him, wondering if I'd be physically shocked when our skin touched. As he reached over to set his empty glass down, his arm brushed mine, and while I did not get zapped, goosebumps erupted across my bare arms.

"Yo, Callie!" Lila came up and grabbed my arm. I smiled at her, grateful for her presence, perhaps saving me from selfcombusting in Julien's presence. I introduced Lila to the group, and they asked her some questions about how she had wound up living here. Philippe shifted nervously, in a way he had not a few minutes earlier, hands shoved deep in his pockets. Philippe's characteristics were classically French, but he was cute in his own way. He stood quite a bit taller and leaner than Fred, and kept his eyes focused downward, periodically shoving his glasses back higher on his nose. He didn't offer any information unless asked a direct question. I couldn't tell if he was shy or if there was just no opportunity for him to talk, because Fred seemed to never stop talking.

Lila, turned from Fred, asked Philippe, "Were the trains crowded?"

"I imagine they were, but we came in on a flight," he said, and blushed.

"You did?" I asked, looking to Lila who looked equally surprised. It was no more than a four-hour train ride to Paris from Strasbourg, maybe six if you got stuck on the slow commuter trains that stopped everywhere.

"My sister works for CrossAir," Fred piped up. "So she got us cheap tickets, and it saved us from wasting most of the day on the train."

Philippe nodded in agreement and looked back at the ground.

"That makes sense." Lila nodded her head. "The trains get so crowded anyway. When Callie and I went to Amsterdam, we had to sit on our luggage in the corridor. I imagine it's brutal with the big New Year's festivities." She took a sip of her drink. "So, what do you all do in Strasbourg?"

They shared the same things they'd told me, but Philippe opened up as he talked about his internship with the European Court of Human Rights and I knew he'd just hit the jackpot. Lila's eyes grew huge, and she started filing a million questions at him. "Did Callie tell you I spent two months in Africa before coming here, helping build schools and working with orphans?"

"We didn't really have time to get into all of that," I laughed.

Lila nodded and turned back to Philippe, excited to have someone else to talk to about her passion for important causes and desire to end human suffering. It was one of the many reasons I absolutely adored her. But while I have been known to geek out for hours on the topic of global politics, my current interests boiled down to one thing: learning more about Julien.

Philippe and Lila gleefully compared notes on the latest global tragedies, and Julien and Fred merged with the group of people behind them, who were having a livelier discussion. Unable to find a subtle way to join the conversation happening between Julien, Fred, Zara, and the others, I busied myself by reorganizing snacks on the table and making sure everything was well stocked.

Periodically, I turned my gaze to Julien hoping to make contact. When I finally caught his gaze, I gave him my most charming smile. I stepped timidly in his direction just as Zara squeezed in beside him. Jealousy and fear that he might choose to spend the evening with her buzzed through me, but rather than be an awkward intruder, I moved over to the window. I pulled out a cigarette and lit it, taking in a slow drag.

"That stuff will kill you," I heard from behind me. Turning, I found him standing close to me, and I briefly closed my eyes to breathe in his sexy scent. My blood pulsed forcefully in my neck as my body stiffened. With my tongue paralyzed again by his unexpected presence, I shrugged my shoulders. I wasn't sure if he was joking or really was one of those hardcore anti-smokers. But the warm smile on his face made me believe he was likely teasing, not berating me for poor life choices. He moved to my side, standing by the window with his arm not quite touching mine.

My shoulders relaxed a little and I was able to find my voice again now that he wasn't looking directly at me.

"Yeah, it's on my list of New Year's resolutions. Return to the US. Quit smoking." I tried to make light of the situation, but my tone was as heavy as my heart. Peering out the window and unsure of where to take the conversation next, I concentrated on enjoying my cigarette.

After an awkward pause, Julien spoke again. "So, when exactly do you go back to the US?"

"Four days from tomorrow." My shoulders slumped and I leaned out of the window to flick the ashes from my cigarette.

"Oh, that *is* soon." His eyes darkened, and this time I was certain he looked disappointed. He crossed his arms and stepped back slightly.

"Yes, but I've been here since July, so I'm kind of ready to get back home." I put out my cigarette in the ashtray and leaned out the window again to get some fresh air.

Julien stepped up to join me at the window again, our bodies touching in the small space. I shivered, but not from the cool air.

"Wow, that is a long time to be here. I've never left France," he admitted. He turned to face me. Our faces were only inches apart, and I was relieved I'd popped that minty freshness into my mouth moments ago.

Our eyes met, and for a moment, the entire world stopped. All that mattered to me was figuring out what was happening behind those blue eyes. I held my breath and my palms got clammy. It took every bit of willpower to not pull his lips to mine. Unable to handle this tension for another moment, I stepped back.

"What? Well, you have to fix that! Traveling is my favorite thing!" I gushed.

"Isn't it a bit, I don't know, scary to be so far from home? On your own?" He tilted his head, those beautifully clear blue eyes searching mine.

I squirmed, fighting the urge to run my fingers through his hair, which fell invitingly across his brow.

"Sometimes, but honestly, it's been amazing. Lila, Emilie, and I have made some incredible memories." I told him about some of the trips we had taken, including a weekend to see the Normandy beaches and a visit to the beautiful Mont St. Michel, the famous abbey on the west coast of France that becomes an island when the tide comes in and surrounds it with water.

"Wow, you've probably seen more of France than I have."

"Well, that's a shame, Julien, you have a beautiful country."

We were finding a comfortable pace and chatting easily until Emilie swooped in, forging a space between us. She held her hand out in demand for my lighter.

"We need to get ready to leave if we're going to find a good place with any hope of a view of the Eiffel Tower for midnight," she said as she lit her cigarette, her brown eyes flashing with that same look of annoyance I'd seen earlier.

I nodded, ignoring her undertone, but trying to gauge if she was truly irritated with me or just anxious about getting down to the riverbanks. We'd been watching the days count down to the Year 2000 on the tower for months. This was not a sight any of us wanted to miss. Disappointed that we didn't have more of a chance to talk alone, I gave Julien a small smile, then turned and wandered over to Lila. She and Matt were cuddled up in the chair in front of the fireplace, Lila's legs draped over the arms of the chair, head leaned back on Matt's shoulder. She held her wine glass in one hand, with her other arm wrapped around Matt's neck as she whispered something in his ear. I almost didn't want to interrupt their cuteness, thinking about how much I'd missed the moments like this in being a couple.

"Come on lovebirds, it's time to go see the show," I said.

Everyone knocked back what was left of their drinks, and we took turns retrieving our coats from the bed and bundling up for the chilly evening before making our way out of the apartment. Before Lila closed the door, I remembered something.

"Wait, Lila, the champagne!"

Her eyes lit up, and she hurried back into the apartment, grabbing a bag and stuffing in the three bottles of cheap champagne we'd purchased to have in the streets at midnight. Matt grabbed the bag, and she gave him a smile of appreciation as we followed the rest of the group down the four flights of stairs and into the chilly Parisian night.

You'd never have known it was 10:30 at night, not with the amount of light and noise and the crowds of people outside of Lila's apartment building. Normally this part of the city would be silent and dark, but everyone's doors and windows were open, people milled in the streets, and the energy flowed. Despite the scarf, hat, coat, and gloves I was wearing, I shivered in the brisk air. With my hands shoved deep into my pockets, I followed Lila and Matt, suddenly worried that I'd missed my chance to connect with Julien. But there was always hope for a kiss at midnight, right? And then we'd be heading to a nightclub. Keeping Julien in sight, I caught up to the rest of the group while strategizing my plan of attack.

5

To shorten the walk, we and what seemed like half of Paris hopped on the metro for a few stops. We emerged into a sea of enthusiastic people. The whole city bustled, filled with people on a varying scale of drunkenness who were also making their way toward the riverbanks of the Seine. Whistles blew and people stumbled through the streets, coming out of apartments and bars, all moving in droves to get a good view of the fireworks display at the Eiffel Tower, who looked stunning as she prepared for her big moment.

We followed Emilie, who looked pretty kickass in her snug black pants, black biker boots, and black leather coat. With her short haircut and tiny stature, sometimes she really did remind me of a pixie fairy. But she was all business right now. She knew exactly where she wanted us to stand for the countdown and how we needed to get there, and she recognized if we didn't move quickly, we might lose our opportunity.

Emilie's concern for finding the perfect spot was not unappreciated, but the rest of us were also kind of gobsmacked by everything happening around us. The environment was both riveting and overwhelming, and I found it difficult to focus on finding the perfect place to stand when there was so much to take in around us. The people and activities around us. The performances. The laughter and the noise. Lila and I hooked arms, our eyes not knowing what to take in next with all the wild displays all around us.

Matt, Lila, and I had separated slightly from the rest of the group, so I leaned in close to her. "What do you think of Julien?"

"I think he's been eyeing you all night."

My cheeks hurt from the smile that stretched my entire face. "Really? Did Matt tell you to say that?"

"What? No!" she said.

I glanced at Matt who raised his eyebrows, shaking his head back and forth as he pulled his beanie over his ears. His nose was red, either from the chill in the air or the booze. Maybe both. He looked like a true mountain man in his big coat, jeans, and hiking boots.

"I have seen this with my own two eyes, truly," Lila said. I wanted to hear more about her thoughts, but the mini circus acts along the street distracted us.

"Oh my gosh, wow!" I said. Jugglers, singers, dancers, and mimes, all in sparkling costumes, moved to the music, lights flashing. All of Paris's finest filled every possible space, drawing the eyes of the many people crowding the streets.

"Look at that!" Matt said, and pointed as flames shot out of the massive metal pipes of an organ playing deep, dark tones, something I'd certainly never seen before. The organ's eerie sound reverberated through its pipes, capturing my full attention. Rooted in place, I barely heard Emilie's plea.

"Guys, we're never going to get a good spot!" Emilie continued to herd us like cats in the direction of the riverbanks. We didn't have far to go, but we moved slowly in the crowds.

Emilie bridged the gap between Julien, Philippe, and Fred in front of her and Matt, Lila, and me in the rear. Emilie's work friends had already broken away and gone off on their own, perhaps annoyed at our slow progress, so it was down to the seven of us.

Fred looked back over his shoulder at us. "Shall we grab a drink here?"

Emilie shook her head emphatically against the idea, face scrunched in distaste. The bar was crowded, with standing room only as loud and happy partiers crammed into every possible open space, and I had our doubts about how quickly we'd get served. But outnumbered, Emilie rolled her eyes and followed us as we shoved our way in, peeling off our hats, coats, gloves, and scarves. The idea of spending a few moments in a warm bar, especially if this meant Julien and I would be able to chat some more, appealed to me. And then there was the issue of needing the toilet.

"I need to use the bathroom, Em. How about if the guys get in line for drinks and maybe we can visit the ladies' room? Hopefully by the time we're done, they'll have drinks? We'll be quick!" I promised, hoping that would indeed be the case.

Reluctantly, Emilie agreed, and Fred smiled at me appreciatively. We handed Matt our coats and the bag with the champagne we'd brought for midnight. He spotted the one barstool in the vicinity that was open and piled our items around it.

"Thank you, lover," Lila crooned at Matt, and kissed him quickly. I kept my eyes on the ground as we separated from them, not wanting to make eye contact with Julien, convinced he'd see my own desire to kiss him. The three of us pushed our way through the crowd to find the bathroom.

The line to the bathroom was long, so while we waited, I

quizzed Emilie. "So, what's Julien's story? Is he single? Is he straight? Is he a psycho?"

Emilie smiled, more relaxed than she had been earlier. "Nothing exciting, yes, yes, and possibly."

"You didn't answer before, in the kitchen. Why have you never introduced me to him?"

"You never met him when we were in school?" While she phrased it as a question, we both knew the answer was no.

"I'm sure I would remember."

"He was in Strasbourg most of the time. I guess he didn't really come see me that much when we were at the Uni," Emilie said flatly.

I unwrapped a fresh piece of gum and popped it into my mouth, offering a piece to Lila and Emilie. My mind whirled, fighting feelings of—dare I say, betrayal?—that she had this perfect specimen of a brother and she'd never even mentioned him. Shouldn't all besties be trying to hook their friends up with their family members? Then, if it worked out, we'd be related! Did she think I wasn't good enough for him? Chewing my gum so hard I thought my jaw might break, I wondered why I was so upset about this. After all, I'd just met Julien. It wasn't like we had a chance at any type of future anyway.

"I think he's super cute," Lila pitched in, squeezing my arm, her eyes twinkling. "You should go for it. A New Year's Eve fling is fun."

"I'm not sure if he's really fling material," Emilie said icily. Then staring directly into my eyes, she said, "And neither are you, for the record."

My mouth dropped open.

Emilie sighed, shaking her head. "You're gonna do what you're gonna do, but just don't break his heart."

"Break his heart? Moi? In one night?" I said, sarcasm oozing in my voice. "You know I am the one who always barely gets out alive anyway. Need I remind you of poor Gavin?"

That did the trick. The ice officially melted as the three of us burst into laughter, Lila pretending to hide behind Emilie from "Stalker Callie."

Emilie squeezed my arm, her brown eyes filling with compassion. "I just don't want to see either of you get hurt," Emilie replied, softly.

"Well, we're making a lot of assumptions about a situation that so far has not shown any real promise," I reminded her as we inched our way forward.

"Finally!" Lila shouted. All three of us crammed into the tiny room and took turns in the bathroom, with no further discussion about the situation.

After we finished up, with Emilie growing visibly agitated about the time wasted here, I chucked my gum in the garbage, and we returned upstairs where we found the gents proudly holding their beers. Matt held out a beer for Lila and one for me. I kissed him on the cheek.

"You are the best bonus boyfriend ever!" I said.

Lila playfully pulled him toward her and kissed his other cheek as he slid his arm around Lila's waist and nuzzled her neck with his nose. "This lady's all I can handle," he slurred. Maybe we'd prepartied a little too hard, I thought, as his hands maneuvered down to her bum, squeezing her playfully, and she squealed.

"Okay, okay, I get it. I don't need to see it."

I met Julien's gaze and raised my glass. He did the same, smiling. Tingles spread over my skin and a warning went off in my brain. *One night of fun, Callie. That's all you get with this one.* I struggled to tear my eyes away from him as I imagined his lips on mine and then hid behind my beer mug before anyone else guessed my thoughts.

"Come on everyone, drink up quickly," Emilie urged. Truthfully, I was also anxious to claim a good spot. After all, we were in Paris, on the last evening of the millennium. And of all New Year's Eves, I did not want to risk missing the countdown and the incredible show they had been hyping up at the Eiffel Tower. Any anxiety about terrorism or Y2K—although I *had* withdrawn all of my money from the ATM the day before, just in case the entire world shut down!—had completely dissipated, and now all I cared about was drinking, watching fireworks, and partying.

We weren't making much of an effort to leave, so Emilie started throwing our coats at us. We pulled on our gloves, hats (sadly Julien covered that cute mop of his), and scarves, even though the chill of the air no longer bothered me as Emilie dragged us back into the street.

Approaching the banks of the Seine, it became increasingly difficult to travel in a group, but we managed to stick together, forcing ourselves through the crowds. *It was loud.* Horns and cheers, screaming and singing, it was wild, and adrenaline flowed through me. I made eye contact with Lila. We both smiled.

"I love you," she mouthed, and I repeated it back to her. Gratitude soared through me.

The large clock on the glowing Eiffel Tower counted down. We had just under fifteen minutes left of this year. I wondered if my friends and family would watch the New Year arrive in Paris on TV.

We pushed forward until it was impossible to move any further. Barricaded alongside a bus stop, we were still at least five rows of bodies back from the river, and I was struggling to see over the crowd. Even in my three-inch boots, I was still shorter than most of the people in front of me.

Scanning the crowd, I noticed a girl across the street

climbing onto the top of the bus stop. Coincidentally, we were also standing next to a covered bus stop. Hands on my hips, I assessed the situation above me.

"I'm going up!" I announced.

"Up where?" Emilie asked.

"There." I pointed to the top of the bus stop. The structure seemed sturdy enough. It was about seven feet high, with a metal roof and plexiglass sides, and big enough to accommodate a couple of benches. The plexiglass did not go all the way to the ground and was rimmed with metal that protruded out several inches along the bottom of the plexiglass. It looked like a good foothold for someone who might climb the structure.

"You're nuts!" Emilie laughed.

"No, I'm short! And I want to see better. Don't you want to come with me, Em?"

She rolled her eyes. "Um, not on my wildest day," she said, and turned back to watch the tower.

Placing my foot on the metal rim for a boost, I attempted to heave myself up. But I wasn't strong enough to pull myself up onto the top of the structure, so I clung to the side of the structure like a spider monkey.

"What's going on here, Callie?"

Julien was suddenly beside me, smiling at my predicament. I was only a few feet off the ground, but hunched over like I was, we were face-to-face. He shook his head back and forth, amusement plain on his face.

"I want to go up! I need a better view."

"I see that. Need a boost?" he asked.

Dang, he was sexy. Before I could reply, his arm was wrapped around me with one hand on my backside.

"Huh?" I was concentrating on not falling, my head was spinning a little from all the alcohol, and at first I wasn't sure who was touching me. Turning toward him, I found myself about a head taller than him from this position, and I just wanted to leap into his arms.

"What are you doing?" I squeaked, not that I minded his hands on me. I liked this position, and I imagined climbing up Julien, rather than the bus stop, and turned my face quickly before Julien read my thoughts.

"I'm helping you go up! That's what you wanted, right?" He winked at me. "On the count of three, you pull, I'll push."

Julien planted his hand firmly on my ass and pushed. One good shove and I heaved myself up over the top of the bus stop. For a moment, I just lay there, thinking about the sensation of his hands on my legs, wishing they had stayed there longer. Then, as water soaked through my pants, I regretted my decision to climb up. The afternoon storms, although they had passed and no longer threatened the upcoming pyrotechnics display, had left small puddles of water on the top of the bus top.

"Awesome," I said. I carefully rolled over, realizing this was higher than it looked. How stupid would it be if I met my death by collapsing the thin metal roof and crashing to the ground? I lay there for a minute, staring at the cloud-covered sky above me before scanning the tops of the magnificent buildings lining the streets along the Seine River. Then, rolling from my back to my stomach, adrenaline pumping, I climbed onto all fours, and slowly rose to my feet, wobbling at first like a baby calf standing for the first time. The roof was not cracking or creaking, which was good, and it held my weight as I balanced myself.

Cheers rose around me, mostly from Fred and Julien, as though I'd just summited Mount Everest. I looked down and grinned, giving them a slight curtsy. That was a pretty cocky move, considering my recent wobbles. I glanced back at Julien and, suddenly emboldened, winked at him. *Who am I right now?*

"How do you like me now?" I hollered out at my good friend, Eiffel. She glowed magnificently, certainly visible from outer space. "Yeah, okay, you win!" I relented, grateful that there was so much noise, no one else would hear my words.

"*C'est magnifique!*" I yelled to no one in particular.

"Callie! Be careful!" Lila looked a little concerned, as a good friend would be when their intoxicated best friend is standing on a plexiglass structure seven feet off the ground. Giving her a little wave, I looked down to see if Julien was watching. He was not. He was engrossed in a conversation with Philippe and Fred, and my heart sank a bit that he was not interested in my actions. I stumbled a little and crouched back down on my knees.

"Oh crap, Callie, cops!" Emilie shouted at me. One pushed his way through the crowd, red-faced, blowing his whistle and gesturing wildly.

Uh-oh, he meant business. I lowered myself down to the roof, slithered backward on my belly, and dangled my legs over. Then, stuck, I panicked. If I dropped from here, I'd likely twist my ankles in my high boots.

Strong hands clamped firmly around my thighs, sending a shock coursing through my body. I slid down the last little bit, guided by Julien's hands, and once on the ground, I stumbled backward into him. His arms still held me, firmly wrapped around my hips, and I didn't move a muscle. His hands seemed to linger slightly before he dropped them, and I fought the urge to grab his hands and return them to their previous position. I turned around, shyly lifting my gaze to meet his. Clear ocean blue. *Breathe before you pass out.*

"*Merci,*" I whispered. *What do I do now?* I pecked him quickly on the cheek. He nodded, staring at the ground, and turned back to his friends. My lips tingled from brushing against the stubble on his face. Sneaking a glance in his direction, my heart jumped a little when our eyes met.

The crowd shifted, shoving us together. Julien turned back to me and wrapped his arms protectively around me as I tucked myself into him, hands at his waist. Chills traveled the length of my body, appreciating the physical contact. We were no longer being pushed, but he hadn't released me either.

"Callie, ça va?" he asked.

"Yes, I'm fine." More than fine. My hands were still on his hips. I looked up, and for a moment, our eyes both searched the other's for answers. What was happening here? Before either of us spoke, the crowd erupted in noise. I turned, dropping my hands, and immediately regretted letting go. Horns buzzed, people cheered and sang, and the noise made it impossible for normal conversation. The energy from the crowd made the air practically sizzle with excitement as we counted down the last few minutes before the end of the century. The crowds condensed even more as people pushed to get closer to the tower. Someone handed me a bottle of champagne and I took a big swig before passing it to Emilie, who also took a big pull. Her dimples showed as she laughed.

Leaning in toward Emilie, I slurred, "I love you," in her ear. She pulled me in tightly and said nothing. I knew she loved me, too, she just wasn't the type to say it. Closing my eyes briefly, my thoughts wandered to Julien, and I shifted to look at him. Julien stood not far behind me, at an angle from where I surreptitiously looked over my shoulder and snuck a quick glance. Julien, Fred, Philippe, and even Matt talked animatedly, their words lost to me in the roar of the crowd.

The collective surge of the crowd pressed all of us tighter together and Julien moved in behind me again, pressing up against my back almost protectively, hands on my shoulders. The scent of his Hugo Boss wafted to my nostrils, causing me to shiver. Snuggling back into the heat of his body, I never wanted to move from this spot. Ever.

"Five minutes!" Julien shouted, still pressed up behind me. I hoped he would stay close and wrap his arms around me again. Frozen in place, I dared not move an inch, afraid he'd drop his hands. Turning my head slowly, I made eye contact with Lila, who stood next to me, pressed against Matt, and I waggled my eyebrows. She gave me a thumbs up, eyes twinkling, nose scrunched up in a smile. *Don't get too excited, Callie. He's probably just smushed up to you because there's literally nowhere else to go.* But he certainly made no efforts to put space between us either.

Boom!

I jumped, and Julien laughed.

"*Ça va?*" he asked me for the second time. His protective response thrilled me. Eyes wide, I looked up at him, nodded, and we both turned our attention toward the direction of the noise.

A crackling noise hissed across the river and a blaze of light erupted around the entire base of the Eiffel Tower.

"What's happening?" Philippe yelled.

"Eighty thousand lights is what's happening!" I screamed back over my shoulder.

I covered my ears in response to the deafening noise as the bright light exploded outward. Slowly, moving up from the base, the lights climbed the tower. One tier after another lit up, lights ascending the tiers rung by rung, until the tower was fully lit all the way to the top.

My mouth dropped open in awe at the mesmerizing scene unfolding in front of us.

"One minute to midnight!" Matt yelled, standing to my left with Lila and holding his bottle of champagne high in the air. As if on cue, the fireworks also increased in intensity.

I cheered along with the crowd, peering back quickly at Julien. He squeezed my shoulder, giving me a grin worthy of melting even Medusa's heart. My stomach fluttered, wondering if Julien would kiss me at the New Year.

My gaze darted to Lila on my left and then at Emilie on my right, both of them mesmerized by the incredible sight. Paris had outdone herself tonight. *You are certainly in your glory tonight, Tower.*

"How are they even doing this?" I screamed. I glanced back at Julien and he was smiling, transfixed by the sight in front of us.

Boom! Pop! Crackles all around.

Another surge of explosions started at the bottom and raced up the tower, shooting fireworks out the sides. So much light. The colors! Purples, oranges, and then all white fireworks.

Matt turned, shoving a bottle of champagne into my hands, then shook another one vigorously and popped it, spraying champagne everywhere.

"Happy New Year! *Bonne Année!*" we all yelled, pulling each other in for hugs. Rather than going straight for Julien, and still woozy from the idea of kissing him, I squeezed Emilie tight. After Matt kissed Lila, I pulled her in for a big hug and a kiss as Matt opened another bottle.

Sucking in a deep breath, I turned around and locked eyes with Julien. He grabbed me into a big hug, kissing each of my cheeks.

"*Bonne Année*, Callie."

Before my disappointment settled in, he grabbed my face in his hands and brushed his lips lightly on mine before quickly turning back to Fred and Philippe. Stunned, I hardly realized what was happening as person after person hugged me and kissed my cheeks. Julien had kissed me. JULIEN HAD

KISSED ME. Yes, it was quick, but he'd purposefully kissed me on the lips. He liked me too!

Emilie's shout interrupted my thoughts. "That was amazing!"

"Absolutely..."—I sighed—"... amazing," I replied, not just talking about the lights.

The bells from all the nearby churches began chiming loudly, adding to the jubilee of noise surrounding us. I grabbed Lila's arm and rested my head briefly on her shoulder, taking it all in, with a smile plastered on my face.

It was officially the Year 2000! Time for a New Year, new plans, new life, new love interest. And apparently, we still had power!

And then, in an instant, it was all over. The crowds thinned out quickly, people scattering like cockroaches in the kitchen when the lights turned on. There were post-New Year parties to get to or beds to be found after the long night of festivities. I could have stood and stared at the Eiffel Tower all night, but Emilie grabbed my arm and tugged me away in the other direction.

6

WE MADE our way back through the streets, still ridiculously crowded with people trying to get home or to their next party stop. Not wanting to get separated as we snaked through the drunken and over-excited crowd, I reached behind me and grabbed Lila's hand. Then, putting my fears of rejection aside, I reached in front of me and also grabbed Julien's hand. My heart lurched when he glanced back over his shoulder and gave me that delicious smile once more, his eyes crinkling at the corners. I had gloves on, and I wasn't about to drop his hand to take off the glove, so we did not lace our fingers. But there was something incredibly comforting about his larger hand wrapped around mine. He grabbed Emilie's hand in front of him, and we moved forward slowly, like a single-file train.

Talking was not an option as we forced our group through the rambunctious crowd. I was perfectly content to just hold his hand and revel in the moment, unconcerned with the drunken and wild people celebrating in the streets. Despite the frigid air, my body warmed as he glanced back every so often to check on me, as if he was genuinely interested in my well-being.

Finally, the crowd broke, allowing us the space to discuss our plans. While everyone else except for Matt and Lila dropped hands, Julien didn't let go of mine. Instinctively, I snuggled in a little closer to him. Even with my high-heeled boots, he stood several inches taller than me.

Emilie glanced down at our hands and quickly averted her eyes. Her poker face was solid, and if she had any thoughts about this progression of things, she kept them hidden. Her words flitted through my mind. *Just don't break his heart.*

"Um, guys, we have a slight problem," Emilie said. "Manu got six tickets to the club, and including him, there are eight of us. We didn't know you guys would be coming when he asked how many." Emilie looked at Julien, her nose crinkled and brows furrowed.

Lila yawned and tucked herself in more closely to her beau.

"Matt and I will make the sacrifice," she said. She looked up at Matt with big eyes and he shrugged in agreement.

"Yeah, clubs aren't really my thing. Especially if Manu got the tickets!" Matt said, chuckling. Manu, one of Emilie's and my best friends from French University, had rather eccentric tastes. He liked edgier things, painted his fingernails black, and loved the shock value of anything beyond the ordinary. It was highly unlikely that we'd be going to a run-of-the-mill nightclub.

I giggled. Julien turned toward me, his eyebrows raised.

"Don't worry, it will be fine," I reassured him. I was already envisioning us dancing closely when I had the sudden realization that Lila had just opted out of going—on our last big night together. I turned back toward Lila, lips pursed in a pout.

"Oh, please come with us and see if we can figure something out," I begged. I hated the thought of missing out on the rest of the night with her.

"We don't have to take the tickets," Philippe spoke unilaterally. "You should be with your friends tonight," he said sincerely to Lila.

My heart sank. I hadn't thought that through either. We didn't have enough tickets. If Julien's two buddies didn't come with us, I was sure he would go with them, and then I'd just be with Lila and Matt. The fantasy of having my hookup with Julien, my magical New Year's Eve fling, would be cut woefully short of anything fantastic. No passionate kisses on the dance floor or secret rendezvous in a hidden booth in a dark corner. This was a lose-lose situation. Although I had only known him for four hours, I was not ready to say goodbye. But I also wanted this night with Lila.

"No, really," Lila insisted. "You guys go on. I have my whole flat to pack up tomorrow and I don't want to be out all night. Besides," she looked directly at Philippe, smiling, "you came to Paris to have a big experience. You should do that! And we're not really clubbers anyway." She tilted her head toward Matt.

"You can say that again," Matt said, nodding in agreement. Matt hated nightclubs. He hated the loudness, the overcrowding, and the expense of the drinks. "I insist you take the tickets."

Philippe looked quickly at the ground, giving a slight nod of his head to acknowledge their comments.

"That's really kind of you, Lila and Matt," Julien said.

Lila leaned in and gave him a kiss on each cheek. "Lovely to meet you, Julien." She then kissed Fred goodbye, and finally Philippe, who blushed as their cheeks brushed. "I enjoyed our conversation earlier and I hope you're able to find an amazing job."

"Thank you," he said softly before shoving his hands in his pockets and taking a few steps back.

Finally, she grabbed me in a big hug. She whispered in my ear, "Do something with this. And tell me all the details tomorrow."

I squeezed her back, tightly. "It's not going to be the same without you tonight."

She did something so Lila then. She grabbed my head with her hands, pulled me toward her, and kissed me on the forehead, like a mama would.

"Happy New Year, Callie. Happy New Millennium. I love you."

"Happy New Year, Lila. I love you too."

Breaking our embrace, Lila turned to Emilie and pulled her into her arms. "I guess this is goodbye for us, my friend." Lila's eyes welled up with tears. She and Emilie didn't let go for several long moments, and I threw my arms around both of them, squeezing tight.

"It's not goodbye. It's just till we meet again," Emilie replied, wiping tears from her eyes.

Lila nodded and faced me again. "See you later, babes."

My hands balled up tightly, I stood rooted in place, holding back tears as Lila and Matt walked away. After a few steps, Lila glanced back over her shoulder. Waggling her eyebrows at me, she mouthed, *Romeo and Juliet!* I smirked and shrugged my shoulders. *Maybe?* I mouthed back.

I watched them for a moment longer until they were lost in the crowd. Over the last couple of hours, I'd been able to push off any thoughts about our separation. But now, my lip quivered and I blinked my eyes rapidly, trying to keep the tears at bay. I wasn't ready to say goodbye. Julien gently put his hand on my shoulder, pulling me out of my moment.

"On y va?" Shall we go? His eyes searched mine, holding my gaze.

I nodded and smiled back, silently promising to make tonight worthy of a good story for Lila and Matt tomorrow.

He grabbed my hand, and I turned to follow him as we squeezed through the crowds to walk down the Champs-Élysées.

7

We strolled down the beautiful street in the city of love, hand in hand. Our hands fit together. I had removed my glove on the right hand, and his fingers covered mine perfectly, keeping them mostly warm. I'd take frostbite for this feeling.

Sneaking a glance in his direction, I admired his profile. His strong jaw, the sharp but not pointy nose. Not perfect, but sexy as hell. Squeezing his hand, I sucked in a deep breath, determined to stay fully present in this enchanting moment.

And yet, it didn't seem real. Was this really me, holding hands with a gorgeous and sweet French man, the cool air and wind biting at my nose and ears? Should I pinch myself? Was there a way to pause time right now? Or at least slow it down drastically?

People tumbled out of every nook, space, and cranny on our walk down the Champs-Élysées. We moved slowly, stopping frequently to admire the festivities. Performers of all kinds lined the streets. Mimes, musicians, jugglers. Even Emilie relaxed a bit and took in the magnificence of the evening, walking between Philippe and Fred and giggling at their silliness. Fred offered commentary on just about every sight we saw along the way, and there were many.

"Can we just take a moment to talk about these Ferris wheels?" I asked.

Julien smiled at me. "They're incredible, aren't they?"

These were not your typical fair-time Ferris wheels. Instead, spread out along the Champs-Élysées were these magical, enormous wheels which featured dancers and acrobats and even musicians playing full concerts positioned on flat platforms that rotated slowly up and around. I had never seen anything like it before. The piece de la resistance was definitely the grand Ferris wheel, positioned opposite from the Arc de Triomphe at the other end of the Champs-Élysées. It was mesmerizing to watch the massive, fully lit wheel spin round and round.

Emilie called back over her shoulder, "It's the cows I want to talk about! Why all the cows?"

I giggled, as it was a question Lila, Emilie, and I had posed many times over the past few months. The trees lining the Champs-Elysée had beautifully painted papier-mâché cows adorning the trees. These were not small cows either. They were enormous, glorious cows. I loved the French.

We shuffled along at a snail's pace. I stared hard at everything, trying to memorize every detail of the sights and art along the route. The bright lights strung in the trees formed a well-lit path to the Arc de Triomphe, and Christmas decorations still hung in the windows of the small shops, adding to the charm. I tried to imprint in my brain the smell of champagne and warm crêpes from the pop-up stands and the sound of the party horns, not wanting to forget any details of this night. Some rambunctious passersby, clearly unaware of my presence, bumped into me as they made their way down the street past us, kicking up the confetti that littered the streets in piles. I smiled at them and leaned in closer to Julien. He stopped, turned to me, and took my face in his hands. I waited expectantly, gazing into his eyes, hoping he'd kiss me again. Gently, he leaned in, his warm lips grazed my forehead, and I breathed in that delicious smell of his.

My lips quivered, waiting for his to touch them. When no kiss came, I blinked my eyes and asked, "What was that for?"

His adorable dimples popped as he smiled, nearly melting me into a puddle on the ground. Those dimples. Reaching out, I traced one with my finger, wanting to explore everything about him.

"You just look so beautiful. Smiling, so happy." Tucking my hair behind my ears, he placed both his hands on my face and shook his head back and forth as I tried not to have a nuclear meltdown on the inside. "I think most people would be annoyed by drunk people practically knocking them off the sidewalk, but you're smiling at them. I thought that was cool."

I sucked in a deep breath. Once again, I needed a reality check. Had I passed out from all the champagne and entered a dreamland? I mean, who was this guy? He spoke like he was in a movie. I could totally imagine this exact moment happening in a romantic rom-com movie, where the guy acknowledges this specific character trait of the heroine's and is so moved by it, he stops in the middle of the street to kiss her. Only instead of on the forehead, it would be a perfect kiss on the lips, and *Cut!* Fade to black. As my heart nearly burst with appreciation for Julien, I smiled shyly, hoping he'd take my cue to continue.

"Mm-mmh." The sound of a throat clearing caused us both to turn. Emilie was standing next to us, clearly annoyed. "We're almost there guys. Come on." Her eyes pleaded with me, and clearly anxious to get to the club, she tugged on my arm.

Giggling and still a little drunk, I saluted Emilie and pulled

Julien along with me, trailing behind her. Sadly, another kiss from Julien would have to wait.

We turned off onto a side street and Emilie stopped in front of a very nondescript building. Not super fancy or presumptuous, two silver and blue doors opened outward onto the sidewalk, framed by a slight canopy. Manu stood at one of the doors, talking to the bouncer, and then looked over and saw us.

"Hello, bitchesss!" he purred, leaning down to peck each of my cheeks."And who are these guys?" He flicked his piercing black eyes briefly over Julien, Philippe, and Manu, arching a perfect brow, right hand on his hip, not waiting for an answer before focusing on Emilie. She introduced everyone.

"Where's Lila?" Manu asked.

"Matt and Lila went home so we'd have enough tickets for Em's brother and his friends," I said.

"Brother?" Clearly, I wasn't the only one in the dark. Manu and Emilie had been friends for even longer than I had known her. He turned back to the guys and studied them closely. "Ok. They'll do," he said, pursing his lips. Then he turned his attention back to me. "We are so lucky to actually have enough for all of us! Everything sold out months ago, you know," he said, and in a dramatic fashion, pulled the tickets out of his pocket. "But I got these!" He fanned the tickets in front of all of us.

"So glad you worked your magic!" I said. And I was. How could we celebrate New Year's Eve in Paris without going clubbing? Having never been to this club, I wasn't really sure what was in store for us. I'd actually only been to two or three different nightclubs in Paris. Lila and I had found the one we liked the most, Le Loco, and being creatures of habit, we tended to default to that one. Dancing was our favorite weekend pastime.

Manu nodded his head and gestured for us to follow him. He handed the tickets to the bouncer, and we filed in. Per the usual routine, we shoved our hats, gloves, and scarves into the pockets of our coats, checked our coats, and made our way into the main bar area and dance floor. I shivered, wishing I'd brought my bag and stuck my little sweater in it. My halter top looked great, but until some more bodies brought their warmth to the room, it was freezing.

Julien moved in close behind me and rubbed his hands up and down my arms. I took in the whole scene around me, smiling, adrenaline coursing through my body.

Fog filled the mostly empty room, the smell a strange mix of something sweet and pungent. The smokey haze hung eerily in the air with no one on the central dance floor, like we were about to watch the making of "Thriller," and multicolored lights swept across the stage, ricocheting around the room. In each of the four corners stood an elevated cage, circular with gold metal bars running from top to bottom, waiting for those who dared to climb in and demonstrate their dance moves. I made a mental bet on who would be the first in our group to get in one, quickly eliminating Philippe, Julien, and Emilie. My money was on Fred. Fast techno music pumped, the beat thumping through my body. I fought the urge to move with the rhythm as the music reverberated through me.

"Well, this is something special, Manu. But where is everyone?" I asked as I looked left to right across the mostly empty dance floor. The center dance floor would accommodate many sweaty bodies, with the large DJ stand centered at the front.

He leaned in, placing both hands on my shoulders and his mouth directly next to my ear so he didn't have to shout over the music. "Honey, the queens rarely come out before 1 a.m. Don't worry, it will be packed in here soon."

Queens?

A tall, well-chiseled man with long, flowing golden locks walked by, wearing nothing but a thong and high heels. His chest glistened, and as he strutted across the room, chest puffed out, long hair flowing behind him, I imagined him as a centaur. Just behind him, another man in a silky robe and high heels pranced by us, heading to the bar and giving a flamboyant flip of his hair over his shoulder as he passed.

Emilie raised her eyes at me, both of us scanning the room once again.

"Ohhhh," I said, turning, raising my eyebrows even higher, if that was possible. I looked at Emilie, the realization striking both of us at the same time. We were in a one hundred percent gay nightclub.

The laughter rolled out of me, a solid belly laugh, and Emilie joined in. Well played, Manu. Manu was my only gay friend and he'd always gone wherever we went. I'd never been in a gay nightclub before, but so far, other than the male-to-female ratio and the "centaur-esque" beautiful men, it didn't seem that much different from anywhere else. And selfishly, I knew I wouldn't have to worry about competition for Julien. Unless he liked guys, which I supposed was a possibility.

Julien, Philippe, and Fred stood on the edge of the dance floor, taking in the scene around them, expressions unreadable. Fred's head bopped to the beat of the music. Manu leaned into me and Emilie as he studied the guys.

"Are these three going to be okay in here tonight? They look a little shell-shocked." He cackled, and as Julien looked over, Manu winked at Julien. Julien winked back, and I exhaled, relieved that he didn't seem to be annoyed by the situation.

"We'll be fine," Julien replied. Fred and Philippe nodded their heads. This was one of those moments that shone a bright light on people's dark places. Would this night be a nightmare for them? Would they become irritated that our big New Year's Eve plans had landed us in a gay club? Or would they roll with it and have fun anyway? Julien's good-natured wink at Manu told me everything I needed to know about him. He seemed completely unbothered by the fact that we might be in the gayest place in Paris.

"Anyone want a drink?" he asked, placing his hand on my arm.

Nodding, I reached out for Emilie's hand. "When in Rome?"

She shrugged, reaching back for my hand, and we all moved to the bar, Manu throwing his arms around Philippe and Fred's shoulders as he started chatting away at them. Julien chuckled, grabbing my other hand and pulling it up to his mouth for a kiss.

The space leading up to the bar was empty, which was a pleasant change from having to fight our way through the crowds earlier in the night. Three bartenders waited for the imminent crowds behind the black countertop, and the shelves behind them looked to be stocked with every type of liquor imaginable.

"Vodka cranberry, please!" I ordered, handing over my drink ticket. Emilie and Manu ordered the same, and we clinked glasses while the boys waited on their beers. Once everyone had their drinks, we moved back to the edge of the dance floor, which was still empty. The DJ, ready to fill the empty dance floor, turned to face us and invited us to start the dance party. I waved and pointed to my still-full drink. We'd be dancing soon.

Observing my friends, new and old, as we stood in a small, sheltered group near the edge of the floor, excitement pulsed through me. I was itching to get on the dance floor. Manu flitted off to say hello to some friends that he saw enter the room, turning briefly to yell something back at us that wasn't audible above the music, so I just smiled and nodded as he blew me a kiss. Philippe yawned. Uh-oh.

Another gorgeous, scantily clad man pranced over in our direction. Apparently, the gold thong and high heels were the floor servers' uniforms. He was truly a marvelous sight with his golden hair flowing at least halfway down his back. He balanced a large tray at shoulder level, full of shot glasses. I waved him over.

"I'll take six!" I paid and distributed the pinkish mystery shot to everyone in the group, waving Manu back to join us and get his.

"To a new century, new adventures, and friends!" I shouted, and knocked back my shot.

Some of the centaur men climbed into the cages. Their bodies moved sensually, gyrating with the beat, arms sliding up and down the cage bars, grinding their hips. As more men arrived, they stood appreciatively in front of the cages, but the dance floor remained empty.

"At first I was afraid, I was petrified..." belted out over the speakers. I squealed, put down my drink, and dragged Emilie and Manu onto the dance floor. We'd danced to this song so many times, we practically had a routine. The dance floor started to fill quickly after that, especially when the DJ followed "I Will Survive" with "It's Raining Men." It was so cliché and yet so French. I'd yet to have a club night during which these two songs weren't played at some point in the evening. But if it ain't broke, don't fix it, right? The crowd loved it. We jumped around, screaming the lyrics and laughing.

"It's literally raining men!" I screamed at Emilie and Manu, who both laughed. Manu grabbed my hands, swinging me around on the dance floor, and then Emilie, while still making eyes at other guys in the process to remove any doubt about his sexuality despite dancing with two girls. I laughed as he blew a kiss at a guy dancing not too far from us, and then shimmied up to the group of guys. Emilie gave me a knowing glance and I grabbed her hand and twirled her in a circle.

As Emilie and I twirled around, singing at the top of our lungs, I snuck glances at Julien while he chatted away with Philippe and Fred. Why wasn't he picking up on my mental invitation for him to come dance with me? The half smile on his face as we locked eyes sent tingles up and down my body. I slowly rocked my hips, hoping to draw him out on the dance floor, but the three of them stood there, rooted in place, fresh drinks in hand.

After several crowd-pleasing favorites, the techno beat picked up, and I waved at the guys but Philippe shook his head no. Julien shrugged his shoulders. Fred seemed oblivious, smoking his cigarette. I danced my way over to the edge of the floor.

"Come join us!" I screamed over the music, waving my arms for them to come toward me and Emilie. When none of them moved, I danced on up, grabbing Julien and Philippe's hands, and literally dragged them to the dance floor, Fred trailing behind.

Once he was out on the dance floor, Fred was a treat. His exuberant personality came out full force as he moved ridiculously, oblivious to our roaring laughter. Sometimes squatting down to the ground, sometimes jumping around, his flailing body parts reminded me of a Mexican jumping bean. While I enjoyed every second of this, I kept my distance so I wouldn't get whacked across the face.

On the opposite end of the spectrum, Philippe barely moved. He kind of swayed to the music, smiling at us every time we looked in his direction. He kept close to me and Julien, probably trying to send the message that he was not available to the menfolk. The boys formed a loose circle around Emilie and me, and Fred kept trying to move in close to Emilie, but she kept playfully shoving him off. I giggled as he moved toward her again, unfazed by her continually moving outside of his reach.

"I'm going to get another drink and have a smoke," Emilie screamed into my ear. "Do you want to come?"

I shook my head. I was in a groove and not ready to take a break just yet. Philippe followed Emilie out, and I realized I'd lost sight of Fred. And then I saw him. He'd climbed into one of the cages and was sliding his hands down the bars, squatting down low to the floor and then pulling himself back up.

"Does he like guys?" I shouted at Julien.

"If he does, this is new info to me! But he always dances like this."

"He's crazy!" I laughed. His moves were no better in the cage than they were on the dance floor, but there was no doubt he was having fun. And alone or not, he was making the most of his New Year's Eve.

The music shifted from a fast techno beat to what I like to call "get your groove on" techno. It was a slower rhythm that oozed sex. The beat thumped through me, lights flashing all around, emboldening me to move more provocatively. I placed my hands on Julien's hips and watched as his eyes lit up. He smiled, pulling me in closer.

Finding it hard to maintain eye contact without melting into a puddle on the floor, I turned so Julien was dancing behind me, and faced Emilie and Fred. Avoiding eye contact with Emilie, I concentrated on moving with the strong techno beat that pulsed through me. The lights flashed wildly and the room grew warmer. I raised my hands in the air above my head, completely taken by the vibrations of the music. The sensation of fingers running down my arms and the sides of my body sent thrills through me, electricity shooting through my limbs as

Julien placed his hands firmly on my hips and his warm body moved in tightly behind me. Turning my head ever so slightly, I smiled up at Julien, raising my right hand up and placing my fingers on the back of his neck, moving in sync with his body.

Song after song, we danced together. Our bodies communicated through the rhythm of the music, without needing words. Moving my hips seductively, I turned around to face him.

"You're a good dancer," I screamed over the music.

"I was thinking the same about you," he replied, his eyes darkening. He chewed on his lower lip as he placed his hands on my hips, gyrating his hips in time with mine. Placing my hands on my head, I closed my eyes and swayed back and forth with the sensual beat. When I opened my eyes, desire flared in Julien's eyes. He ran his arms down mine and settled his hands on my hips again, pulling me in tighter and turning my body so he was pressed up against my back. We moved to the rhythm together, my heart rate climbing with every beat. Once the music picked up its pace, we separated and jumped around with everyone else in the club, never losing eye contact. I wondered if my eyes reflected the same desire as his did, and I shook my head to break the trance I had fallen into, afraid of doing something rash in the heat of the moment.

I had lost sight of Emilie, Manu, Philippe, and Fred, and found I didn't even really care what they were doing as I stared into Julien's eyes. But after several more songs, I scanned the room and located Manu not far from me, dancing with a group of guys I didn't recognize. He gave me a big thumbs up, smiling happily as he nodded back to the guy behind him, and waggled his eyebrows at me. *Good for Manu.* I finally located Emilie, Fred, and Philippe camped out in a booth. They appeared to be engaged in conversation and enjoying themselves.

Eventually the music slowed again, and Julien grabbed me and pulled me in close to him, arms wrapped tightly around my waist, my arms around his shoulders. I tucked my chin into his chest, and swayed, wrapped tightly in his arms, body to body. He rubbed his chin on the top of my head and I trembled.

Pulling back, I stared at Julien, taking in every detail of his face. His sharp nose, the bright-blue eyes that looked questioningly at me, his full lips. And good grief, those dimples. If the enticing smell of his cologne didn't drive me crazy, those dimples would. He was more than just a hot guy though, wasn't he? In just a few hours he'd demonstrated his protectiveness, shown he had an open mind, and was kind to others. And had I mentioned the super-hot bod? Icing on the cake, y'all. Delighting in the sensation of his hands rubbing up and down my back, my lips tingled, begging for him to kiss me. He didn't kiss me, so I tucked my head back onto his chest and swayed with him, hoping I'd not misread the signs. Maybe he was less for a public display of attention than me, my inhibitions severely limited by the amount of alcohol we'd consumed. But when you are drunk on a dance floor and you close your eyes, no one else can see you either, right? No? Shoot.

The music picked up its pace again, and we separated, hopping around with the others to the music as all the uncoupled dancers flowed back onto the dance floor.

Emilie made her way back to us, but my heart dropped as soon as I saw the bored look on her face. She yawned, pulling in closely to me and yelling over the music. "I'm tired and want to go home."

"But it's so early," I complained, yelling in her ear over the music, as we moved toward the edge of the dance floor. "Please stay longer!"

Julien leaned in to be part of the discussion.

"It's almost 3:30 a.m.," Emilie piped back. "Fred and Philippe are ready to go too."

Panic set in as I realized Julien and I might be separated

now, before we'd had a chance to fully connect. What now? Shifting my gaze from Emilie, back to Julien, I searched his face for answers. Emilie shoved her hands in her pockets and turned, leaving us on the dance floor.

Julien shrugged, grabbed my hand, and yelled, "Come on!"

Shuffling off the dance floor, which required a bit of squeezing and shoving through the now fully packed, sweaty dance floor, we walked back to the table where Philippe and Fred were waiting. Fred gave me a little wave, and Philippe looked visibly relieved that Emilie had succeeded in her mission.

"What do you want to do? I'm not ready to say goodnight," Julien said, gently grabbing for my arm as if he was worried Emilie might pull me out and away from him.

Relief washed over me. I wrapped my arm around his waist, stretching up to kiss him on the cheek. "Me either."

Emilie stood with her hands on her hips in front of me, tapping her foot, waiting for me as I racked my brain for potential ideas.

I pressed my fingernails hard into my palms, desperate for a solution that would please everyone. "Nothing will be open. There aren't many options. It's a long walk to my place and there is no public transportation open now."

Julien nodded his head, disappointment clouding his features.

"But what do you think about just walking around for a little bit? Paris by night?" I asked.

His face lit up in a smile. Swoon. Would I ever be able to see those dimples without my legs turning into a pile of jelly?

"That sounds great," he said.

Emilie rolled her eyes and huffed. "Fine."

Panic hit me. "Wait! I need to say goodbye to Manu!" This was the last time I'd see him before leaving for the States.

"We'll go get the coats. Give me your ticket," Emilie said, holding out her hand, and I gave her my claim check before searching the crowd for Manu. He was still dancing with the same guy from earlier. I pulled him away and explained we were leaving.

"I might not see you again before I return home, Manu."

Manu wrapped his arms around me, pulling me in tight. "Come visit me soon! And don't let that hottie get away!" Manu winked.

"I don't intend to!" I shouted over the music, blowing him a kiss as he disappeared into the sea of men.

The others waited near the entry with our coats and belongings. Fred and Philippe offered to walk Emilie home on their way back to their hotel. As a group, we sluggishly bundled up and headed into the quiet Parisian street.

"We'll see you back at the hotel, man," Philippe said, and gave me one more shy smile. Fred pulled me in for a big hug. Apparently, dancing had bonded us.

"Still on for tomorrow night?" I asked Emilie.

"Yeah, sure. See you then. Don't forget to grab the food from Lila's!" She turned to go, and I pulled her back in for a quick hug.

Alone for the first time, Julien and I stood on the street.

"Now what?" he asked.

"Let's go this way," I said, pointing in the direction of the brightly lit Arc de Triomphe. Julien reached down for my hand, lacing his fingers through mine, instantly warming them.

I had no idea where this night would take us beyond the Arc de Triomphe, but it didn't matter right now, not if we were together.

8

PULLING my scarf tighter around my neck, I walked slightly faster to stay warm as we walked toward the Arc de Triomphe. Now that we were alone, I didn't quite know what to say. We knew practically nothing about each other. We hadn't exactly done a lot of talking in the club.

"So have you visited Paris often?" That seemed like a good starting point.

"Not really. My dad visits often for work, and sometimes, like Emilie, I'll tag along, but we usually spend our time in restaurants meeting with his clients, or in swanky hotels. We've never made much time for sight-seeing."

"That's a shame, it's such a gorgeous city. So much history. So much to see."

Julien turned to me. "How lucky am I to have an American tour guide for the evening, to show me the best of the city?"

Chuckling, I pointed to the storefront on our right. "We're currently passing by my favorite music store, the Fnac. This is where I've been developing my pictures the last four months, and where Lila and I bought our tickets to see the Red Hot

Chili Peppers at Bercy, as well as the opera *La Bohème*," I said, mimicking the prim, precise tones of a tour guide.

"Eclectic tastes," Julien snickered.

Pulling him off the sidewalk and into the road, I twirled him around on the Champs-Élysées, reveling in the silence of what is normally such a busy boulevard.

Julien's eyes widened. "What are we doing?"

"When else will you ever get to dance in the middle of the Champs-Élysées?" I replied, spinning around, arms in the air. We stood for a few moments in the middle of the street, staring down at the Arc de Triomphe, the massive white stone structure resembling a giant H, with an enormous arch across the top. The monument sat in the middle of a massive roundabout where the five largest boulevards of Paris converged. Traffic was generally so bonkers you had to go under the street to get there safely. But tonight, the roundabout was eerily empty.

Still in the role of tour guide, I pointed ahead and said, "Our first destination, the lovely Arc de Triomphe, is one of Paris's most well-known monuments. Under the Arc de Triomphe, you'll find the Tomb of the Unknown Soldier and a fire that burns 24/7 to commemorate the soldiers lost in WWI."

"Now that I actually did know," Julien said, looking pleased with himself.

"Well done!" I joked. "But did you know it took thirty years to build and was actually constructed in memory of the soldiers lost in the Napoleonic Wars?"

"That's not nearly as impressive to me as your wealth of knowledge about this particular French monument," he said, looking me over as if seeing me for the first time. "I may have underestimated you, Callie, um, what is your last name?"

"Sparks." I blushed. What did he mean he had underestimated me? Had he summed me up as a silly American?

"Callie Sparks," Julien repeated.

I loved the way it sounded coming out of his mouth. "I assume your last name is Reynard, like Emilie's, since you have the same dad?"

He nodded.

The chill spread further through my body, my breath visible in front of me, and it was time to move. Julien gently tugged on my hand, leading me back onto the sidewalk, and we continued walking briskly toward the Arc, our free hands shoved in our coat pockets, heads bent down to keep the slight breeze off our faces. Searching my brain for something interesting to say, I drew a blank. I'd already told him everything I knew about the Arc de Triomphe, and the other sites between us and the monument were mostly storefronts and business offices, with apartments above them.

"Want to hear about something cool that happened to me the last time I visited the Arc?" By this point we had arrived at the flame for the unknown soldiers. We stepped closer, grateful for the warmth from the flame.

"Of course I do!" Julien said, and I cocked my head to see if he was mocking me or truly interested. Not yet able to decipher what his facial expressions meant, I continued, hoping he was actually interested and not just humoring me.

"Lila and I were standing right here in early November. We were taking pictures and taking this all in." I raised my hands to frame the arch above us. "Two of the volunteers came up and asked us if we were American. We thought we were about to be scolded for being too loud, but when we said yes, their eyes lit up. They said they had fought side by side with American soldiers in WWII. The older gentleman had served as a very young soldier at the end of WWI as well."

"That must have been a really special moment," Julien said sincerely.

"Yes!" I eagerly agreed. "They were so cute, wearing their full military garb so proudly."

"I'm sure 'cute' is exactly how a battle-proven World War veteran would love to be described," Julien chuckled.

"Yeah, probably not," I said, blushing. "Especially considering all the medals that decorated their coats. They shared some of their memories, gushing about how much they appreciated and loved the Americans. Made us both feel really good, especially after some of the run-ins we've had with some Parisians who are not so appreciative of Americans."

Julien raised his eyebrows. "Have you faced a lot of that?"

"Not too terribly much. A few incidents, and Lila's boss, who was absolutely horrible to her."

"Poor Lila, she seems so nice!" he empathized.

"She is absolutely amazing! Like a sister. Anyway, the best part happened next."

He turned to me, waiting for me to continue.

"Okay, so the younger veteran had tickets for the upcoming service commemorating Armistice Day, or what we Americans call Veterans Day, and he offered two to us!"

"That's pretty cool."

"So, on November 11, Emilie and I had the privilege of being here, with fewer than 100 other people." I dropped his hand to indicate where we'd been that day, "They'd closed down the entire Champs-Élysées, which is far more impressive when it's completely empty during daylight.

"Just over there," I pointed to the left of where we were standing, "they set up some chairs and small bleachers for the guests, and we watched as a massive military parade of tanks and jeeps and trucks and soldiers rolled down the Champs and circled the Arc as they passed in review before the senior leadership."

"The senior leadership?" Julien asked.

"Yes, now this part was so cool." I clapped my hands together in excitement. "We sat fifty feet away from the defense minister and not much farther away from Jacque Chirac himself!"

"That's cool. I can't imagine visiting the US and being invited to an event where I was so close to the president!" He looked around as if he was imagining the scene playing out and what it might have been like for me.

Nodding my head, I said, "It truly was an unbelievable moment. I absolutely loved watching the military parade."

With the details still fresh in my memory, I recalled my experience from that day. We had sat in bleachers facing the Arc de Triomphe as a full military parade and review passed, giant tanks and jeeps rolling down the cobblestone streets and rows of soldiers marching behind. I had sat so close to two of the most important men in France, who both gave speeches before the parade.

"Yes, you Americans do seem very patriotic." The words were not condescending, rather admirative. "With your military presence, I understand."

"It's more than that for me," I continued. "My dad is a retired fighter pilot, so I have a special love for the military."

"Woah, your dad is like Tom Cruise in *Top Gun*?" Appreciation showed on his face.

I chuckled. "Similar, but he was Air Force. Maverick was a Navy pilot." Smiling, images of my dad yelling at the TV during all the parts of the movie that were "absolutely impossible!" popped into my head. He most certainly would not appreciate being compared to Maverick. But then again, maybe my dad would get a kick out of the comparison, seeing that Julien thought he was so cool for being a fighter pilot.

Julien nodded and lifted my hand to his lips. "That's a cool story, and unlikely to be a memory most Americans can ever share with you. I'm glad you had that moment," he said, kissing my hand.

I looked back to the spot where the festivities took place, my thoughts drifting back to that day. "It's not the most exciting story if you're not into military history, but I'm grateful for the experience," I said, shrugging and slightly embarrassed at how worked up I'd gotten while retelling the story.

"No, I think that's cool. I like that you're interested in so many things." He moved in front of me, grabbing my hands, and stared directly into my eyes. "Actually, I think it's sexy as hell."

His beanie covered most of his hair, with just a few wisps poking out around his ears, further enhancing those eyes. Knees wobbling a little, I blushed, blinking my eyes. Neither of us moved, but stared into each other's eyes intensely. I stepped back before I melted into a puddle of goo.

"Shall we keep walking?" Julien asked, reaching for my hand.

Nodding my head, I looked around, deciding where we should go next.

"Let's go this way," I said. From the Champs we took Avenue Marceau back toward the Seine River. We walked in comfortable silence, taking in the architecture. Most of the buildings were four or five stories, housing storefronts or office buildings on the lower levels and apartments on the upper levels.

"Whoa, watch your step!" Julien maneuvered me around a street sign I'd nearly collided with. I'd been too busy staring up to pay attention to what was in front of me.

"I really adore the architecture in Paris. It's so different from anything you'd see in my hometown." I pointed up. "Take those for instance. All the Juliet balconies. You might find these in big cities, but not like this. These are so ornately designed. I love how beautifully these white stone buildings look with the black steel window dressings." I sighed.

We stood there for a moment, Julien examining the buildings through my eyes. "Yeah, really different from the architecture in Alsace as well."

"Mm-hmm. I could stare at these buildings all day."

"Or all night, apparently," Julien joked, tugging me forward.

A few steps later, I halted once again. "What is this?" I asked, rhetorically, because it was clearly a cathedral of some sort, but it appeared centuries older than anything around it. The steeple climbed so high I wondered if the architect thought the spires might actually touch God. The stones, darker in color than the buildings built next to it and attached on either side, indicated this church was ancient. Julien shrugged and I examined the stone carvings of the disciples in the wall facing the street.

"Do you ever wonder how they were able to carve such intricate details in this stone and build soaring buildings so long ago?" I asked.

"Look at this," Julien pointed out. "They built this church, Saint Pierre de Chaillot, in the eleventh century."

My jaw dropped. "My stars. Old, where I live, was built in the eighteenth century!"

Julien squinted his eyes at me.

"What?" I asked, suddenly self-conscious.

"You're just..." he placed a hand on my cheek. The intensity of his gaze burned through me. This was an exquisite type of torture. *Breathe, Callie, breathe.* I cleared my throat. Julien dropped his hand from my face and moved his arm around my shoulder. "Shall we?"

The silence of the normally busy streets weirded me out a bit. There was no one anywhere. Few sounds, no movement.

My imagination transported us into a horror movie. I expected a zombie attack at any moment. And my ideal apocalypse scenario would definitely include a hot guy by my side. How would Julien and I fare in battle together? I was completely opposed to violence and had never even been in a physical altercation, so I hoped Julien wasn't counting on me to save him. Or maybe I'd have some badass dormant fighting skills and I *would* save him. Yes, I liked that idea. We needed more lady heroes. I wrapped my arm around Julien's waist. His presence comforted me and made me feel safe. I still promised myself that if a zombie jumped out around the next corner, I'd put up a good fight.

I giggled, and Julien tilted his head toward me.

There was absolutely no chance I'd share my thoughts with him. I had to ease him into my silly side slowly. I quickened our pace and stared forward.

"So, what do you have planned for your final days in beautiful Paris?" Julien asked.

"Hmmmm. Well, I have a lot of super fun things to do. Like eat more *pain au chocolat*, because no one can ever eat enough *pain au chocolat*."

Julien laughed, shaking his head back and forth.

"And there is the matter of packing everything, cleaning my apartment, meeting with my super-friendly landlord and hoping she gives me back my deposit."

Julien laughed. "Well, that seems like a tragic way to finish out your trip. I mean, *pain au chocolat* notwithstanding."

"Isn't it?" I giggled. "There is this one thing I've had on my list."

"What?"

"I hate to admit it, but I still haven't climbed to the top of the Eiffel Tower. And I really want to check that off my list before going. I'm probably going to do that on my very last day. Have you been there yet?"

"Yes, but I've never climbed the stairs. Are you actually going to do the stairs or take the elevator?"

I feigned shock. "Elevator? Really? That's for wimps. I'm climbing the 674 stairs. Care to join me?"

"Only 674? I thought it would be more. Manageable." He shrugged.

I smiled, turning to him. "Well, there's actually 1,665, but the stairs to the top level are closed to the public."

Julien raised his eyebrows. "You sure are full of random facts."

I playfully punched him in the arm.

"Hey! I think it's cute that you're nerdy too."

I continued walking. I'd just been called nerdy by a literal computer science geek.

Julien grabbed my arm and pulled me close against him. "But don't worry, I find smart to be sexy."

Flutters started in my stomach and climbed to my heart where they bounced around like a ball in a pinball machine. Pulled tightly against him, staring into his blue eyes, everything else around me disappeared.

"You haven't discovered yet that I'm full of all kinds of useless knowledge?" I whispered.

His brow furrowed and he looked directly at me saying, "Nothing you've told me so far has been boring or useless. I'd love to know what else you've got in that head of yours." His voice was low and scratchy, and neither of us moved, other than the rise and fall of our chests from heavy breathing as he ran his fingers down my jawline.

The world stood still. We faced each other, Julien reaching for both of my hands. Lost in his eyes, my chest heaved up and down. Why, crazy universe? Over the last five hours, I had transitioned from seeking a fun fling to reconsidering my life trajectory. His protective embrace as the crowd tried to crush me, the way he gently brushed my hair from my face, his fun dance moves—he'd shown me so much in a few short hours. Most importantly, he listened to me and engaged in deep conversations on topics beyond weather, sports, and pop culture. And yet, timing had failed us.

"Callie," he murmured, nuzzling his nose on my neck, nearly causing me to explode. Just as I thought we'd kiss, he released me and started walking again.

What was that? What just happened? Why didn't he kiss me?

He moved slightly away and jammed his hands into his pockets. I shoved my tingling fingers deep into my pockets too, stinging from this shift in mood. We walked in silence for a few moments, my brain running in circles trying to understand the shift.

My default mode in awkward situations is to chatter incessantly, so I returned to talking about how much I wanted to climb the tower and see the full view of Paris before returning home.

"Speaking of home, what state are you from?"

"South Carolina. Have you ever been there? Or to the US?" I turned to see his response.

"Never. I thought about visiting Emilie last year when she was studying there, but it never worked out." He shrugged noncommittedly, hands shoved deep in his coat pockets. "Maybe one day."

"I think you would like it. It's a massive country, and it's so different from one state to the next. So much to see. Did Emilie tell you about her cross-country trip?"

"Yes, she did."

"They drove all the way from coast to coast and back. I've

never even done that. I mean, I've driven across the United States with my parents, but it was not to stop and see sights along the way. We drove out to visit my uncles in California."

"Los Angeles? Hollywood?" he asked enthusiastically.

"Nah, didn't really go there."

"I would love to see Hollywood." He turned to me, eyes widening at the idea. "We have so many American movies here, I want to know if it's really like that."

I snorted. "I guess it depends on the movie." Should I invite him to visit me? My heart thundered as I thought about him, with me, back home. Feeling the pressure building inside, I let out an audible sigh.

We both faced forward again and continued walking briskly down the street, two people side by side, the magic of our intimate moment completely gone. I shifted the conversation to family.

"Do you have siblings?" I asked.

"I have a thirteen-year-old brother and my sister, who is seventeen. And of course, Emilie."

"So, how old are you?" I asked.

"Twenty-two. You?"

"I just turned twenty-three."

"Mmmm. An older woman!" He laughed. "And you? Siblings?" he asked.

"Mm-hmm. I have a sister," I said, nodding.

"Let me guess, you're the youngest?"

"Should I be insulted by that question?"

Julien laughed. He stopped walking and turned toward me. "Well, was I right?"

"Yes," I chuckled. "I'm practically an only child, because she's eleven years older than me."

He nodded his head as if that made all the sense in the world to him.

Pondering why he would guess I was the youngest, I asked, "What made you think that?"

"You kind of remind me of my little sister. She's got the same, I don't know, vulnerability, innocence about her."

Innocent? If he'd heard the thoughts that'd been flitting through my mind since the moment I laid eyes on him, he'd reconsider that assessment. And vulnerable. *What did that mean?*

Nodding, I kept walking, lost in my own insecurities. From the corner of my eye, I saw him turn his head toward me a few times, and it seemed as if he might want to say something, but he never did. We continued in silence.

Finally, the cross street dumped us out to Avenue New York. Julien looked at the street sign. "How appropriate."

In front of us stood the massive the Pont d'Alma bridge. My eyes darkened. "This is where Princess Diana died in a car crash. Well, actually under there," I said pointing to the tunnel.

He looked around. "So sad."

We walked a few steps over to the large golden statue of a flame. Originally intended as a monument to represent the friendship of France and the US, it had been taken over as a memorial to Diana. Pictures of the Princess and her boys lay on the ground, surrounded by flowers and a few candles.

I said a quick, silent prayer, and turned back to face the river. Julien stood silently by my side as we both took in the beautiful sights.

But it was the Eiffel Tower that won the night.

"Well, you've outdone yourself tonight, lady," I whispered. We were very close to the Eiffel Tower from this position, and she was still sparkling brilliantly, hours after the end of the New Year's celebration. Bluish lights glittered all the way from the bottom to the top of the tower. I imagined her chanting, "What do you think of me now?"

"Absolutely stunning," I said.

Julien nodded his head in agreement, and we stood silently, paying homage to the tower. I leaned forward, resting my arms on the stone barrier along the river walkway, and Julien moved in behind me, wrapping his arms around me, chin resting on my shoulder. Sighing softly, I hoped the tower recognized my gratitude. Once again, her magic had saved the evening and Julien seemed to be over whatever issue he'd had earlier.

For a few blissful moments, time may have actually stood still. Neither of us spoke, but stood wrapped together, breathing in sync, his breath warm on my ear. It would be difficult to ever recreate a more perfect moment. Then, without a word, we both started walking again.

The magnificence around us struck me. Paris, at night, with no tourists, no cars, no buses. Just the trickling sound of the water. Bridge after bridge spanned the calm, dark water, light from the streetlamps reflected off the dark water below us and provided a beautiful ambiance to the quiet, calm early morning hours. Reaching a smaller bridge, I turned and he followed me.

"Callie," he started, reaching to turn me to face him. He brushed my hair away from my eyes, then grazed my cheek with his finger. Confused by his hot and cold moments, I wanted to lean into this.

"Yes?" I asked, hopefully.

"You're really cute," he said after a pause.

Not what I expected, but I'll take it. Blushing, I replied, "Thank you. I think you're cute too."

"I didn't expect this tonight."

"What did you expect?"

"Just a fun night in Paris with my friends. I didn't ever imagine meeting someone so..."

"So what?"

He reached for my hand and pulled it into his. "So... you."

Nervous giggles erupted. "Well, I am... me."

Julien looked out toward the water. He took his time before continuing.

"You're so different from anyone I've ever met before. You have this vibe of not really caring what the world thinks, and yet, vulnerable, but not in a needy way. More like," he paused, searching for the right words, "more like you have this goodness about you that somehow, this crazy world hasn't managed to squash. And I have this urge to protect you, yet I also feel like you're fully capable of protecting yourself."

I let his words sink in. He had seen all of this in less than eight hours? Guess I wasn't doing a good job of being mysterious at all. They were the kind of words women dream to hear. Also, they were the kind of words that are often followed by a "but." I held my breath, waiting for him to tell me it's been fun, have a nice life.

He continued, "And despite those naughty, naughty moves on the dance floor tonight, you still strike me as innocent."

Squirming a little in discomfort at his compliments, no words seemed to be the right ones to follow this. I wanted to spill my guts, to tell him I was falling for him and that I was terrified that this was just a fun night for him, but I turned back to the water in silence. Placing his arm on my shoulder, Julien gently turned me back around. His eyes searching mine, he reached behind my neck and pulled me closer to gently place his warm lips on mine. Slowly, gently, his lips increased in intensity as our embrace deepened and our tongues found each other's. My hands wrapped around the back of his neck, pulling him tighter into me, pressing his body against mine. I'd died and gone to heaven, I was sure of it. His thumb traced my neck and I ran my hands down his back, finding the bottom of his coat and shoving my hands under the coat and his shirt. He jerked as my cold fingers touched his back, but I barely had time to mutter, "Sorry," before his lips were on mine again. Time was irrelevant. We explored each other's mouths slowly and cautiously. My heart took me to places I hadn't allowed it to go in so long, imagining the potential love story we could have if only I weren't leaving in four days. Scratch that. *Three days now.*

He finally released me, both of us panting, and I held my breath as he traced the line of my jaw, around to my ear, and down my neck to my scarf. My eyes closed, waiting for his lips to find mine again.

"I can't fall for you," he whispered.

And there was the "but." Like a ton of bricks, my heart dropped to the ground and tears pricked my eyes. There was no response to those words, especially after the kiss we'd just shared.

I expected him to start walking again. To end our evening. Instead, he stood next to me, laced his fingers through mine, and for several minutes we stared deeply into each other's eyes, saying nothing. The questions raced through my mind at a million miles per hour. Was he concocting a plan to end this? Thinking about a potential future for us? When he didn't kiss me again, I stepped back and stared at him intently, tracing his features with my eyes.

"What are you doing?" Julien asked.

"I'm taking a mental photograph."

"Huh?"

"I'm trying to commit every detail of your face to memory." I looked down at the ground, suddenly embarrassed.

"Why don't you take a picture with your camera? Or did you leave it at Lila's?" he asked.

Shoving my scarf out of the way, I undid the first button of my coat.

"What's happening here?" he asked, his finger tracing a line down my skin to the low cut of my halter top, eyes darkening. My body tingled as I reached inside my coat to my secret pocket, where I dug out my small camera.

Holding it up, I smiled devilishly. "Strike a pose!" and snapped a picture before he turned.

"Give me that."

He pulled me toward him and turned the camera to face us. "Smile!"

A night, a memory worth cherishing forever. I imagined my future self, clutching this picture, reliving the experience, telling the story to anyone who would listen about the night I met Julien. But I'd have to wait until I got the film developed at home and who knows what the story would be at that point?

Tucking the camera back in my pocket, I bundled up again. We stood in silence on the bridge, Julien once again behind me, arms wrapped tightly around me. As I stared at the beautiful tower, sparkling away as though everything was perfect, I willed myself to forget that he'd ever said he couldn't fall for me and focused on the fact that for now, he was still holding me close.

9

No MATTER how many yawns affronted me, I did not want to budge from this space. I turned so that my back was against the bridge railing, with Julien directly in front of me. Adjusting his scarf to cover his exposed skin, I then slid my hands up under his jacket, resting my hands on his hips. We stood face-to-face, his hands on my shoulders.

Staring deeply into his eyes, feeling pressured by the limited time we had together, I wanted to know everything about him. What made him tick? Noticing his ears were no longer covered by his beanie, I brought my hands up and tugged down on his cap to keep him warm, eliciting a smile and those incredible dimples. Replacing my hands on his hips, I asked, "So, Emilie said you're at Uni in Strasbourg?"

He nodded. "Yep, I'm in my final year studying computer science."

"Oh, so you're a computer geek?" I teased.

"You won't think it's so geeky for long when computers take over the world and us geeks are millionaires."

I liked this self-assuredness. "Fair point. What kind of job do you think you'll get?"

"Probably working for a tech company in Paris."

I pulled him in closer and gave him a soft kiss on the lips before continuing. "The only reason I ever need a computer is to check my Yahoo account and send emails home to my friends and family. I can't imagine wanting to be on a computer all day."

His face lit up as he launched into a description of all the cool things happening in the computer world. Dropping his hands from my waist, he took a small step back, gesturing in excitement about the expansion of the world wide web, gaming systems, and social networks. His enthusiasm, and how absolutely adorable he looked, was getting even me excited about computers.

"You just wait, Callie. Within ten years, almost every house will have a computer. You'll be so plugged in, everything you do will be connected to computers. You'll rely on emails, and one day that will be replaced by video chatting," he said.

For now, I was fine using my computer for emails and hanging out with online friends periodically on AOL. But video chatting. Holy smokes. Even though I was baffled by the technology behind it, my imagination soared. An international relationship stood a chance with the ability to video chat regularly!

Julien's eyes sparkled, and he pulled me closer into a hug. His breath warm on my neck, he continued.

"But the impacts are so much bigger, Callie. Think about medicine and banking and... there are just so many cool things that technology can do to improve our lives."

The wheels in my brain whirred. "Your courses must be really hard." Horrible memories of lines of os and 1s and coding from the computer science and web building courses I'd struggled through flashed through my mind.

"It's not very difficult for me. I love it." He lifted his finger to my face and ran it along my jawline, studying the details of my face.

Teeth chattering, I asked, "So, what do you do when you aren't studying?" I removed my hands from his waist to retrieve my black beanie from my pocket and pulled it down over my ears, immediately returning my arms to his waist.

"Mostly I stalk the American girls on campus."

Smirking, I playfully shoved him back a little from me, shaking my head. He laughed and leaned in, whispering, "I'm just kidding. I play football. We train a lot." While his lips were near my ears, he kissed my neck a few times, melting the icicles forming throughout my body.

Soccer. My hands ran up and down his abdomen, his chiseled stomach confirming his dedication to sports. He nuzzled my neck again, moaning as I shifted in toward him. A firecracker show, not that different from the one we'd watched a couple hours ago, set off inside me as I moved my hands from his chest to his back, feeling the ridges of his muscles.

A comfortable silence settled around us. Warmth moved up my body, and despite the flames shooting through my abdomen, the whirring in my brain would not stop. Did he feel as drawn to me as I did to him? Was he plotting ways to extend our time together? Or was he just living for the moment? Was it absolutely insane that the thought *How do we make this work?* had just crossed my mind?

Emilie's words crept into my mind. *Just don't break his heart, Callie.* Would we be doomed from the beginning?

His mouth stretched open into a big yawn. I yawned even bigger, stretching my arms over my head.

"Geez, it's almost 4 a.m. Maybe we should start walking again? So we don't pass out on the street?"

He nodded, suppressing another yawn, and reached for my ungloved hand. His fingers interlaced with my freezing fingers. Frostbite seemed worth this exchange. I glanced quickly over my shoulder and whispered *good night* to the tower, and we turned to walk in the opposite direction, toward the Louvre.

"How did you wind up here in Paris anyway?" Julien asked as we walked.

"Well, that's a long story."

"I have nowhere else to be," he laughed.

"Let's keep walking down the river," I said. I released his hand and pulled his arm around my shoulder, wrapping my arm around his waist.

"Okay," he agreed. "But you're going to tell me, right?"

My eyes blinked rapidly. What would I tell him? The story did not shine a super positive light on me. Running to France to be with a man who discarded me like a used hanky? Nope. An idea popped into my mind. "Have you ever played the game Two Truths and a Lie?"

He raised his eyebrows, not understanding how this question related to his. "No, I don't know that one."

"Oh, it's fun! I will tell you two things about me that are true, and then one lie. You get to decide which one you think is the lie." Briefly, I became aware that he might think this was the dumbest idea.

He looked at me questioningly. "Okay, I'll play along."

What would I tell him? I hadn't thought this far ahead.

"So, are you going to tell me some stuff?" he asked after a long silence.

"I am, I just want to make sure I pull the best things, so that it won't be so obvious."

"Good idea. But since I know pretty much nothing about

you except you enjoy crawling onto tall, dangerous places and you can move your body on the dance floor, like a pro—oh wait. *Are* you a pro?"

I giggled, playfully tapping my fingers on his chest. "No, just lots of practice."

His eyebrows furrowed together. I flicked my hand as if to dismiss that topic for another time.

"Okay, here we go." I stopped and turned to him. Then I turned my back to him. I peered back at him over my shoulder. "I'm a terrible liar, so I don't want you to see my face when I tell you."

I heard him chuckle.

"Okay. I have four cats. I love history. I came to France to marry the love of my life."

"I really hope the lie is not the cats! Because I already know you love history, thanks for throwing me that bone. And that last one..." his voice trailed off as he probably imagined a sad story of heartbreak.

I turned to him. He looked so cute, hands stuffed in his coat pockets, hat pulled down over his shaggy brown hair, waiting expectantly.

"OK so the history one was too easy. I like cats, but I draw the line at two. So, yes, I came to Paris for love."

His face fell. "Um, so follow-up question. Were you actually with this guy? Or were you just hoping you'd meet someone here?"

Sucking in a deep breath, I contemplated how much I wanted to share. "It's a little embarrassing."

He looked down, shuffled his feet, and then returned his gaze to me. "I'm assuming you aren't still with him?"

"Oh, he's waiting for me back at my apartment. That's why I haven't invited you back to my place."

He pulled in a sharp breath and, as I laughed, realized I

was joking. "That wasn't funny," he said, face reddening as he stared down at the ground. Did I detect some jealousy?

My heart quickened. I shifted uncomfortably, wondering what lay behind that strong response. "No, I'm not with him. He actually dumped me right after I arrived in Paris."

This time Julien stopped dead in his tracks. "What?"

He watched me. "So, you moved to France to be with your guy, and he dumped you right after you got here?"

"Sadly, yes. Ok your turn!"

He turned, a quizzical look in his eyes. "Uh, you can't drop a bombshell like that and then just move on." He paused, turned to me, and grabbed my hands in his, searching my eyes. "Unless it's too painful for you to talk about."

Closing my eyes for a minute, I bit my lip, searching for the right words. The very last thing I wanted was for him to feel pity for me. Should I tell him all the details? Would he think less of me that I had given up everything for a guy who then dumped me, leaving me on my own in this city?

"Well, like I said, I came here believing I was going to marry the love of my life. But he ended it." I shrugged. After a night with Julien, the need for answers about Vic's behavior had dissipated. But despite my fears of Julien's judgment, the words tumbled out of me. I found myself telling him the whole story about how I had met Vic one night in a club as an exchange student and how we'd stayed in touch until I could return to France.

"I can understand why he'd be attracted to you, after seeing you dance tonight," Julien quipped, with a sly smile.

"Well, attraction or not, as soon as I got back to France, he told me it was over, left me in my hotel room, and I haven't heard from him since."

Julien whistled in disbelief, pulling me in for a quick hug.

"How terrible," he breathed into my ear, before stepping

back to look at me. "So, you left your life for him, showed up in Paris, and he just ended it? Just like that?" Julien reiterated in disbelief. When I nodded, he pulled me back into a tight squeeze, rubbing his arms up and down mine lovingly, with no judgment toward me. I relaxed in his arms, head against his chest, again breathing in the smell of his Hugo Boss cologne.

After a few minutes, I stepped away and stared off at nothing in particular. "The worst part is that I'd convinced myself we were absolutely destined for each other."

"How so?"

Shrugging, I thought about it for a minute before continuing. "Well, the night he and I met, my friends had to convince me to even go. And apparently, he and his friends chose that particular club randomly. So, it was kind of a fateful turn of events that even landed us in the same place at the same time. Destiny, I thought." *Kind of like tonight*, I thought. Was this destined for similar heartbreak, like Emilie had warned me?

"So how long were you two together?" Julien asked.

"Almost two years, but most of that was long distance after I came back to the US to finish my degree."

Julien nodded, a faraway look in his eyes. Had I shared too much? Or perhaps he had experienced something similar and this was a triggering story? Or had I just confirmed his thoughts about vulnerability? Although to be fair, I had actually met Julien at a party, not at a nightclub.

"So, when he dumped me, I had two options. Go home or make a life here on my own." Yay for Plan B.

He nodded his head, his expression thoughtful. "How long ago did this happen?" There was that tinge of jealousy again. I kind of liked that he seemed bothered by the knowledge I'd been with someone else, although, haven't we all? I knew exactly what he was feeling, because I already loathed all of his ex-girlfriends.

"I arrived in July."

Julien shook his head, absorbing the story. "French men are dicks," he deadpanned.

I laughed out loud.

"Yeah, it wasn't the best day of my life. But I was lucky. I've had the most incredible six months here. I met Lila. Emilie's, um, I guess your dad, introduced me to Gerard, who needed a bilingual secretary. And the rest, as they say, is history."

He kissed me gently on the forehead. "You're impressive. This is not an easy city for outsiders. I think most people would have just gone back home. But here you are."

"Here I am." I twirled around and curtsied, completely leaving out the details of the misery of those pathetic first few days after the breakup, when I called Vic about eight million times, begging him to change his mind, or how I stalked him outside of his apartment. I'd made a real fool out of myself, trying to convince him we were meant for each other. My eyes unexpectedly filled with tears.

Julien encircled my waist with his arms. "In all seriousness, that guy was a jerk. I hope you know you didn't deserve that?"

His breath was warm against my face and I trembled in his arms. Pulling back to look at me, he said, "No one deserves that kind of treatment."

I leaned into him, and neither of us spoke as he held me, rubbing my back. After a few minutes, he released me, grabbed my hand and we silently continued our walk. Trailing the fingers of my free hand along the stone wall barrier lining the riverfront, I stared down at the river. Several homeless people had made their camps in among the small monuments and statues that lined the grassy section, though the grass was dormant in the winter. The Musée d'Orsay loomed impressively on the left bank of the river, across from us.

"That building," I said, pointing across the river, "used to be a train station. Now it's an art museum, holding a wonderful collection of almost exclusively French art."

"You really should stay in Paris and get a job as a tour guide," Julien said.

A simple suggestion holding a million questions within it. Could I stay in Paris? Would I want to stay? Was this him suggesting I should stay because he wanted me to, or just a comment based on my level of knowledge and love of Paris?

Staying *had* been the original plan, but I'd adjusted everything in the last six months. I'd spent the last month preparing to return home, mentally and emotionally, but not much physically. My room vouched for that statement. I had applied for some internships and my parents had made plans. I even thought my parents had expected this turn of events, never fully believing I'd spend the rest of my days in Paris. They wanted me home. And I missed them.

But Paris! Paris held my heart, certainly. No doubt France powered the eternal flame in my heart. I'd consider coming back permanently. One day. For the right reason. Maybe.

My gaze fixed on the beautiful golden, winged horses, mounted on enormous stone columns on all four corners of the bridge that appeared in front of us.

I sighed. "The Alexander III bridge is quite possibly the most beautiful bridge in Paris," I said, stopping for a moment to take it all in. Julien wrapped his arms around my shoulder, smiling down at me before gazing at the beauty surrounding us.

A motorcycle buzzed by, reminding us that we were not the only people in Paris. Slowly walking along the edge of the river, I stopped at a set of stairs that descended from the road down to the edge of the river. "Want to walk down there a bit?"

Julien nodded and followed my lead. The cobblestones along the edge of the river were uneven, and he steadied me as I tripped on a stone that jutted out above the others. I smiled sheepishly at him and we continued, walking quickly under a bridge that had a raised platform serving as a homeless encampment and smelling strongly of urine.

A little farther down, I stopped and faced the water. The trickling sounds of the water soothed me. Julien wrapped one arm over my shoulder as we stood quietly, taking in the beauty of the quiet setting.

Time dominated my thoughts. The numbers 4:25 blurred in my tired vision on my watch. Our plan had been to walk until the metro started running again at five. Then we'd go our separate ways. Would the magic end at that point?

10

AT THE NEXT OPPORTUNITY, we climbed the stone stairs returning to street level onto the intersection with Rue de Rivoli. The empty Place de la Concorde loomed in front of us. Only hours earlier, we'd said goodbye to Lila and Matt here, surrounded by thousands of people still celebrating the New Year, but now it stood deserted and silent. *So much can transpire in such a short time.*

The pain in my feet shot up and down my legs, numbed only by the serotonin pumping through my body as Julien rubbed his thumb on my fingers. Fueled by the hope that this night would last forever, I kept my focus on Julien rather than the fatigue as we continued our walk. Neither of us spoke, at least not out loud, but our hands communicated desire through our soft touches.

"It's so beautiful," I whispered, as the Louvre came into sight. "I walked past the Louvre every day on my way to work, and yet, even seeing it daily is not enough for it to stop taking my breath away."

Julien leaned over and kissed me on the forehead. "She is a

beautiful sight," he whispered, staring at me, not the Louvre. Pulling me in closely, we continued to walk slowly, arm in arm.

"My European history teacher told us that the basement is so large, the king and the noblemen used to have hunting trips in it. Can you even imagine?" I asked, turning in his direction.

Julien raised his eyebrows, stopping to examine the building more closely, as if he were trying to work out if this was possible.

"I've never found anything to back up that statement, but of all the weird things the French monarchy did, that scenario seems believable."

"I've never visited the Louvre, so I wouldn't know."

I stopped abruptly, dropped his hand and threw my hands up in the air. "How can you be *French* and never visited the Louvre?"

He laughed. "When I move to Paris, I'll add it to my list!" Julien grabbed my hands and placed both our palms together, lacing his fingers with mine. "You can be my tour guide." His voice low, he leaned in, kissing my neck and my ear.

I gasped, tilting my head back. "Mmmm. I'd like that."

In no real hurry, we slowly continued down the street. It was magically quiet and calm, with the exception of the clanking from the boats anchored along the side of the river below us.

Now slightly delirious from fatigue, I blurted out, "I love water."

"Ok, we'll talk about water now," he said, half smiling. "I like water too. But I prefer the ocean. My parents have a little house on the coast, and we spend time there each summer."

"That sounds nice. I live about three hours from the ocean, so I spend a good bit of time on the coast as well. I'm thinking of moving to the coast when I go home."

"I know I'll likely have to work in Paris, but I'm really

hoping it doesn't take me long to have enough money to buy a house in the South of France." As soon as Julien mentioned having a house in the South of France, his entire disposition changed. A dreamy look crossed his eyes, a look I understood as a lover of the coast myself. "Life is slow and sweet down south. Even if I'm working there, I'll always feel like I'm on vacation if I can walk at the beach every day."

A vision played out in my mind. A cute little house near the coast, fresh bread and coffee on the terrace in the mornings before leaving for work, preparing dinner together in the evening and drinking wine until dusk. Making love before falling asleep, only to repeat this happy scene the next day. I sighed longingly.

Snap out of it!

We'd known each other for approximately eight hours, and four of those hours had been spent dancing or walking in crowds with few or no words exchanged. Completely sober by this point, my logical brain took over. *Happily ever after is probably not in the cards for you and Julien.* At least, not with each other.

A loud yawn escaped.

"I'm so sorry!" I did not want our time together to end, but my body was starting to betray my heart. Sleep called to me.

"Me too," Julien said, struggling to suppress his own yawn.

"It's not much further," I said, squeezing his hand. He responded with a kiss on the top of my head, reenergizing me slightly. Lifting one foot and then the other, my feet ached from the activity of the last fifteen hours, which had not included much sitting. A bus stop came into sight. "Oh, thank goodness," I said, releasing an enormous sigh of relief. "This will do," I said, leading him to the bus stop only a few feet away. "We can sit here and wait for the metro to open. The station is just there." I nodded to the entry not far from us.

Julien nodded, following me to the stop.

Dropping onto the bench, another yawn escaped. "Sleeeeep," I mumbled.

"I think I can keep you awake," Julien grinned devilishly, dimples popping out at me, and wrapped his arms tightly around me, nuzzling my ear with his nose. I sunk into him, leaning my head against his shoulder, allowing my eyes to close.

"What are you thinking, Callie?" he asked softly, bringing my hand up to his lips and gently kissing my fingers.

"Home," I mumbled, half asleep.

His posture stiffened. "You're thinking about home?"

Okay, Callie, that was a stupid thing to say.

"Not because I want to be there but because I'm leaving soon and I don't want this to end," I murmured. I'd tried the long-distance thing already, and I didn't intend to watch the sequel. Most sequels suck.

"I can't believe I'm going home in four, well, three days." I lifted my head and shifted to face Julien, sticking out my bottom lip. He reached out and ran his finger along my lip. I resisted the urge to playfully bite his finger and kissed it instead.

"So am I," he replied. "Well, actually two."

Two days! That was an impossible amount of time for this to become anything more than a fun fling, even though tonight rated epic on the scale of romantic encounters. I leaned my head back against him, pushing away thoughts of separation.

"But your home is four hours by train and still in France. My home's across the ocean and very much *not* France," I murmured drowsily.

Julien rubbed his hands up and down my arms, protectively, comfortingly. "You're so different from the girls I know, Callie. I wish we'd met sooner," he whispered, once again kissing the top of my head.

His gentle caresses lulled me further into a docile state, but my brain pinged my conscious thoughts. Who exactly were these "other" girls? Smacked by an unwarranted pang of jealousy, the thought of him with anyone else pricked my heart. I softly replied, "You're different too, Julien." So different. The, "Let's throw caution to the wind and fall in love four days before I move back to the United States," kind of different.

No longer fighting the pull of my eyelids, I closed my eyes as my head rested on Julien's shoulder. My brain juggled random thoughts. Bed. Love. Packing. Sweet kisses. Airplanes. Bed. Julien's smell.

"Hey sleepyhead. The metro is opening up. Ready?" Julien asked, gently shaking me awake.

Yawning again, I slowly stood and leaned on Julien, dragging my leaden legs the short walk to the metro station.

Our time together expired as we took the escalator into the bowels of Paris. At the point where our tunnels diverged to our separate trains, Julien stopped walking and pulled me into a big hug. Snuggled tightly against him, I felt like a crowbar might be necessary to pry my arms from him. Was this the end? My legs ignored the message to turn and walk away from him, rooting me solidly in place.

He squeezed me tightly and kissed me on my forehead, cheeks, nose, and finally softly on the lips. "I will see you tonight."

"You will?" I released my arms and looked at him, blinking my eyes in confusion. Good grief I was tired.

He smoothed my hair back off my forehead. "Emilie's invited us round for dinner. I assumed you'd be there? Since I heard you ask her earlier if it was still on."

"Oh, yes! I will be. I just didn't know you would!" I squealed a little, a second wind hitting me as I realized we would have at least one more evening together. Of course he'd be there. He was her brother. "I can't wait."

Julien pulled me into his arms. I wrapped my arms around his neck and we held each other tightly, swaying back and forth for a few moments. Resting my head on his chest, I breathed in his scent. Couldn't we just stay like this forever?

Julien finally broke the embrace, dropping his arms, and I dropped my hands to my sides. He interlaced his fingers with mine, leaning in, peppering my forehead with kisses.

"*Allez*," he said softly, indicating it was time to go. We kissed each other multiple times quickly on the lips, his soft lips lingering for just a moment, before he dropped my hands, smiling a little, and whispering, "*À demain.*" See you tomorrow.

As he turned to walk down the tunnel toward his train, I grabbed his hand and pulled him back to me for one last hug. "Thank you for a really perfect night," I whispered hoarsely, afraid I might cry.

"*Bonne nuit, ma chérie.*" His sweetheart. One last quick peck on his soft lips and I turned in the opposite direction before losing all my resolve. A quick glance over my shoulder revealed Julien, hands shoved in his pockets and a goofy grin on his face, watching me walk away. Butterflies swarmed in my belly as I darted around the corner and out of his sight.

Nothing short of falling on the train tracks and being tragically run over by the metro could have ruined this night for me. The lines from a song from one of my favorite musicals, *South Pacific*, fought to burst from my lips. "I'm in love, I'm in love, I'm in love, I'm in love..."

I chuckled as I boarded my train, imagining myself spinning around the platform singing these words. That probably would have resulted in the aforementioned tragic scenario, so I refrained. My heart and reality were likely both headed down on a collision course, but I'd deal with that later.

Cold air funneled through the quiet hallways in the metro as I changed to the Green line. I stood up in the middle of the car, gripping a strap, afraid I'd fall asleep if I sat. When the train finally arrived at my stop, I exited and trudged the half block to my apartment building. Buzzing myself in, I crossed the entryway, groaning slightly as I looked up the back stairwell. *Eight flights of stairs*, I told myself. *You can do this.*

Placing a hand on the railing, head down, I slowly huffed my way up. My heart was pounding as I stumbled up the last few steps into the cold, stark hallway with seven other doors just like mine. Finding my door, I pulled my key from my pocket and unlocked it, and entered my tiny room. I pulled off my boots and clothes in the six steps between the door and my bed, and then fell into the twin bed, pulling my down comforter tightly around me. One more glance out my window showed the tower twinkling away as I drifted to sleep, thinking of Julien's soft lips on mine.

11

THE SHARP BANGING of metal pans pulled me out of my short slumber.

"Son of a biscuit," I grumbled. Every time I had a late night, it seemed like Lucy, my neighbor next door, was up early. We shared a wall that was not very thick. I rolled on my side, curling into a ball and pulling the covers tight over my head to try to drown out the noise, but she was making an enormous racket. Prying my eyes open, I tried to focus on the blurry numbers of the clock on my bedside table.

Almost noon.

Now wide awake, I shot up in bed. There was so much to do! I was due at Lila's in two hours to help pack, and in seven hours, I'd see Julien again. I groaned. Why did I have all this stuff? My room was basically a locker, so it didn't take much to fill the joint. It was going to take forever to pack. Dishes, pans, a lamp, and a phone; all the things I'd bought to make my little room "homey." And the clothes. I had twice as many as I'd come with. The walls displayed my favorite memories from both home and my time in France, as well as posters and fliers, souvenirs from my escapades. What if I just grabbed my favorite pics, filled a duffel bag, and abandoned the rest? No, that wouldn't work. I really needed my security deposit back.

Hands on my hips, I scanned the room, trying to decide where to start. My eyes landed on my discarded clothes from the night before and I shivered, replaying the feel of Julien's touch, his dreamy smell, our many kisses, and our sweet conversation. After all these months of loneliness, naturally I had met someone four days before leaving.

Glancing out my window, I blew a kiss at the Eiffel Tower. I forgave her. "Thank you," I whispered, grateful for the magical role she'd played in last night's events. *But now what?*

"Now you pack and clean your room, Callie!" I said. If I wanted my deposit back from the landlord, it needed to be shipshape.

I looked at the clock again and groaned. Somehow, I'd wasted a precious ten minutes standing in the middle of the room daydreaming about Julien. "Get moving!" I told myself.

Combat shower time. I literally had about two minutes of hot water each day, and the shower stall reminded me of a phone booth. So, it was what I imagined a shower at boot camp would be like. I wasn't complaining, though. Not long after moving in, I had learned from Lucy that this was the only room on the floor that had a shower. Better two minutes of hot water than walking six blocks to the showers at the public swimming pool, like the rest of the immigrants that lived on my floor. If I ever gave you the impression I lived in a nice place, imagine having to share a toilet with eight other strangers—most of them men. Thank goodness my grumpy landlord had added a shower to this room. Because *eww*, showers at swimming pools are always full of other people's hair and God only knows what else.

Turning on the water, I rapidly put shampoo in my hair,

scrubbed the makeup from last night off my face, rinsed the shampoo out, and had just enough time to run conditioner through and lather up my body, squealing as the frigid water hit me. Then, teeth chattering, I exited the shower booth, wrapped my towel tightly around me, and dug through a pile of clean clothes. I settled on my most comfy, favorite pair of light blue corduroy pants, a plain t-shirt and a cute sweater, and, for the sake of my aching feet, went with my Doc Martens.

I whipped some gel through my short hair to give it a little sass, threw on some lip gloss and mascara, and I was good to go. The chilly air would ensure my cheeks were nice and rosy.

Not wanting to waste any more of the precious time I had with Lila today, I moved quickly, putting on my coat and scarf and grabbing the box of items to take to Emilie's, then darted out of my living quarters. Eight flights of stairs, one block to the metro, and I was back down in the piss-smelling wind tunnels that I'd left just hours earlier. I shimmied awkwardly through the turnstile with the box and made my way to the platform.

There were very few people in the metro since almost everything was closed on New Year's Day, which suited me fine. I enjoyed having some time to rehash the moments of bliss with Julien. I mentally replayed our conversations, remembering his soft lips grazing across my cheek, neck, and ears. The way he smelled, the warmth of his hands, those adorable dimples. How he had unzipped my jacket, encircled my waist with his arms, and pulled me closely to him. My skin tingled where his hands had touched my bare skin and butterflies beat their wings in a torrent in my abdomen.

Lost in my daydream, I almost missed my stop, only scrambling to get out of my seat and off the train as the alarm sounded forebodingly that the doors were closing. Sweat rolled down my back and my arms ached from carrying the heavy box as I scurried down the long hall. For the love of all things holy, the stupid exit escalators were turned off again.

After climbing out of the dark metro and into the sunlight, I walked two blocks before arriving at the place I'd practically lived the last four months. Lila's apartment had been our jumping-off point for exploring the nearby tourist attractions—Notre Dame, the Pantheon, the Sorbonne, the Luxembourg Gardens, and the Rodin Museum. And even though the shops in Saint-Germain-des-Prés and the neighboring Latin Quarter were way outside our budget, we'd spent many hours browsing through the aisles and giggling about what we could buy if we had extra money—we'd spent what we had recklessly on Paris's nightlife.

Now, as I stood in front of the large green door that had welcomed me for the last few months, tears pricked at my eyes. This would be the last time I'd enter this building. Balancing the heavy box on my hip, I typed in the code to enter her apartment building, pushed open the heavy wooden door, and walked across the courtyard, hollering up at Lila's open window on the way. Popping her head out, she greeted me with a Cheshire cat grin.

"Come tell me everything!"

Unlike the very narrow, straight staircases I had in my apartment building, the beautiful wooden spiral staircase up to Lila's apartment wound around the center support gently. The stairs squeaked and groaned with each step, the railing worn soft from all the many hands that had caressed it on the way up and down. Climbing the stairs, I thought about the many evenings I'd come straight here from my office for our standard meal of pasta, baguette, and brie cheese. Once we'd gobbled down enough to soak up any beer we drank later, we wandered over a block to the nearby English pub, the Frog and the Princess.

Oh, the Frog. So many shenanigans had played out there. Lila had worked there for a very short time as a waitress, and we'd gotten to know the staff quite well. Trivia night, sports night, quiet just-drink-a-beer nights, the Frog was our version of *Cheers*. Everyone knew our names.

Lila stood in her door frame, hands on her hips, long hair pulled back into a low ponytail, and her head covered with a bandanna. Even in a faded-out Grateful Dead t-shirt and a pair of old corduroy pants, she looked adorable. Eyeing the large box, she said, "Honey, I'm moving out, what on earth did you bring over?"

I chuckled. "It's for Emilie, don't worry."

She nodded her head, relieved. I set the box down just inside the doorway and peeled off my coat, hanging it and my bag on a hook in the hallway and grabbing her in a big hug, choking back my tears. "I can't believe this is our last afternoon together."

"I have no time for ooey gooey sadness right now. Give me the deets! Stat!" Lila shoved me back playfully, raising both her eyebrows expectantly.

"Oh gosh, I don't even know where to start. In summary, he's charming, cute, and so sweet. And funny!" I sighed deeply, arms hanging limply by my sides.

"Uh-oh."

"Uh-oh, what?" Matt sauntered in from the main room and grabbed me in a brotherly hug.

We moved from the hall into the main room and I flopped on the bed, a large "oof" of air coming from my lungs.

"Uh-oh," Lila repeated. She and Matt exchanged glances like worried parents.

"Yeah," I said softly. I sat up and looked at them both. "You guys, he's perfect." I sighed again. My thoughts drifted to the way he'd so gently kissed me, held me closely, explored me.

Was he replaying every moment in his mind too, desperately wishing away the time until we'd see each other again?

Once again Lila and Matt exchanged looks.

Lila sat down beside me and put her hand gently on my thigh. "You're leaving in three days, Callie. Be careful. You don't want to get too invested if..." Lila trailed off.

"If he's not in the same place..." I threw my arms over my head and flopped back on the bed. "I know and it sucks."

"So what happened last night?" Matt asked, pulling up a chair. Sometimes he really was just one of the girls.

I turned on my side, propping my head up on my hand and turned to look at both of them. "Well, we danced a lot at the club. Then everyone else went home and Julien and I walked around Paris until the metro opened. We talked about everything. It was so romantic."

"Okay, sister. That's the boring version. Any kissing?" Lila asked.

A shy smile crossed my face as I nodded, but I didn't share anything more. The details were only for me.

"Did he go home with you?" Matt asked, eyebrows raised.

"No. We said goodbye and went our separate ways. But he'll be at Emilie's tonight." I beamed at the thought of seeing him in a few hours.

"Tell me all the details while I pack," Lila said as she stood, holding out her hand to help me off the bed.

As I helped her sort through what to throw out or take home, fold her laundry, and cram every last thing we possibly could into her suitcases, I told them about the entire night. Occasionally, one of them would ask a question or interject something, fully invested in the story.

"Pause for a second, Callie. I need your help." Lila sat on her suitcase and Matt and I pushed down and worked together to get the zipper to close. Huffing and puffing, we managed to secure it.

After accomplishing this major feat, I sat on the floor next to Matt. "I'm scared."

Wiping her brow, Lila sat down next to me and took both my hands in hers. "Callie, you know I want you to be happy more than anything in the world. But you're going back to the States, permanently, in three days. And the look on your face tells me you're smitten."

It was true. My friends had criticized me in the past for how hard and fast I fell. Emilie had teased me about progressing from stranger to wedding with Vic. She and I saw the world very differently in this aspect. She never hesitated to walk away from a guy without regrets, whereas I plowed full speed ahead, determined to find my happily ever after. That was probably the reason Emilie had acted so weird last night.

"Should I not see him tonight?" My voice quivered, surprised at the depth of sadness this idea evoked.

Matt jumped in. "I think you should find happiness in every moment you can in your last few days here, Callie girl, but from a guy's perspective, no matter how awesome he is, he's probably only thinking about how he can screw you before you leave."

Lila cut Matt a sharp look, and while Matt's words hurt, I knew he probably was right.

Lila rubbed my back as I contemplated my next words. "He just doesn't seem like that kind of guy. He never asked me to come with him last night or asked to come home with me. If he was just in it for sex, wouldn't he have tried last night?"

Matt shrugged his shoulders. "Not all guys are dogs, but even if he didn't just want a one-night stand, I doubt he's thinking about anything with you past Tuesday."

My body deflated like a sad balloon. He was right. Of

course, he was right. Four—no, *three* now—days in Paris. Nothing else.

Lila squeezed my knee. "I'm sorry you met such a great guy right at the end."

"I know. It stinks."

Lila scrunched her eyebrows, deep in thought. Sucking in a deep breath, she said, "Callie, you're a 'yes' girl."

I furrowed my brow, waiting for her explanation, unclear as to where she was going with this.

"We have had some of the greatest adventures together here, and you're always willing to try new things, to find adventure. It's one of your greatest qualities. So, follow your gut. If this feels right, go for it. You know the potential for heartbreak, but what if he feels the same way? Don't you owe yourself the opportunity to explore that?" Lila paused as I contemplated her words. "Yes, you may get hurt. But you already know you can survive and move on if it doesn't work out. But what if it does?"

I tucked my knees into my chest, thinking about what she had said. *What if it does?*

Lila patted my back, stood, and walked into the kitchen. She returned a few moments later with two bottles of wine and three glasses. "No room to take these in my luggage. Shall we?"

12

Despite the two bottles of wine, Matt, Lila, and I still had to finish packing and cleaning up her apartment. As we drank and chatted, listening to Jamiroquai and other funky beats, we reminisced about our adventures. Lila put the items she wanted to take home in the bag, chucking the garbage in a big bag. Matt cleaned, while I removed pictures and memorabilia from the walls, bookshelves, and tables.

I laughed as I picked up a framed picture of Lila and me, arms around each other, dressed in our hippie gear with scarves tied into headbands pulling back our hair.

"The Haunted Hostel!" I turned to Matt. "Did we ever tell you this story?" He shook his head no.

"We stayed at this hostel on our way to visit Mont St. Michel." Lila and I took turns telling the story. We had completely winged our trip, stopping in a town between Normandy and Mont St. Michel. Our guidebook listed several acclaimed hostels in the area, and we had decided on a quaint hostel, which sounded much nicer than many others we'd visited. But when we'd arrived for check-in, the hostel was unlocked but totally unattended.

After we had waited for a little while, Lila and I started to consider finding a different place, but then a group of travelers about our age entered the hostel.

"Waiting for the attendant?" a blonde girl with an Australian accent said.

We both nodded.

"Well, she's gone for the night," she replied.

"At 5:00?" I exclaimed. Lila and I looked at each other. It was just getting dark outside, but it was cold and rainy, and neither of us wanted to go back out to find another place. As I reached down to grab my bag, the blonde Aussie continued.

"But she left everything open. The keys, the cash box. We've just been self-checking people in as they arrive." She nodded toward the office, which was open.

"We thought maybe the attendant had gone on a break or something, but after waiting awhile and with no one coming, we decided to check ourselves in," Lila giggled. "Just like Jennie said, the office was open, the room keys were there, and when we opened the drawer, all of the cash was just sitting there. Jennie told us there were plenty of beds available in her room, so we added enough to cover the cost for the two of us, got keys to room three, and followed Jennie."

"I mean, how crazy was it that absolutely no one was there to run the place, and they left the money drawer unlocked?" I threw my hands up as I asked the question.

"I think the crazy part is that you two broke-ass girls didn't *take* all the money from the money drawer!" Matt added. Lila and I both laughed. Neither of us were the type to steal, no matter what our situation was. In fact, we had left money for the nightly fee, and a little extra for the food we'd eaten.

"That place was so creepy, there was no way I was stealing

anything. I'm sure it was being watched over by something," Lila said, and I nodded my head in agreement. The building was really old, to start with. Everything creaked and groaned, lights flickered, and it was bone-chillingly cold. Despite all of this, it was also very charming.

Matt looked back and forth between the two of us as we shared the details of that evening. About eight other students from Australia and England had come in throughout the evening from their various adventures. We'd scoured the kitchen for food, opened some bottles of wine, and hung out in the common area. Despite the odd environment, we'd spent the evening in deep conversation with this group of strangers. I'd spent almost the entire time with this adorable couple from Australia. They were traveling Europe for six months after they'd finished their studies. It was their premarriage voyage. If they still liked each other after a no-frills budget trip, they knew they were right for each other.

"That's an interesting concept," Matt chimed in, as he wiped down the surfaces in the living room. "How was that working out for them?"

I stopped peeling tape off the back of some photos and turned to face him, leaning back on the wall. "They seemed to be great when we saw them," I said. "They were always touching, looking at each other and sharing inside jokes. It was disgustingly cute." Lila nodded her head in agreement.

My thoughts wandered back to Julien and how he'd pulled me in close, almost always touching me in some gentle manner. How would we fare on a six-month, low-budget backpacking trip to a bunch of unfamiliar countries? Would we weather language barriers and frustrating public transportation and budget issues without cracking? Or would we discover we were 100 percent incompatible? Furthermore, would he even be interested in a trip like that? I knew so little about him.

Matt was still waiting for my reply, so I continued. "They said they'd had their ups and downs, but they were learning a lot about each other. The guy, for example, knew not to give tickets and important papers to his lady, because she had a tendency to misplace things." I laughed, thinking about the stories they'd shared with me about their trip.

Matt looked at Lila, raised his eyebrows and chuckled. "That would be the complete opposite scenario with us." He nodded his head in Lila's direction. "She takes anything important."

My thoughts returned to the Australian couple. They'd clearly been in love, holding hands, gently caressing each other's arms, his hand resting on her knee. Even when recounting the parts of their trip that seemed strained, they talked as if it'd been the funniest thing ever. I remembered at the time that I'd never had that with Vic. That absolute camaraderie, respect, and desire to do anything and go anywhere with your special person. That encounter, with this couple whose names I didn't remember, opened my eyes to what it looks like when you find the *one*.

———————

Lila's bags were finally packed, the apartment cleaned. Standing in the center of the room, I scanned the room, trying to commit everything to memory, replaying some of my favorite memories that happened here. Especially last night. Staring at the window, I visualized Julien leaning into me as we had our first conversation, drinking in the smell of his cologne. Tears welled in my eyes. I wasn't ready for any of this.

Matt and Lila sat smoking at the table by the window, satisfied with their work, and I joined them. When we'd finished our cigarettes, Matt stood, walked over to the pile of luggage, and began staging it in the hallway. Lila walked slowly around the room, running her fingertips across the surfaces, checking in the nooks and crannies for misplaced items. But from the faraway look on her face, I knew she too was rehashing precious moments. Before moving to the hallway to grab my coat and belongings, I turned back once more to the window, where Julien and I had had our first meaningful conversation.

Lila tapped me on the shoulder, indicating it was time to go, and we grabbed each other's hands. Tears pricked at my eyes as I realized our life together in Paris was coming to an end, and both of us were moving into the complete unknown. Lila had been my everything for the past few months. My travel buddy, my cheerleader, and my counsel as she'd listened to all of my challenges, fears, and problems. She was the person who knew me the best in this world. And now we were going our separate ways.

We said nothing but held hands quietly.

After a moment, I said, "Thank you for the amazing memories!" to both Lila and the studio. I dropped Lila's hand, turned and moved to the hallway while putting on my coat, and grabbed the bag of stuff I'd left the night before and the box for Emilie. Lila put on her coat and followed me out, locking the door behind us, and the two of us silently descended the stairs for the final time.

Brushing away tears, I helped them load their bags into the back of the waiting taxicab.

"This isn't forever goodbye, you know that, right?" Lila comforted me as I tried to hold back the flood of tears.

"I know, but it feels like..."

"I know what you mean," she whispered, grabbing a tissue out of her bag to dab at her own eyes. "It feels like we're leaving a part of our lives we'll never experience again." She reached into her bag again and pulled out her beret, putting it on her head. "We'll always have these."

I laughed, pulling her into another hug and we continued to hold each other close until Matt cleared his throat. "It's time," he said.

Matt pulled me into a tight hug. "Come visit us anytime, Callie girl." He crawled into the back of the cab and gave me his lopsided grin.

Lila wrapped her arms around me. "I hope your last couple of days are magical."

My tears flowed openly now. "I'm so glad I stalked you after our chance encounter!" I blubbered. We both laughed.

"Me too, babe, you're my sister now." Lila, a little bit hippie and a lot of love, smiled and ducked into the cab. She turned, waving wildly, and as the cab pulled away from the curb, a loud sob erupted out of its window.

The cab stopped. Stunned, I watched as Lila jumped out and ran to me.

"You realize that you and I are not in a rom-com movie, right?" I joked, as I wiped away the tears. "You've already got me. You don't have to come running back to profess your love."

She snickered and moved in closely, grabbing both of my hands in hers. "Callie, I think I know you better than anyone else in the world right now."

I nodded, sniffling. My connection with Lila was stronger than most of my relationships.

"I want you to hear me now. You're amazing. You're smart, you're young. Don't be afraid to just be you. Even if it means being *alone*. This idea that you must be with someone to be complete, well it's just bullshit."

I cocked my head to the side, unsure as to whether she was complementing or chastising me.

Despite the loud honking of a car that was blocked behind the taxi, Lila continued. "Say yes, always, Callie, when it feels right. It's your nature and it's how you'll find your way," she said, her voice wavering. "So, if you feel this is worth pursuing, go all in. Leave nothing on the table. But, if you have any doubts at all, if you're just afraid of what is next for you, if this isn't exactly what you want, don't do what you did with Vic. Don't put the rest of your life on hold because you're trying to fulfill this fantasy of falling in love and staying in France."

Her words struck hard. A loud gong vibrated inside my head. She was giving me permission to go full speed ahead, and yet, also the permission to abandon ship if that's what I needed to do. Lila knew that I often grabbed onto something and held tight, like a vicious pitbull, even if everything inside of me knew it was wrong.

I nodded slowly.

"Be careful with your heart, okay?" Lila kissed me on the cheek, gave one last squeeze, and jogged back to the car, smiling sweetly at the driver who was honking and gesturing wildly for them to move.

She blew one last kiss in my direction. Tears streaming down my face, I waved until the taxi left my sight. Alone on the sidewalk, I was left with a different kind of broken heart, a bag full of leftovers, and a box of memories to leave with Emilie.

13

WIPING AWAY TEARS, I dragged the box and bag back to the metro station, following the route I'd taken many times over the past three months, from Lila's apartment to Emilie's. A five-minute walk, four stops on the first line, a train switch, three more stops, and another five-minute walk. It gave me plenty of time to think about Lila's words.

While I wanted nothing more than to lose myself in romance, truthfully, Julien and I didn't really know each other. A few hours of fun and conversation barely cracked the shell of who we were. Did I really want to throw myself into a guy, only to face certain heartbreak and sadness? But the fear of missing out on the greatest love of my life pulled stronger at me than the fear of being hurt.

The weight of my robust to-do list pulled on me. While it wasn't a long list—pack, spend time with Emilie, check off a few remaining bucket list items—it would still be difficult to do it all *and* spend time with Julien. My skin warmed at the memory of his touches, and the tourist sites that seemed so important for me to see before leaving suddenly paled in comparison with my desire to explore more of my connection with Julien. The monuments had survived thousands of years and two world wars. They'd wait for me to see them another time, right?

My arms ached from the heavy load I was carrying and felt like they might actually break off if I continued much further. Thankfully, Emilie's building appeared in front of me and I set the box down for a moment, wiping the sweat from my brow. Unbuttoning my coat, I fanned my sweater out a few times, desperate for cool air. My heart pounded in anticipation of seeing Julien, and I hadn't even started climbing the stairs yet. All these freaking stairs. Emilie lived on the fifth floor, and one would think I'd be in great shape with all the stair climbing I did, but the bread, wine, beer, and smoking certainly hadn't helped. Willing myself to get this part over, I picked up the box and bag of food, entered her building, and started climbing. Huffing, I knocked on the door to Emilie's apartment, anxiety tearing at my innards.

Emilie flung the door open and smiled, dimples like Julien's flashing at me. That was the end of their similarities. Tiny Emilie looked adorable in her jeans and an oversized sweatshirt. She pulled me in for an awkward hug around the box and bag.

"Lila and Matt all packed up?" she asked. "I know that it was hard to say goodbye. You okay?"

I nodded, afraid that if I said anything, the waterworks would begin. The box dropped with a thump on the ground and I handed Emilie the bag.

"Oh good, you remembered the food!" She grabbed the bag and delivered it to her kitchen.

Relief filled me when I saw Emilie and I were alone. I pulled off my coat, hanging it in the small closet. Her small studio—a huge room with a balcony, a small bathroom, and a kitchen off to the side—put my shoebox to shame. Her bed, a pullout couch, could be stowed away during the day, creating a large open space, in front of which sat a large rectangular coffee table where we ate. A cherrywood bookshelf on the opposite side of the room overflowed with books of all shapes and sizes, many of them for her coursework at the Sorbonne. The top two shelves held her stereo and equally impressive CD collection. The studio was cozy yet allowed multiple people to gather.

"What's all this?" Emilie asked, perusing the contents of the box. She pulled out some cookware, smiling since she had so little kitchen gear, as well as the terry cloth robe she'd lent me, and a few other odds and ends that I'd collected that couldn't travel home with me.

"I can vary my daily menu now!" She lifted one of the skillets above her head in celebration and took the pans to the kitchen. "Drink?" she asked, showing me a bottle of unopened wine.

I nodded. "Please. I'm just going to wash my face quickly." Wiping down my face and neck with a cool washcloth quickly, I checked my appearance, teased my hair a bit, and then joined Emilie in the small kitchen just steps away from the bathroom.

"So did you have a great time last night?" She bit her lip as she asked, avoiding eye contact, and suddenly busied herself putting snacks into small dishes and pouring wine.

"Yes, it was amazing," I replied dreamily, leaning against the small counter space.

Emilie raised her eyebrows and turned to face me, handing me a glass of wine, which I accepted gratefully with a smile. "What did you do?"

My cheeks flushed and I told her about the evening, walking all through Paris. "Emilie, we talked all night long. Literally, all night long."

"Really?" She looked surprised.

I shook my head enthusiastically. "All night long."

"What did you guys talk about?" Emilie turned her back to me and went back to the food preparation.

"Everything. He's so fun and interesting and sweet..." my words drifted off.

When I released a deep sigh, Emilie glanced over at me and set down the knife she was using. "Oh, geez."

"Oh, geez what?"

"I've seen that look on your face before," Emilie said.

"What look?" I asked.

"You're lovesick."

"Would that be so bad?" I asked Emilie.

She wiped her hands on a towel, and moved to my side, linking arms with me. We stood in silence for a few moments, leaning on the kitchen counter, sipping our wine. Finally, she asked, "Can you help me prepare the rest of the food?"

I nodded my head, grateful for the distraction from the whirlwind of thoughts and emotions threatening to knock me over. The Coldplay album came to an end and Emilie moved into the living room to change the CD. She put in a French group, Noir Désir, shifting the mood as we hummed along to the upbeat rock music.

My tummy rumbled as I spread smoked salmon paste on small toasts, organized little pickles on a tray, and poured pretzels and chips into small bowls, sneaking in a few bites here and there. The tiny pretzels struck me as a good visual representation of my nerves, which were also wrapped up as tight as I awaited Julien's arrival.

When the danger of a meltdown faded, I placed my hand on Emilie's arm and said softly, "He's really a neat guy, Em. Why haven't you introduced me to him sooner?"

She stopped and looked at me. And said nothing. I

squirmed, waiting for an uncomfortably long time before she finally spoke.

"I didn't really want you to meet him."

Not what I'd expected. "Why not?" My hurt and confusion matched each other.

Emilie breathed in slowly and turned back to the dish she was preparing.

"Emilie, why?" I insisted, moving closer to her.

"Because I believed you'd break his heart. Or he'd break yours," she said softly.

Stunned, I wasn't quite sure how to respond. "Why would you think that?"

Again, she paused, taking her time to choose her words carefully. My heart was racing, and nausea crept in.

"Well," she began, "for one, all you've talked about the last couple months is Vic. How much you loved him, how much he hurt you, your fear of never loving anyone that hard ever again."

"Okay," I said, placing my hands on the countertop to stabilize my shaking legs. Emilie and I didn't often have disagreements and the tension physically impacted me. I let out a deep breath. "That's a fair assessment, even though I think you know I'm well over Vic by now. But what about before?"

"What do you mean?"

"We spent four months at Uni together before Vic was even in the picture and you never introduced me to him then, either." I stared at the ground. Was this really worth getting worked up over? It was not Emilie's duty as my friend to find a romantic partner for me, and really, who wants to set their friend up with their brother anyway?

"Well, that's a little easier to explain," she said. She wiped her hands on the tea towel and turned to face me, crossing her arms as she leaned back on the counter. "The whole time we were in Mulhouse he was also in a very serious relationship, so there was no need to introduce him to any of my single friends. And then you met Vic, and you were madly in love and busy every time Julien was around."

"Mm-hmm," I nodded.

Emilie continued. "I didn't introduce you because, well, I knew you wanted a relationship with a French guy, and maybe I didn't want to take a chance that you'd develop feelings for him. You fall easily and I don't want to see either of you get hurt."

A whooshing noise started in my ears, and they suddenly felt like they were on fire. I turned and walked into the main room, grabbing my cigarettes from my bag on the way. Lighting one by the balcony door, I took in a deep drag, needing a moment to compose myself. Her concern for her brother was understandable, but it stung that she didn't trust me. Why would she assume I'd just hurt Julien? Did she think so little of me?

Emilie came over to my side and lit her own cigarette, staring out at the building across the street for a moment before she spoke.

"Look, don't take it personally Callie, I wasn't doing it out of malice. It's complicated on Julien's end too. And you kept talking about going home and starting over. It didn't make sense to introduce you to him." She paused. "Please know I thought I was doing what's best for both of you." Her voice was filled with compassion, concern showing in her brown eyes.

My hands shook as I lifted the cigarette to my mouth, considering her reasons for purposefully avoiding introducing us. Deep inside, I knew Emilie was telling the truth. She hadn't wanted to set us up, not only to protect me, but also her brother. And I'd certainly done my part in telling her I was not interested in starting anything new here. Over the past few months, I'd given her the same message over and over.

I'm strong. I'm independent. I have my whole life ahead of me. It's time to focus on me, not finding a love interest with so little time left in France.

We'd spent months talking about how I'd perhaps forced a relationship with Vic because I was more focused on achieving my goal of spending my life in France instead of looking for any red flags that would have indicated it was not a good match. But now that I'd met Julien, I wondered how things would have played out if I'd met him sooner.

I put out my cigarette and turned to Emilie.

"I understand your perspective. But I want you to know, I believe Julien and I shared a real connection. It was more than just a physical attraction or a meaningless hookup. In fact, after we left the club, other than holding hands and hugging, he didn't even kiss me again until we'd been walking and talking for a very long time." Emilie raised her eyebrows at this. "But once he kissed me, it ignited something in me different from anything I've experienced with anyone else. Not even Vic. If we'd met sooner, who knows..." My voice trailed off.

A banging on the door interrupted us, sending my heart into my throat. A new fear settled in. How should I greet him? Should I kiss him on the cheeks like friends do in France, or should I go in for a kiss on the lips? What if he avoided my kiss if I tried to do that? Speaking of kisses, cigarette breath, yuck. I pulled a mint from my pocket and popped it in my mouth.

I stood planted in the middle of the room as Emilie moved to open the door. As the door opened and I saw him, tousled hair flopping down on his forehead, coat unzipped to reveal a blue shirt the color of his eyes, and perfectly fitted jeans, I bit my lip and sucked in a deep breath. My whole body buzzed with excitement, wanting nothing more than to run into his arms. Instead, playing it as cool as possible, I gave a casual little wave, betrayed by the enormous smile on my face. To my relief, I saw the same emotion reflected followed by a big smile. It was the kind of smile that obliterated any good-girl thoughts and made me completely second-guess my decision to go home alone this morning.

Julien pecked Emilie on the cheek and beelined it across the room in my direction, pulling me into a giant hug and kissing my neck.

"I missed you today," he whispered. Breathing in the smell of his cologne, I rested my head on his shoulder, feeling at home in the crook of his arm. Pushing Emilie's warning away, I whispered, "Me too."

Philippe and Fred removed their coats, handing them to Emilie, who hung them in her small closet, and I broke away from Julien to greet the other two. Philippe winked at me. *I think he's rooting for me.*

"Anyone want a drink?" Emilie asked, moving to the kitchen, avoiding eye contact with me. "Food's there," she said curtly, pointing to the table where we'd laid out the spread of appetizers for everyone to enjoy.

Not knowing what else to do, I moved to the kitchen in a daze and helped Emilie get the drinks, neither of us saying a word.

14

By the time we returned with the drinks, Fred had devoured a plate of brie toasts with smoked salmon as if he hadn't eaten in a week.

"Mmmm, this is so good," he mumbled, crumbs falling on his, of all things, Guns N' Roses t-shirt.

Emilie rolled her eyes. "Eat much?" She picked up the empty plate and walked back into the kitchen.

"Don't mind him, he's an animal," Philippe piped up, politely placing a tart in his mouth and smirking at Fred. Fred grunted in reply and we all laughed.

The three boys were on the couch, so I pulled a chair up next to Julien, reaching for a handful of snack mix as I plopped into the hard, uncomfortable chair. I crossed my legs and that didn't work. Next, I crossed my ankles. Nope. This was a bum-numbing chair. Julien's lap looked far more inviting. I sipped my drink and tried to just sit quietly.

"So, Callie, how did you and Emilie become friends anyway?" Philippe asked, wiping his mouth with a napkin. His warm brown eyes exuded kindness behind his glasses.

"We were in the English program together when I came over as an exchange student two years ago," I said. I glanced at Emilie, who'd put a chair on the opposite side of the table. She took a sip of her wine, avoiding eye contact.

"Wait, you were in Mulhouse?" Philippe asked in surprise, pushing his glasses up on his nose. Julien also looked surprised.

"Yep. So close to you guys," I said, catching Julien's eye. Mulhouse, where I'd gone to school, was only about an hour away from where they lived in Strasbourg. Strange how many times I'd been to Strasbourg, and been so close to Julien, and how many times he'd been to Mulhouse, yet we'd never crossed paths.

"So why were you, an American, studying in the English program?" Fred asked. "Don't you already know all that stuff?"

I chuckled. It did seem a little silly. "All the international exchange students went into the English program. But we were working on the French part of the translation, as opposed to the English part. So, my grades reflected how well I translated in and out of French, as opposed to English."

Fred nodded his head. "That makes sense."

"I had mostly English and French translation classes, but I also took Japanese for a couple of weeks."

"You speak Japanese?" Julien's jaw dropped.

"Ha, hardly! I don't know what I was thinking when I added that as a class! I barely spoke French." Everyone laughed as I recounted how long it took me to first translate the assignment from French to English and then into Japanese. "I dropped the class after about two weeks!"

"My head hurts thinking about it!" Fred lamented.

"Your head hurts just from thinking!" Philippe teased him, punching him lightly in the shoulder. Fred grabbed Philippe by the head and tried to maneuver him into a headlock, as they both laughed.

"You guys are going to knock over the table!" Emilie snapped.

Conceding, Philippe threw his hands up, and Fred released him.

"What's your degree in?" Philippe asked me, cheeks red from being chastised.

"Callie is actually a political science graduate," Julien said, a smile crossing his face. He reached over, placing his hand on my leg as he said this. Was that *pride* I heard in his voice? Cocking my head, I smiled warmly, pleased that he'd remembered personal details.

"Politics, huh?" Fred asked. "I have so many questions about American politics."

Philippe snorted, then hid behind his beer as Fred looked questioningly at him.

Emily and I shared an amused look. "Ask away. It's my favorite topic," I said. I shifted to get more comfortable, pulling both of my legs into the chair and crossing them, leaning forward, elbows on my thigh, ready for anything he might throw at me.

Fred chuckled. "Well, it's not really that deep of a question. Just wondering what you thought about your president?"

Squinting my eyes at Fred, I tapped my pointer finger on my chin and leaned in further. I knew enough about Fred now to know where this was heading. "You mean, about the cigar? Or the pizza? Or the dress?"

Emilie snickered. "Seems like you understand Fred well enough."

"Come on, Fred. Sex scandals are standard in French politics," Julien said, shrugging his shoulders.

Fred threw his arms up in defense. "Still, I wondered if all of that was true. I thought Americans were more prudish," Fred interjected.

I snorted. Bill Clinton was certainly not prudish. "It appears to be true. And yes, especially among conservatives, people were shocked, or at least they feigned shock for the purpose of having a reason to criticize Clinton. And for the record, it's not that it doesn't happen, it just seemed to be hidden better from the public, or perhaps ignored in the past." Reaching back toward the table, I swiped up a handful of pretzels and popped them in my mouth, enjoying the salt and crunchiness.

Philippe stood, raising his empty beer bottle. Walking to the kitchen, he said, "The US seems like such a massively interesting place."

"Well, if you ever decide to come, you'll have to plan on visiting me!"

Philippe nodded his head.

"Grab me another too, will ya?" Fred asked him, spreading out in the newly opened vacancy on the couch.

Julien turned in my direction. "Are you ready to go home?" Julien asked, leaning in, rubbing his hand on my leg. A curl lay adorably on his forehead, and I brushed it to the side before covering his hand with mine, rubbing his thumb gently. I longed to kiss him again, to be closer to him rather than sitting on a little chair to his side.

I didn't want to think about going home. I was definitely more interested in alone time with him.

"I still have a lot of packing to do," I whined, dropping my hand from his and raising both hands to my face, as if I was trying to hide from the inevitable.

"And we have plans to see some things on her list of must-dos before leaving," Emilie interjected. Her voice was a little strained.

"What's on your list?" Philippe asked as he took his place back on the couch, handing Fred a bottle of beer.

"Oh, the normal stuff. I want to ride the giant Ferris wheel. And I've been wanting to get back up to Sacré-Cœur, hang out a bit in the Artist's Square at Montmartre, and I never did go through the Salvador Dali museum that's there," I said.

"I've never been to those places," Philippe admitted.

"Nor have I," Julien said, turning to Fred, who nodded in agreement.

"Maybe you can join us?" I looked quickly at Emilie, trying to gauge if she would be upset now that I had invited them.

Julien, Philippe, and Fred shared a glance and then Julien turned to Emilie. "Em, is that okay with you?" he asked softly.

Emilie shrugged her shoulders. "Why not? The more the merrier." Her tone was flat.

"You sure?" I asked. Although the idea of spending another day with Julien thrilled me, it was important for me to spend some time with Emilie too.

"Yep. I don't get off work until noon tomorrow, so you guys should do the Ferris wheel first, since I already rode it. I'll meet you after work."

I nodded and gave her a small smile. Avoiding eye contact again, she busied herself gathering empty bottles and plates.

"When do you leave, Callie?" Philippe asked.

"My flight is in three days." My head dropped low. It was coming so fast. A huge yawn escaped me and I clapped my hand over my mouth.

Philippe chuckled. "Are we that boring?"

Tucking my hair behind my ear, I looked back, grinning sheepishly. "I'm sorry. It was a really late night last night."

"So we heard," Fred quipped, standing. "I think we need some livelier music." He walked toward the stereo on the other side of the living room.

Squirming in my seat, I wondered how much Julien had

told them about our night. I stood up abruptly. "Well, my glass is empty. Can I get anyone another drink?"

Fred, who was rifling through Emilie's CD collection, turned. "Me!"

"Dude, you literally just got another drink," Julien quipped.

"It will be gone shortly!" Fred took a big swig and burped.

Shaking my head, I grabbed the rest of the empties and joined Emilie, who was busy stacking dishes in the kitchen sink.

"You sure you're okay about tomorrow?" I asked.

She nodded, turning to refill the plates with extra food she pulled from the fridge.

I placed my hand on Emilie's arm to get her attention. "We can uninvite them if you want?"

"Don't be ridiculous." She turned toward me, an unreadable expression on her face. "It'll be fun to go in a group." Her voice didn't match her words, but I knew better than to push. After a moment of silence, she stopped what she was doing and turned to me. "I don't want things to be weird between us. We only have a few days together."

Wrapping my arms around her in a big hug, I whispered, "Same."

We both turned as loud music blasted from the living room. Fred danced around the living room and Emilie and I giggled as we refilled our wine glasses and grabbed beers for the guys. Handing beers to Philippe and Julien, I leaned forward and gave Julien the briefest kiss on his forehead. He smiled, placing his hand gently on my hip as I shimmied back to my chair.

Philippe leaned forward on the couch, chuckling at Fred's moves. "It's a bit loud!"

Emilie shook her head in agreement and beelined it to the

stereo, turning the music down a little. Fred joined her and they shuffled through her CDs together, discussing her collection of music.

Julien glanced at me, then indicated to Philippe to scooch over. Julien slid to the middle of the couch, patting the seat next to him. Accepting his invitation, I joined him on the coach. He put his arm around me, and I nestled into the crook of his arm.

After dancing around a bit, Fred plopped down in the chair I had vacated, and the guys launched into an animated discussion about sports.

Rolling her eyes at me with a playful smile, Emilie excused herself to the bathroom and my eyelids closed for a moment, content in my current position.

Julien's mobile phone ringtone interrupted the conversation. Julien smiled apologetically as he removed his arm from around me and I shifted, allowing him to dig his phone from his pocket. He silenced the call but had barely put it back in his pocket when it started again. Julien tapped the end call button again.

Emilie came back into the room and claimed the chair next to me.

When the phone started to ring a third time, Fred piped up, "She's not going to stop. You should probably answer."

She? My heart rate quickened as I turned to face Julien, my eyebrows raised, Julien shot a look of death toward Fred, and quickly looked back at me, his face flushed. I sat there, stunned for a moment, then turned to Emilie, who cast her eyes downward. Fred seemed to realize he'd said something wrong and tried to dance around it. "Um, I mean, it's probably not important. You, er, you don't owe her anything."

Julien gave him a look that pleaded for him to just stop talking. My stomach gnawed on itself with anxiety. Who was calling, and why? Rubbing my sweaty palms on my pants, I watched as Julien silenced the call again. My eyes darted to Philippe who was suddenly busy studying the label on his beer. Emilie sighed, shaking her head, and shot Julien an irritated look before turning to me, eyes clouding over.

The atmosphere in the room suddenly seemed oppressive. No one spoke. I stood quickly. "Ok, um, I need to, um, use the bathroom!" Although I was unclear about what was happening, I had a few ideas, and none of them boded well for the happily ever after scenario I'd been concocting. Closing the door behind me, I leaned back on the door and took several deep breaths, willing my hands to stop shaking. Then, fighting the sickening feeling in my belly, I placed both hands on the white sink basin and stared at myself in the mirror. Red blotchy patches covered my face and my eyes were red. I splashed some cold water on my face while questions ripped through my thoughts.

Maybe I'd imagined it all. The deep connection, the romantic gestures. Had I ever even asked him if he had a girlfriend? Or had I just assumed by the way we interacted that he was, in fact, single? And if he had a girlfriend, wouldn't Emilie have mentioned that?

I recalled her earlier words. *It's complicated with Julien, too.*

It's only been one day of fun, Callie. You're doing it again. Getting far more invested in a situation, creating fairy tales where they don't exist.

The cool water helped take away some of the heat and stinging, and I patted my face with the towel, trying to calm myself. Wiping away the mascara that had run a little under my eyes, I fussed with my hair, breathing deeply. After my heart finally returned to a normal rate, I opened the door slowly, planning my next move. Afraid to look at the guys, I made eye contact with Emilie, who smiled sympathetically.

Julien was nowhere to be seen.

"What's happening?" I asked, hoping I sounded normal.

Attempting to defuse the situation, Emilie shrugged her shoulders, saying nonchalantly, "Julien took a phone call and these idiots are talking about football."

Emilie's attempt to lighten the mood didn't stop the intense pulsing of my heart. Trapped in this small apartment, I wanted to grab my belongings and run. But to do so, I'd have to pass Julien. So I did what every girl does in this situation. Picking up a plate of toast with salmon spread and pickles, I popped one after another in my mouth and washed it all down with several large gulps of wine.

"I'm going to smoke a cigarette," Philippe announced, grabbing his jacket and retreating to the small balcony.

That seemed better than staring at Fred and Emilie, and if I continued to drink, I'd be plastered on the floor in no time, so I joined Philippe, closing the door behind me and squeezing in next to him on the tiny balcony.

Philippe shifted back and forth on his feet. Neither of us said anything for a moment. This was decidedly awkward.

"So, how about them Cubs?" I asked, half under my breath.

"Huh?" Philippe raised his eyebrows.

"Sorry, just something stupid we Americans say, when we don't know what else to say." I didn't really want to explain the whole baseball thing, and he just nodded, not asking for more.

"He's not with her anymore," he finally said, turning his lanky body so that he had his back against the balcony railing. Even in this position, he still stood quite a bit taller than me.

"Hmm," I said, sucking in a long drag. I didn't know why Philippe decided to share that information. "It doesn't matter. I'm leaving in a couple of days."

Turning toward me, Philippe exhaled and pushed his glasses back up his nose. Running his free hand over his short hair, he said, "Yeah, that does complicate things, doesn't it?"

Complicated. Yes. I nodded and gave him the smallest of smiles. Once again, Philippe's kind demeanor shone through. Scrutinizing him as if for the first time, I realized he was pretty cute in his own way. While he wasn't my type physically, he wasn't bad looking either. His rounded nose and the dimple in his chin gave him a Clark Kent vibe when combined with those glasses.

His brown eyes were filled with compassion when he turned to look at me. Cigarette to his mouth, he paused for a minute before blowing out the smoke. "He told me about what happened to you with your jerk of an ex. I can imagine that was really tough."

"Yeah, I seem to be great at attracting men who just aren't as into me as I thought they were," I said, flatly. *No, let's not play the self-pity game, Callie.*

"I wouldn't be so sure about that."

I focused my attention on the street below us. Cars were crammed tightly into the spots along the street. There might have only been inches between some of them. A van, wedged into a spot below us, tried to work its way out. Philippe snorted as the van backed into the car behind it, shoving the car backward to gain a few more feet. After a few tries, surprisingly, the driver succeeded.

"And this is why we do not drive to Paris," Philippe joked, eyes still focused on the street below.

Turning in response to the sound of Emilie's door closing, I saw Julien was back in the apartment. He gave me a half smile, and while my heart lurched at those beautiful dimples, I turned back toward the street view, glancing quickly at Philippe, who was studying me quietly.

4 Days in Paris

After we smashed our cigarette butts into the ashtray, Philippe opened the door for me and we rejoined the others, the mood decidedly different from the lighthearted atmosphere moments earlier.

15

As PHILIPPE and I reentered the room, Fred stood up and stretched, shirt lifting to show a bit of his pudgy abdomen.

"I'm getting bored." He turned to Emilie, "No offense, Emilie, but is there someplace we can go that might be a little more..."

"Exciting? With more girls?" Emilie filled in.

"Yes! That!" Fred nodded eagerly.

Philippe rolled his eyes at Fred's behavior. Philippe definitely didn't give off the vibes that he was interested in any short-term flings or hookups. He seemed far more interested in meaningful conversations and finding someone with the same interests in saving the world. If Lila was single, she seriously would have been a perfect match for him.

"I don't know what you'll find open on January first, but I can give you some ideas of places to look."

"You're not coming?" Julien asked.

"I have to get up really early for a morning shift, so I think I'm done for the evening," Emilie replied.

"I think I'm going to call it a night, too," I announced, suppressing another yawn.

Julien's arms flopped down to his sides, like a deflated balloon. "You're leaving so early?"

Glancing at my watch, I realized it wasn't even nine in the evening yet. "I'm sorry, but I need to get a good night's sleep if we're going to hit all of those places tomorrow." That was assuming we were all still going.

He nodded slowly, pouting.

"You girls are lightweights," Fred joked, putting on his coat.

Ignoring Fred completely, I turned to Emilie. "I'll help you clean up before I go, Em."

"Let me grab those," Julien took the plates I held, so I picked up the bowls of chips while Emilie pulled out her map to show Fred and Philippe the places with the best nightlife.

In the kitchen, Julien set down the plates and faced me. "Are you leaving because of what just happened?"

"No."

He didn't look convinced. "Let me explain," he started, eyes pleading, reaching out to touch my arm.

"No, you really don't need to," I interrupted, moving out of his reach, though I desperately wanted to feel his touch just as much as I wanted to reach out and brush his floppy locks off his forehead. "We had a great night last night. Let's just leave it at that."

He stepped back, eyes darkening. "Was that all it was to you?"

I shrugged my shoulders, leaning back against the kitchen counter, and crossed my arms across my chest. It had been far more than that, but I was afraid to admit it. Julien stood there patiently, hands shoved in his pockets, waiting for me to say something. I wanted to reach out and trace his jawline, feel his skin on my fingertips, as I had done last night. I shook my head slowly, trying to ignore the enticing smell of his cologne. That stupid cologne and its magical powers of attraction.

"No. That's not all it was." He might run away if I told him I was already planting the seeds of a future with him in my heart. Suddenly very warm, I wiped my clammy palms on my pants and shoved up the sleeves of my sweater.

"I don't want you to leave tonight not knowing how amazing last night was for me," Julien said. He grabbed my hands, then pulled me in, wrapping his arms tightly around my waist, pulling our bodies together as he nuzzled into my neck. "I want more time with you." Shocks of electricity coursed through my body, and, despite wanting to fight this urge, I wrapped my arms around him as well. We said nothing, just held each other. This felt so right. And so wrong.

Fear caused me to push him away, but I reached for his hands. "Julien, I ..." My words were garbled, my tongue stuck, and no words came.

Julien brought my hands to his mouth, kissing them both gently. "Please come with us tonight."

I pulled my hands away. "I can't. It's been such a long day, helping Lila pack and saying goodbye..." my words drifted off. Had that really been just a few hours ago?

His face fell. "Okay. But we'll still spend the day together tomorrow, right?"

I nodded emphatically, pleased to see his smile return, popping out those dimples. "Yes. I have to pack in the morning, but I can meet you at the Ferris Wheel at the Place de la Concorde at 11:30?"

"I'll take what I can get," he said, giving me a soft peck on the lips.

My heart lurched. Curiosity about the phone call was eating at me, competing only with the gnawing fear gurgling in my gut. I was afraid to know that there was someone else, no matter what their current relationship status was. If she was still calling, it wasn't done. And I refused to get further entangled in what would likely lead to a broken heart. I returned my attention to putting the remaining pretzels back in their bag.

Julien shook his head and then joined in. We scraped plates and stacked the dirty dishes in the sink, tidying up all the leftovers.

"Ready to go?" Philippe asked, popping his head into the kitchen.

"Yes," I whispered, and made my way to the closet for my coat and bag, glancing back over my shoulder at Julien, who followed me out and grabbed his coat silently.

Hugging Emilie goodbye, I confirmed I'd see her the next day, and the four of us put on our coats and left her building. As we exited onto the street, Julien grabbed my gloved hand in his, and we walked together to the metro. Neither of us said anything, listening to Fred and Philippe argue over which area of town they should go to for a bar.

When the moment came for us to go in different directions, Julien bent over and kissed me gently. As our lips parted, I turned and walked away, fighting the urge at every step to run back to him.

16

I OPENED MY EYES SLOWLY, still trying to work out my dream from reality. Groggily, I shielded my eyes from the sun streaming in the window, and sat up slowly, touching my lips, which tingled at the memory of Julien's kiss.

"I have nothing to say to you!" I said to the Eiffel Tower, who stared back at me in judgment through the window. Flopping backward, I rolled on my side in the other direction, not quite ready to leave the warm cocoon of my bed.

My thoughts turned back to Julien. My emotions were muddled together in a big ball of confusion. Should I worry about the phone call? Was it really nothing, as Philippe had suggested? Volleying back and forth between these thoughts, and despite the little alarm bells that wanted me to run, I shivered with excitement thinking about seeing him again. We'd managed to have a mostly fun evening the night before, and it was probably best to just keep things light and fun. Was I capable of that?

I had today to figure that out.

Sliding out of the bed, my feet hit the cold floor and I scurried to grab my robe and slide into my fuzzy slippers. What I needed now was a hot tea, and I'd figure out the rest later. Despite the small wall heater that was usually ample enough to keep the room warm, it had seemed to shut itself off overnight and the room was frigid. I'd be out of this sad excuse for a studio apartment in two days and returning to the comfortable world of central air and heating! But it would be a world with no Julien.

The mess of my unpacked items strewn about the tiny room taunted me, and I shifted piles from one place to another so I had space to heat the kettle. Why had I waited until the very last minute to pack? *Because, Callie, procrastination is the name of your game.*

Turning from the hot plate and walking the two steps across my room, I moved another pile of clothes from the chair to my bed, making room to sit down at my tiny table and drink my tea. Sipping slowly, I looked at the clock and bolted to my feet. There were just two hours until I needed to meet the guys and I needed to pack at least *one* suitcase before leaving for the day.

Glancing around, I didn't know where to start. My clothes were strewn everywhere, souvenirs in piles. Packing was the worst part of going home. Once again, I just contemplated throwing it all away. That was tempting, but I didn't have the money to replace my entire wardrobe.

Okay, let's get to it. I set my teacup in the sink, rinsing it quickly, and turned to sift through my clothes on the bed. My wardrobe consisted of a combination of, "What would the Frenchies wear?" mixed with hippie casual, influenced by Lila, and my "American" clothes—sweats, t-shirts, and comfy clothes. I crammed the American clothes into a bag I pulled from under the bed. Then I grabbed my hamper. There was no point in doing laundry again before I left, so I dumped all my dirty clothes into the bag too.

"Have fun with this, Mr. Customs officer," I joked aloud, and then really hoped they didn't dig through my dirty clothes.

"One bag down!" I pumped my fists in the air. Digging through the clothes that remained on the bed, I selected my cutest jeans, a soft blue V-neck t-shirt, and a warm sweater, anticipating the chilly temperature outside. Glancing at the clock, I saw that only thirty minutes remained before I needed to leave. Using the small mirror over the four-drawer dresser that filled the space between my twin bed and my "kitchen," I applied a touch of mascara so that I didn't look eyelashless and a small amount of lip gloss. A quick brush-through of my hair and I was ready. Glancing back in the mirror, I was happy with what I saw. Even a small amount of mascara made my brown eyes stand out a little bit.

In the few minutes that remained, I tried to clean out some of the stuff I knew I wouldn't want to pack to take home. It was mostly souvenirs from my time here: letters, posters I'd hung on the walls, stuff I'd purchased that was basically just junk. In a few short minutes, after attacking the room like a Tasmanian devil, I managed to fill an entire garbage bag.

An impressive amount of stuff collected in six months, Callie.

Despite my efforts to purge, my room was still littered with stuff that would need to be shoved into one of my four remaining bags, but that would have to wait. Grabbing my small backpack purse, I heaved the heavy garbage bag into the hall, locked my door, and carefully traipsed down the eight flights of stairs. The garbage bins were in the courtyard at the bottom of the stairs, and I deposited the bag and gave a slight smile to the concierge, who was peering through her window. In response, she snarled at me. She'd never been very friendly. I wouldn't miss her.

Arriving at the metro station, I searched through my bag for my ticket and descended the stairs. The smell of the subway never disappointed. The combination of dank must, urine, and plastic affronted my senses as I power walked through the tunnels. In larger stations, where there was room for small shops, there might also be a good whiff of baked goods, which really confused the olfactory senses. I snickered, realizing I would even miss waiting in the smelly, windy metro. Maybe I wouldn't miss the smell, but I'd definitely miss the convenience of public transportation and the ease of getting from place to place, never needing a car.

Climbing the stairs out of the station two at a time, I burst out to the above-ground world, filled with sunshine and blue skies.

Playing my own personal game of frogger, darting between the traffic across the Rue de Rivoli to get to the Place de la Concorde, I scanned the square for Julien, Philippe, and Fred, who were nowhere to be found. Checking my watch, I realized I had made great time and was about fifteen minutes early. *Whew! Plenty of time to catch my breath and walk around for a few minutes.*

Stuffing my hands in my jacket pockets, I slowly circled the space, smitten by the gorgeous sights of the Place de la Concorde. The huge fountain triggered a memory from when Lila and I had witnessed a wedding photo shoot in the square. The bride had worn one of the most beautiful dresses I'd ever seen, strapless with a formfitting bodice, the dress flowing out into a long trail behind her. Attendants and photographers had flocked around her and the groom, posing them in a bazillion different ways, yet she kept her amazing smile in place despite what looked like a nightmare situation to me. Her wedding party, on the other hand, did not look so thrilled. Lila and I had pinky swore to each other that we'd never put our friends through hours of photos when we got married.

Large wrought iron gates, tipped with gold and flanked by two grand marble pillars with the statues of the two figures riding Pegasus, beckoned me into the Jardin des Tuileries. I still had a few minutes, so I crossed the street with a herd of tourists and entered the beautiful gardens. The white gravel crunched loudly under my feet. Despite the chilly temperatures, the gardens were full. Children played with their sailboats at the large round pond, pushing them with sticks on the water, which shone in the sunlight.

The smells of fresh crêpes and chocolate wafted through the park, reminding me that I hadn't eaten anything yet, and I hoped the guys would want to eat an early lunch when they arrived. I continued walking through the gardens, passing the Musée de l'Orangerie on my right, where Lila and I had gawked over the breathtaking *Water Lilies* by Monet and incredible artwork by other impressionist artists. Walking down the grand path of the garden, I admired the multitude of marble sculptures, before arriving at another large, round pond. Before me stood the beautiful glass pyramid and the Louvre, and despite having visited numerous times and walked by them daily on my way to work, the majesty of this massive building still took my breath away. Lila and I had spent days in the Louvre and still had never managed to conquer the entire museum.

There was no time for another visit today. I checked my watch and turned back to the Place de la Concorde. Retracing my steps, I exited the garden, crossed to the giant square in the middle of a very busy road, and turned in a slow circle. Still no sign of the guys. Now they were late. Cars honked and people scurried everywhere as I edged closer to the Fontaine des Mers, the Fountain of the Seas, admiring the tritons and the beautiful artwork, the six figures, the fish, the shells. The fountain was a stunning mixture of black, greens, and gold.

Chewing on my bottom lip, I fretted about seeing Julien. Would he be excited to see me? After the events of last night, would we be hanging out just as friends today?

Lost in thought, I startled as a pair of arms grabbed me from behind. With a short scream, I drove my elbow back hard and yelled, "No!" Turning quickly, I found Julien doubled over in pain at the unexpected attack.

"Oh my gosh, Julien!" I clutched my hands to my chest in surprise, leaning in to see if I'd hurt him as Philippe and Fred guffawed.

Julien, still bent over, laughed as he fought to catch his breath. "Wow, you're strong for a little thing!" he panted, hands on his jean-clad thighs. He smiled at me, blue eyes sparkling. His beanie covered his hair, but the black cap made the blue of his eyes stand out even more.

"Are you okay? I'm so sorry!" As I placed my hand on his arm, he pulled me in close and kissed me. His lips, warm and soft, assured me he was more than okay. Tingles traveled through my body as he tucked my hair behind my ear, his finger lingering on my cheek.

"I'll take that as a yes!" I giggled, as I caught my breath.

He kissed me lightly one more time on the lips. "I missed you," he whispered into my ear.

I simply nodded, slightly paralyzed by his physical effect on me. Despite my efforts to keep this light, to not allow any more feelings to develop, and the warning lights pinging in my head, electricity shot up and down my body. Face fully flushed, I stood there for a minute, unsure of what my next words or actions should be.

"Looks like Julien was worried for absolutely no reason about leaving you to take the metro on your own last night and the other morning!" Philippe joked.

"My dad insisted on self-defense training before I left for college," I said. The three of them nodded in apparent understanding, although Fred stared at me as if I might karate chop him to pieces at any moment, causing me to laugh.

"Relax, Fred. You're safe with me."

"I see that I'm safe from others with you, that's for sure," he joked.

Turning to face all three of them, I clasped my hands together in front of me and looked at the guys, giving my best impression of a tour guide. "Okay gents, we have a long list of activities to knock out today! Emilie is meeting us here in forty-five minutes. Shall we get on the wheel?"

"I don't know, is it on your list?" Julien teased.

"Why yes, it is!"

"Then I guess we have to," Julien said with a smile, interlacing his fingers in mine.

Fred and Philippe led the way to the ticket booth, and Julien reached for my hand. As he rubbed his thumb back and forth on my thumb, my body heated quickly. My resolve to keep things cool was rapidly diminishing as very naughty thoughts coursed through my mind.

Waiting in the long line for tickets, the conversation turned to the topic of Philippe's love life, Julien and Fred teasing him about the girl he'd been dating. Pulling myself back into the present tense, which included Philippe and Fred, I enjoyed watching how lively Julien was with his friends. On our walk, he'd been calm, a good listener, somewhat reserved. Now he laughed and joked with the guys, a side I really enjoyed seeing.

"We were all anxiously awaiting Christmas dinner, but after a few hours, we realized she had never turned on the oven. The chicken was still raw!" Julien's whole face lit up as he told the story.

"What did you do?"

Fred jumped in. "Well, we're French, so we had plenty of bread, cheese, yogurt, and of course, wine. By the time the chicken was done late that night, we'd all passed out on the floor."

I snickered, shaking my head back and forth.

"But she's really sweet, just not chef material," Philippe explained, his cheeks bright red.

"I'm sure she's lovely," I said warmly.

Julien resumed rubbing his thumb gently back and forth on my hand as we stood in line, sneaking side glances at each other, and occasionally a quick peck. While my mind kept telling me to back down and make more space, my body took every opportunity to get as close to him as possible. I moved in front of him and leaned back against his warm body. He wrapped his arms around me and rested his chin on my head in a very familiar way.

Finally, it was our turn to load up into the carts. We anxiously waited in the little holding area as the carts arrived. Julien and I climbed into one cart, which rocked back and forth unsteadily as we took our places. The compartments were round and hung from what seemed like a surprisingly small steel bar, dropping from the round umbrella-like cover. We sat side by side and I squeezed his hand tightly as the cart lurched forward. Nothing protected us from the cold wind of the day, and shivering, I maneuvered myself more closely to Julien. He wrapped his arm around my shoulder, pulling me in closely, kissing the top of my head.

"Paris really is beautiful," Julien admitted, as we climbed up, getting a vantage point that was far different from the street level. I nodded, thinking that this city was truly one of the most magnificent cities in the world. So romantic. No wonder it was the city of love.

"You can see so much from here!" I exclaimed as we neared the top. I pointed to a spot far in front of us. "There's Notre Dame."

Julien nodded. I turned, and of course, the Eiffel Tower dominated the scene in the other direction. A treasure trove of delights surrounded us. The Jardin des Tuileries, the Champs-Élysées, the Arc de Triomphe—I pointed out the sites like a small child, and recalled our moments the night before at many of these places.

"This is the best view in the city," he said, gazing directly at me with his beautiful sky-colored eyes. Julien leaned in and brought his lips to mine, kissing me, softly at first, and then with more urgency, his tongue flicking mine playfully. His hand moved down around my waist, unbuttoning the bottom button of my black pea coat so he could slide his hand under. I gasped at the cold of his fingers on my warm skin. His other hand moved to my right thigh, and warmth spread through my abdomen. I wanted to explore more. My body was saying yes, but my poor heart trembled with fear. With all the willpower I could muster, I placed my hand firmly on his, stopping him from moving any higher. He squeezed my thigh, and moved his hand to my face, then behind my neck, pulling me deeper into the kiss. My hands ran through his hair, moving down to his neck. Pulling back for a breath, I wrapped my arms tightly around him, resting my head on his shoulder, my heart thundering as I leaned back to watch the view as we descended back to the ground.

So much for keeping things light, Callie.

Hushing the warning bells in my head, I gave in to the moment, forgetting all about the wondrous sites surrounding us. Dammit, I was falling in love.

17

EMILIE WAS WAITING for us when we disembarked, hands stuffed in her oversized coat, which covered half of her baggy khaki pants. Her black beanie covered her short hair.

I waved, grinning like a Cheshire cat.

"How was it?" she asked when we reached her, smiling as she kissed each of us on the cheeks.

"Cold! Windy! But excellent views!" I enthusiastically replied.

Philippe snorted. "Well, I'm not sure these two saw anything," he said, nodding our way. "But I found it incredible."

Emilie smiled but shot me a questioning look. My cheeks flushed, and I looked down. Julien just chuckled, squeezing my hand.

"I loved it! Let's go to Montmartre!" Fred turned, gesturing for us to follow him, beaming, and I appreciated his enthusiasm. He was getting really invested in my bucket list day. "Come on, you guys!" He turned to Emilie. "Is it too far to walk?"

"It's kinda far," Emilie replied. "But there's a direct metro line from here which should only take us about fifteen minutes." She looked at Fred and Philippe, who both shrugged their shoulders in agreement.

"Besides the obvious Sacré-Cœur, what else is in Montmartre?" Philippe asked as we walked.

"Ooh, so much great stuff!" I gushed. "Montmartre is the district where Sacré-Cœur, the Artist's Square, and the Salvador Dali museum live. I've had the Dali Museum on my list for a long time!"

Hustling to the metro entrance, we descended the stairs and followed the directions to Line twelve.

Stopping at the map, Philippe studied it carefully. "Looks like we'll get off at Abbesses Station and walk a short distance."

Nodding in agreement, I said, "It's pretty easy to get there from here."

Philippe counted the number of stops, reminding me of my earlier days in Paris before I knew my routes by heart, when I would also count the exact stops to ensure I didn't get off in the wrong place.

The train lumbered into the station, squealing as it came to a stop. We piled on in a single file line. As was usual for this time of day, there was standing room only, but I didn't mind being crushed into Julien. He grabbed onto a metal bar, wrapping his other arm around me protectively. The train jerked around a corner, nearly catapulting us into the lap of an elderly couple sitting in the seats near us. I smiled sheepishly at the woman.

Fred, ever the jokester, wrapped his arms tightly around Emilie to catch her when she stumbled. "I got you, babe," he said, as Emilie removed his arms and rolled her eyes in my direction.

My back was to the rest of the group as I leaned into

Julien's chest. I didn't care if it was 100 million degrees in this metro car, I hugged him tightly, resting my head on his chest, but watching through the window as the tunnel zipped by. A huge picture of the Eiffel Tower appeared on the side of the metro tube as we entered the next stop.

Ticktock, she whispered.

A low buzz of fear vibrated in my chest, competing with the vibrations running through me from the floor of the train. Sweat rolled down my back, my heart racing as I realized how little time I had left here. What was I even doing? The more time I spent with Julien, the further I fell and the harder goodbye would be. Why was I purposefully putting my heart at such risk? It didn't feel as if I had any real choice in the issue. No matter what I tried to do, no matter how many times I told myself to slow down, I couldn't seem to force myself to take a step back.

Lila's words replayed in my head. "If you feel this is worth pursuing, go all in. Leave nothing on the table. But, if you have any doubts at all, if you're just afraid of what is next for you, if this isn't exactly what you want in life, don't do what you did with Vic. Don't put the rest of your life on hold because you're trying to fulfill this fantasy of falling in love and staying in France."

Was I doing that? Was I trying to make something happen here for a reason to stay? Or were these feelings legit?

Julien nuzzled his chin on my head, and I tilted my head back to look up at him. His lips found mine, briefly, a quick grazing kiss, not totally inappropriate for our public surroundings, but enough to cause a dramatic physical reaction. My pulse quickened, my heart thundering. We locked eyes and I wondered what he saw. Did he know I was falling in love with him? Did he feel the same? His fingers trailed lightly up and down my back, and the rest of the world seemed to have stopped making any noise at all. What did I see in his eyes?

I needed to trust myself. Leave nothing on the table. I would deal with the repercussions later.

Philippe tapped me on the arm. "Next stop is ours."

The train pulled in, and once we heard the loud buzz of the alarm, Philippe jerked up on the handle, opening the door and leading the way off, followed by Fred, Emilie, and then Julien and me.

"It's this way, guys," I tilted my head in the direction we needed to go, and we moved forward, Julien, Emilie, and I in front, Fred and Philippe right behind us. Exiting the metro station, we had a short walk. As we turned the corner, Sacré-Cœur came into view, causing us to pause for a moment.

"Wow," Philippe said, taking a deep breath.

We continued walking up the crowded streets, stopping periodically to make way for the other pedestrians also making their way around the street vendors, and the tourists that stopped to peer in windows or buy from the vendors, until we finally arrived at the bottom of the base of the hill of Montmartre. Sacré-Cœur, the Basilica of the Sacred Heart, sat high upon a hill, overlooking the northern part of the city.

No matter how many times I saw the beautiful white of the massive cathedral, it remained stunning each time. Made from white limestone, the massive basilica dominated the hill and stood out against the gray clouds that were moving in. A large round dome in the center was flanked by two smaller domes widely set to the left and right. The domes reminded me a little of the Capitol building in Washington, DC. The front of the building was defended by two large statues of soldiers on horses, Saint Jean d'Arc on the right, and King Saint Louis on the left. The bells began to ring, noting the top of the hour, and filled me with reverence. The area bustled with the many tourists who flocked to see the beautiful basilica and the view.

"It's so big!" Julien exclaimed, turning to playfully punch Fred, who hadn't missed the opportunity to add in a crude joke.

Catching Emilie's eye, I shared a warm smile with her. This was one of our favorite places in Paris. Lila, Emilie, and I had visited here numerous times. Every time a friend or family member came to visit us, this was always one of our stops.

"Come on! Let's go up," I encouraged after a few minutes of quiet admiration.

"We've got to climb all of these?" Fred huffed, looking at the staircase that led to the basilica.

"You can do it," I encouraged. "It will be worth it. Just keep your eye on the prize."

I led the group in the direction of the large carousel centered at the bottom of the hill. Then we turned left and followed the curved ramps to the central set of stairs. So many stairs. Emilie and Philippe began the climb, Fred following reluctantly, huffing the entire time. Julien and I exchanged an amused look and followed along behind.

After what seemed like an eternity, all of us gasping, we all made it to the top of the stairs.

"Wow," Fred said, and we collectively nodded, standing in silence, awestruck by the view. The sun, now buried behind a thick layer of clouds, provided no warmth, and the wind whipped frigid air in my face. Tourists milled everywhere, snapping pictures, making memories. Watching the awed expressions on Philippe, Fred, and Julien's faces, I realized that today they were the outsiders. I had shared a little piece of my world with them, even if it would no longer be my home in just a matter of days.

I turned to Emilie and wrapped my arm through hers. "This never gets old!" She nodded in agreement.

Julien stepped closer to me and put an arm around my shoulder. "You've been here a lot?" he asked.

I nodded. "Yep. Lila, Emilie, and I made it a point to visit often."

"I can understand why." He turned back to look at the basilica looming behind us.

"I'm hungry," Fred announced.

My tummy rumbled in response. It was now after one and I still hadn't eaten anything. I imagined the smell of the crêpes and frites and other goodies that we'd find in the Artist's Square.

"Are we going to try to visit the inside first?" Philippe asked.

"The line to enter looks pretty long, so it's up to you. But if everyone is hungry, we can go to the Artist's Square, just over there." I pointed in the direction behind the basilica. "We'll find lots of food options."

Emilie nodded, shivering. "A hot tea and something to eat sounds good."

Julien agreed, took my hand, and I led the way. We walked around to the left of Sacré-Cœur and behind the building, following the flow of traffic. On our way, we passed many shops selling all kinds of paintings, and we stopped to admire a few. Several store attendees tried to offer us the best deals we'd ever see to get us to enter, but we laughingly declined their offers and continued to the Place du Tertre, the famous Artist's Square.

Restaurants lined the outer perimeter of the square, and delicious smells made my mouth water. The inside of the square was filled with artists' stalls, roaming artists, beautiful paintings, and tourists who'd been convinced to get their caricatures or portraits painted. Weaving our way through the dense crowd, I admired all the beautiful watercolors, sketches, and portraits.

Artists floated through the tourists with their sketch pads, demanding we get our portraits painted. Waving them off, we reviewed a couple of menus and restaurants, settling on a sidewalk café facing the square that met all of our needs and had a table for five. I was delighted to sit outside, even on a chilly day, so I could enjoy my favorite pastime of people-watching while enjoying a meal. Thankfully, the restaurant had heat lamps so we wouldn't freeze to death.

"I will certainly miss this," I said, as we sat at our round table, Julien and I cozied up closely together, Fred to my left, Emilie across from me, and Philippe between her and Julien.

"Crowded squares with a bunch of loud tourists?" Philippe inquired, the thought apparently absolutely appalling to him.

"No. The cafés."

"You don't have cafés?" Fred asked incredulously, as if I'd just said we had no food in the States.

"Of course they have cafés in the States," Emilie quipped. "It's just nothing like this."

I nodded in agreement. "Nothing like this. I've spent hours sitting at tables outside, just watching people. We don't have a lot like this, with large outdoor patios. Probably because it gets so hot where I live. And definitely no Artist's Square."

They nodded their heads, but I wasn't sure if they grasped how different this was from my life in South Carolina. The architecture was nothing like it was here, cars were ten times bigger, people, clothes, food... it was all so different.

"What else will you miss?" Julien squeezed my thigh. The touch of his hand sent lightning bolts through my body. As I covered his hand with mine, thoughts of leading him somewhere private filled my mind. Exhaling, I silently created a new bucket list of places Julien and I could...

"Earth to Callie," Emilie snapped her fingers in my face, pulling me out of my reverie.

"Oh." I blushed and cleared my throat. "Hmm. Well, I'll definitely miss the *pains aux chocolats*." I shrugged my shoulders, as if I'd just told them the most obvious answer.

They roared with laughter, shaking their heads in surprise at this being my choice.

Julien pouted playfully. "I mean, I guess they're good, but..."

"Seriously. I've had a *pain au chocolat* every day since arriving. I don't know how I'm going to live without these French delicacies." I glanced around the table, to find Fred nodding his head emphatically in agreement. No surprise there.

Julien's pout deepened. My heart fluttered as I realized he was fishing for something else. I squeezed his thigh and leaned in closely. "I'll miss you," I said softly, before leaning in to brush my lips against his.

"Are we going to have to watch this puppy love all day?" Philippe asked, punching Julien in the shoulder, and winking at me. Shifting in my seat, I scrunched my nose at Philippe, and he chuckled. Smiling back, I realized, *Philippe's rooting for me!*

"For real," Emilie said, rolling her eyes.

"Maybe," Julien replied, leaning in for another kiss. He didn't care if Emilie was annoyed by us. "Do you really have to go? Stay, please?" Julien begged, nuzzling my cheek with his nose.

For the second time I pondered the idea of postponing my return. Did I really have to go home this week? My parents would be so disappointed if I stayed, and I no longer had a job or a place to live. No money. I shrugged, unsure what to say to Julien in reply.

From the corner of my eye, I noticed an artist painting a giant clock. My stomach dropped. *Ticktock.*

"*Mademoiselle, votre cafe au lait,*" the waiter announced, with a twinge of disdain for my large cup of coffee and milk. With all the Americans that visited here, one would think he'd be quite used to Americans loving big cups of coffee with lots of milk or cream. He delivered three tiny espressos to the guys, a more typical French order, Emilie's hot tea, and bustled off.

Philippe laughed. "It's really true that Americans like everything bigger, don't you?"

I blushed. "Sometimes size truly matters. Like coffee cups, trucks, and..." I glanced quickly at Julien. "... but it's not always the most important thing."

Blood rushed to Julien's face as he chuckled and shook his head. After the briefest of pauses, he replied, "Sometimes amazing things come in the tiniest of packages." And we all laughed hysterically.

"He admits it!" Philippe and Fred continued to harass Julien, but he took it like a champ.

We ordered a light lunch of sandwiches and fries, continuing to tease each other. I savored the fresh baguette of my sandwich, which had a lightness and taste that no replication in the States ever mastered. Even average ham and cheese sandwiches, with salty butter and soft brie, seemed so much better in France. The fries were mouthwatering. They had just the right amount of salt and were crispy but not crunchy.

We laughed and joked around through the rest of our meal, and Emilie, who seemed to be warming up to the idea of whatever was happening between Julien and me, joined me in telling stories of the adventures we had had together in our time in Paris.

After all the food was gone, we paid the bill and I stood up. "Okay guys, let's wander." Julien grabbed my hand. The warmth of his hands spread across my fingers and up my arm, causing me to shiver.

"Lead the way, my lady." He bowed and ceremoniously ushered me in front of him, causing me to giggle.

Our next destination was the Salvador Dali museum. Wandering slowly through the Artist's Square, we admired the beautiful paintings and laughed at the caricatures, skillfully avoiding being sucked into our own piece of art as we made our way through the square. Philippe, Fred, and Emilie walked ahead of us, pointing out cool things. Julien and I strolled behind slowly, admiring the varying works of the artists.

Occasionally an artist would ask us if we'd like to have our portraits made. Some were more insistent than others. A tall, thin artist with a mustache and a beret on his head popped out from around a corner, artist pad held in front of him, pencil ready to sketch.

"Come madame, let me capture you and your husband."

I blurted out, "Oh, um, he's not my husband!" I unsuccessfully tried to pull Julien past the artist.

The artist smiled, blocking our way. "Well, I see love. Let me paint your love."

I glanced at Julien, who smiled. "He sees looove," he joked.

But do you? I wanted to ask. It had been two days. There was no denying when I looked at him, talked to him, there was a definite chemical reaction. And when he kissed me deeply, I wondered if I was experiencing a sensation similar to sticking a fork in an electrical outlet. But was that love?

As the artist continued to list the reasons we should get our portraits painted, Philippe magically appeared, grabbed us, and led us away, much to my relief.

18

WALKING down the slope of the hill, we made a slight right onto Rue Poulbot and arrived in front of the Salvador Dali museum. The museum entrance sat at the end of the little street, dead-ended by a brick wall. Mopeds lined the street in front of the simple entrance. Squealing, I dropped Julien's hand and clasped my hands together.

"I had no idea this was such an exciting museum," Julien said, and cocked his head, trying to understand why I was so pumped.

He, of course, didn't know I had been anticipating my visit to this museum for months. But Lila and Emilie and I had never had enough time to go through the museum, and it had continued to stay on the list.

Dali had earned a place as one of the most fascinating people since I'd learned about him in my art history class a couple of years prior. Dali had a knack for creating weird, dark scenery, but also beautiful, haunting images. The melting clocks and butterfly prints drew me in instantly, but it was the haunting Dante's *Inferno* I wanted to study today. I secretly hoped Julien found him as intriguing as I did. While I didn't exactly consider myself a connoisseur, I enjoyed learning about the stories behind the artwork.

After purchasing our tickets, we descended the straight wooden staircase into the museum, which seemed tiny upon entry until we entered the lower level, which opened up into a larger space where the walls were painted black and paintings and sculptures filled the area. Directly in front of the staircase, on the other side of the room, a large section of a cathedral, with glorious archways and architecture, greeted us. Huge sculptures of animals, a giant snail, and other unusual sculptures, like a giant, four-foot-tall green thumb with barren trees growing from the top, sat randomly around the room.

This was a treasure trove of weirdness, and we quickly found ourselves immersed in the weird mind of Dali. Julien and I separated ourselves a little from the group. I could see Emilie out of the corner of my eye, reading all the details on each painting's information label. She glanced back in my direction and smiled, pointing at a picture and raising her palms in the universal, "What on earth is this?" gesture. Thankfully she did not seem terribly irritated that we had extra visitors on what was supposed to have been our day together.

Fred pointed out odd paintings and laughed, no doubt making crude jokes, and Philippe nodded as he tried to read the inscriptions on the labels.

"Some of these are really creepy," Julien commented as we examined the melting faces in the scenes from Dali's *Divine Comedy* suite.

"Mmmm," I agreed, staring at the paintings. "I researched Dali in my art history class. Apparently, he was desperately in love with his wife, but she was a monster. Despite his dedication to her, I wonder if some of these reflect the suffering she caused him."

"Women are known for causing unbearable suffering." He winked at me.

I playfully shoved him, and we moved on. Love, in my experience, didn't exist without pain. It was only a matter of time before Julien and I caused each other to suffer.

Stopping to look at one of the paintings of melting clocks, Julien studied the details.

"I'm no expert, but I read on one of the little cards that the melting clocks symbolize how, when we're dreaming, time passes erratically and unreliably. Feels a little familiar," Julien said, turning to me.

"Time is erratic and weird in dreams," I said softly. *And time was fleeting in real life.* Closing my eyes, I whispered, "I wish I could bend time right now. Make it stretch so much longer."

He moved his hand to my neck and gently massaged it, searching my eyes. I leaned into him, touching my forehead to his chin. Though the ending of our story was undetermined, I wanted as much time as possible to figure it out with him.

"Do you have to leave tomorrow with the guys? Stay one more day?" I whispered, practically under my breath. I wanted to ask him to stay with me, but I was afraid to take that leap.

Silently, he stared at me, shifting a little before shoving his hands in his pockets, and turned back to the painting.

Oh no.

I had misread all the signs. This was just fun for him, and I had just pushed it too far. The world spun a little as I tried to save this moment from becoming super awkward. My face warmed as I stepped back, wondering if he was in the process of trying to let me down gently. I stared at the painting in front of me.

"I mean, um, you don't have to. I just thought it would be nice to spend more time together and..."

Julien cut off my rambling, turning to me. He reached out and caressed my face. "I do want to. I was just thinking through the logistics."

Sighing with relief, I leaned into him.

Julien stroked my cheek. "I'm sorry, Callie. I didn't mean for you to take that the wrong way. You just took me by surprise."

He still hadn't said yes. "What do you have in mind?" I asked.

Julien shrugged. "Not sure, but I am definitely not ready to leave."

"You could, um, ask Emilie to stay with her tomorrow night?"

He looked a little disappointed. "Not with you?"

As much as my body was screaming to take things to the highest level with him, I wasn't sure if my heart was ready. If my attachment developed any further, would I even be able to get on the plane? Or worse, what if he was one of those guys who lost interest as soon as they'd gotten their way?

Taking a beat to consider my response, I finally replied, "I would love to have you stay with me, but my tiny apartment is a huge mess and I'm trying to pack everything up, and I only have a small bed, and..."

Julien cut off my rambling. "None of that stuff really matters to me. But time with you does."

His eyes penetrated mine as he seemed to be searching for answers. There was more to it. It wasn't just about what would happen if he stayed with me, but it was a question of losing myself completely in him.

"Can we see how it goes tomorrow?" I asked meagerly, casting my eyes downward. I didn't want to say yes, but I didn't want to say no either.

Thankfully, Julien nodded his head, offering a half smile, and planted a kiss on my forehead.

But the guilt struck me. More time with Julien meant less time with Emilie. Even if we were all together, if he was with us, he'd be the one getting my attention. I turned to find her. Emilie was behind us a bit, but on her own, examining the paintings thoughtfully.

"I, um, I need to talk to Em too. We were going to spend this evening together..." My voice trailed off. This was awkward. I was torn between wanting to spend more time with Julien and wanting to have these last few moments with Emilie, and I didn't want to bail on our plans of hitting up some of our favorite spots.

"Okay."

To lighten the conversation again, I shifted to running through my to-do list for the next day. "Tomorrow, I have to finish packing up my apartment and clean it. Give the keys to my landlord. So, sorry dude, but if you want to hang tomorrow, there may be some manual labor involved." I touched his arm gently, waiting for his reply.

He pulled me closely to him. "Is this like a test? If I help you pack, maybe I'll get rewarded?"

"It is a terrible request, isn't it? But I have to get it done and I don't want to miss the time with you, either."

"Callie, if it means more time with you, I'll do whatever you want." He bent in and kissed me on the neck, causing goosebumps to spread everywhere.

Smiling the tiniest smile, I broke free from his embrace, reached for his hand, and turned back to the display of disturbing scenes before us. We continued on quietly, occasionally pointing out something interesting in a description or a really weird scene. Dali certainly knew how to capture an audience.

Reaching the end of the museum, we found Philippe and Fred, mulling through the souvenirs at the gift shop placed between the last display and the exit. There were very few other visitors in the small space.

"I hope the rest of your list gets a little more exciting," Fred said glumly, garnering a horrified glare from Philippe.

Julien kissed me. "I'll tell them the plan," he said, nodding toward the guys.

"Ok, wish me luck with Emilie!" I said, inhaling deeply.

"She's easy, don't worry." Julien squeezed my hand before we separated, ushering the guys closer to the exit.

Emilie waited a few feet away in the very small gift shop, flipping absently through the prints that were for sale near the cash register.

"Well, what did you think?" I asked.

"He had quite an interesting approach to art, didn't he?" She looked up at me, eyebrows raised.

"Part of his charm, no? I really wonder what drove him to this level of what appears to be madness. Julien and I decided it was his crazy wife."

Emilie nodded her head in agreement, eyes back on the art she was sifting through. I shifted a bit on my feet, palms sweating as we stood in an awkward silence and I worked up the courage to ask if she'd mind if I invited her brother to stay at her place.

A few minutes passed in silence and Emilie stopped flipping through the prints, turning to face me.

"Out with it, Callie." She knew me too well.

"So, here's what we were thinking." Wiping my clammy palms on my thighs, I timidly explained the plan as she stood there, staring at me, expressionless. I really didn't want things to be weird between us. It was important to me to spend time with her before I left but there was a battle raging in my heart and mind right now and my hormones were winning. Despite my desire to spend more time with Julien, basking in his kisses and gentle touches, the guilt of ditching one of my best friends ate at my soul. Emilie had been such an important part of my life for so many years, and yet I knew I had to find out if there was something more than just a flirty connection between Julien and me. The logical part of my brain screamed I was stupid for doing so, under the circumstances.

"Okay," Emilie said, shrugging. She looked pointedly at me. "But under one condition."

Holding my breath, I waited to hear her request.

"The guys don't get to hang with us all night. I want to stick to our original plan for this evening."

My eyes widened. Reasonable terms. A huge breath escaped me, and I hugged Emilie. "You're the best!"

"I know," she said flatly, returning to the prints.

I wrapped my arms around her back and kissed her on the cheek as she giggled, squirming to break free from my tight embrace.

Julien sauntered up to us, raising his thumb, the universal sign that all was clear. My smile stretched so far across my face it almost hurt. Like two kids that had just pulled off a heist, we were both pleased with ourselves for figuring out this plan.

Emilie stepped away from the prints and put on her coat. "So, what's next?"

"Let's walk down toward Pigalle and see what we find," I said, putting on my coat. I linked my arm with hers, leading the way through the door, where we found Fred and Phillipe waiting, smoking cigarettes.

"Yes!" Fred exclaimed, stubbing out his cigarette and turning. "Pigalle! Let's go. Moulin Rouge, Red Light District, here we come!" He pushed past us and out into the streets, Julien and Philippe laughing in his wake.

I linked arms with Emilie and we trailed behind the guys, who were goofing off in front of us. I loved seeing Julien with his friends. Julien and Philippe trailed Fred, who was on a mission to get to Pigalle. What were they discussing so seriously? Was it too far-fetched to imagine he was talking about me? A more likely scenario was that they were deep into analyzing some recent sporting event.

Descending the hill from Montmartre proved far easier than climbing. The sun was setting, causing any lingering warmth to completely disappear, and I tightened my scarf around my neck and shoved my hands in my gloves. Despite the chill, we walked slowly, examining the wonderful and bizarre sights along the way. Pigalle presented bars, sex shops, and the risqué side of Paris, and Philippe rolled his eyes, shaking his head as Fred pointed out sex shops like a twelve-year-old boy.

"For the record, this is one of the reasons I want to ditch the guys," Emilie said, looking pointedly at me.

"Ditch the guys?" Julien asked, tilting his head.

I turned my gaze to him and explained as we walked. "Oh yeah, that part. Emilie is cool with you staying with her tonight, but in exchange, we're going to do our own thing for a few hours."

His face fell and he stopped walking. "Really?"

Emilie took her cue and caught up with Fred and Philippe.

I grabbed both of Julien's hands in mine. "I not only owe her this, I want some time with her before I leave."

He stuck out his bottom lip, which instantly made me want to nibble it. His eyes darkened a little, and he ran his hand through his hair. Too bad his heavy coat covered what I imagined to be a delightful display of rippling abs as he moved his arm up and over his head.

"Aww, don't give me the sad puppy look," I teased.

He furrowed his brow.

"If you stay with us, I won't pay any attention to her at all." Sighing, I peered at him, hoping he could understand how difficult this decision was for me. My heart picked up its pace, and I nervously tried to anticipate how he would respond.

He pursed his lips, squinting his eyes at me thoughtfully before reaching over and tucking my hair back beyond my ear. "You're right. But you're staying with us for a few more hours, right?"

"Yep!" I reached up and pecked him on the cheek. "Thanks for understanding." We resumed walking, catching up with the rest of the group who stood in front of a sex shop.

"Let's go in!" Fred insisted, pleading like a child in front of a candy shop.

Of course he wanted to go in. Emilie and I rolled our eyes at each other and she put her hand on my arm. "This isn't really my scene. I'm going to go get another pack of ciggies. Meet you back here in a few minutes?"

"It's not really my scene either," I admitted, as I watched Emilie walk away from us.

Julien stepped back and took my hand. "Hey guys, we'll wait for you outside."

"Great, so I get to be the babysitter?" Philippe asked grumpily.

"Sorry man, it's your turn," Julien laughed as Philippe begrudgingly entered the store.

Stepping just beyond the storefront, Julien leaned back against the wall and pulled me into him. We just stood there in silence for a few moments, arms wrapped around each other, and I wondered if he thought I was a prude. I started to apologize, but he interrupted me.

"It's okay, Callie. I think a lot of that stuff is weird too." He kissed me on the top of my head, then my forehead, then my nose, then gently on my lips.

His words reassured me. But my thoughts drifted to his experience with other girls. Was this something he would do with one of them? With the girl who kept calling? Who was she to him anyway? Knowing I might be stepping in some serious poo, I knew if I was going to spend the next couple of days with him, I needed answers.

"So, this probably isn't the best timing, but you were going to tell me about who was calling you the other day, and I stopped you." *No, why Callie? Why did these words come out of your mouth?*

"Hmph." His arms dropped from around me and I took a step back.

Cocking my head to the side, I waited for him to say more, while desperately fighting my urge to brush the hair flopping on his forehead to the side. I crossed my arms, trying to warm myself from the chill both outside and decidedly between us.

He sighed and shifted to put more distance between us. Julien stared off across the street, fidgeting with his scarf. His physical response to the question triggered my alarm bells, leading me to wonder if there was more to the story than just an ex who had bad timing with her phone calls.

Why wasn't he saying anything? Panic rose and a thousand questions attacked my consciousness, but one was more important than the rest. A tingling sensation arose on the back of my neck as I pointedly asked the most important question. "Are you even single?"

"It's complicated."

I took a step back. "It's complicated?" What the heck did that mean? The blood drained from my face, leaving me woozy.

He looked at me, eyes softening, and reached out to place his hand on my arm. "I mean, yes."

"Yes, you're single?" I wanted to make sure I understood.

"Yes, I'm single, but I haven't been for long."

A whooshing sensation traveled through my body, and I suddenly felt light-headed. Emilie's warnings now made sense. Her comments, her looks of frustration, and her concern all flooded through my mind as though it were the first time I was actually hearing her words of warning. While she'd been warning me not to break his heart, perhaps her real intention had been to shield mine?

Needing more, I pushed for answers. "So, it was a bad breakup?"

"Are they ever not?" he asked softly.

Wanting to backtrack, I squeaked out, "You don't have to talk about it if you don't want to." Inside, I was silently begging him to spill the beans. I wanted to know everything about this girl and the breakup. What was I competing with? *Who* was I competing with?

Callie, you're not competing with anyone. You're going back to the United States, five thousand miles away across an ocean, in two days.

"We were together for five years." He looked down at the ground.

There's that whooshing sensation again. *Five years?* He could not be over a girl he'd been with for five years. And clearly, she was not past him.

"Wow. That's a long time." I leaned back against the wall next to him, staring out into the street, pretending I was intrigued by the cars and buses driving by and wishing I'd never asked the question.

Julien also stared at the cars in front of us, but continued. "Yeah. I went to Uni and she is a couple years younger, so she wasn't with me, but we stayed together."

"So, when did..." But before I finished the sentence, the

door to the shop burst open and Philippe and Fred erupted through the door, the cashier chasing behind them.

The smell hit me first—a mixture of roses, cotton candy, and patchouli, and my gag reflexes responded. As I blinked away the tears that sprang to my eyes, I tried to understand what had just happened.

Julien grabbed my hand and dragged me forward down the street, as the cashier yelled about paying. We hustled along, Philippe and Fred laughing hysterically, until we were a safe distance from the store.

"What just happened?" Julien demanded.

"And more importantly, why do you all smell like THAT?" I demanded, fanning the air in front of myself and putting distance between me and the guys.

"Well, this idiot," Philippe pointed his finger at Fred, "was playing 'demo,' dropped the bottle, and well, now we're wearing the lube."

Emilie caught up with us in that moment. "What did I miss?"

I gave her the CliffsNotes.

Emilie rolled her eyes. "Again, this is why I insisted on our plan for tonight."

"Let's find someplace to eat!" Fred insisted, surprising no one.

I wasn't hungry, but a beer sure seemed like a good idea. I hoped Julien and I would be able to finish our conversation.

We started walking, and for the first time in two days, Julien didn't reach for my hand.

19

THE FIVE OF us strolled along toward the pubs, Fred and Philippe rehashing their big sex store adventure, oblivious to the fact that Julien had his hands stuffed in his pockets, head down.

Emilie, seeming to sense the shift in my mood, hung back with me, looping her arm through mine. We walked in silence for a few minutes. The crowded streets made it difficult to participate in a conversation as we wove through the sightseers gawking at the sights of Pigalle.

The wind whipped at my face and tears stung my eyes. I would certainly blame them on the cold wind and my hair, if asked. Teeth chattering, I longed for Julien's arm thrown around my shoulders, pulling me in for warmth. But now only a vortex of chills claimed the space between us.

My thoughts whirled in my mind almost as strongly as the wind. Why had I brought up the topic? We were having such a great day, making plans for tomorrow. Judging by his demeanor, it could all be a moot point now.

There were no shortage of pubs in this area of town, but

for someone who was starving, Fred took his time. We stopped at the first pub, and Fred studied the menu closely. "Nope."

That happened three more times.

Julien planted his feet and raised his hands up.

"Come on, Fred. Just pick a place!" From the looks on Fred and Philippe's faces, I was not the only one surprised by the sharp edge to Julien's voice.

"Hangry or what?" Fred punched Julien in the arm.

"Would you stop with the punching?"

"Okay, okay!" Fred looked down and continued walking toward the next pub.

Well, this was fun while it lasted. Julien was really irritated and I still wasn't quite sure what had happened. As I silently dissected our conversation, trying to find the moment that he'd become angry, Emilie tugged on my arm to pull us back a little from the guys.

"Everything okay?" Emilie asked, brown eyes full of concern.

"He just told me about his ex."

Concern shifted to surprise. "And what did he say?"

I didn't get a chance to reply before Fred stopped abruptly, tilting his head to the sports bar to our right. "This place looks good!"

We followed him in, no one objecting. I sighed, dreading the idea of small talk and a bar atmosphere. As I wrapped my coat on the back of the chair, I just wanted to escape.

"What's with the long faces?" Fred, normally oblivious to the tension around him, finally seemed to realize not everyone in the party was as exuberant as him as he looked first at Julien, then me, Philippe, and finally Emilie.

No reply.

Waiting for Julien to answer, I searched his face for any

indication of how he was feeling. Finally, he looked up. "Nothing, just been a long day."

"Cool, let's eat!" Fred replied.

Excusing myself to the ladies' room, my eyes connected with Emilie's inquiring glance and I shook my head no in response to her silent question if she should join me. Right now, I just needed a moment alone. Maybe I would ride out the remainder of the afternoon there. It seemed safer.

But the freezing cold bathroom, which was about as big as my shower booth, would not offer the shelter I was seeking. Plus, it smelled strongly of pee and was in the dark basement, which really creeped me out.

Crossing back across the bar, I rejoined the others at the round high-top table, crawling up to my chair between Emilie and Philippe, across from Fred and Julien.

"We were about to send a search party!" Philippe quipped.

Emilie looked hard at me, searching for answers.

"Long line."

The guys raised their eyebrows and surveyed the four men seated at the bar and the mostly empty tables. Maybe that lie had been a bad choice. Emilie placed her hand on mine and I leaned in. "We'll talk later," I assured her, and took a long draw from the beer they'd ordered for me in my absence.

It was excruciating, sitting so close to Julien, wishing it was him next to me, imagining him pulling his chair close to mine, placing his hand on my thigh as he'd done at lunch. I wanted to touch him but he wouldn't even make eye contact.

Knots of nervousness built in my stomach as I twisted my hair and pretended to smile and pay attention to the conversation at the table. My mind ran through the options available to me, resulting in two potential plans of action. In Plan A, I let my stubbornness prevail and wait for him to make the first move, guided by a sense of injustice that I'd done nothing to deserve the cold shoulder treatment. Or, Plan B, I could admit that if I didn't get answers, it would fester and ruin my evening with Emilie because I'll be obsessed with trying to figure out what happened and fretting about fixing it. Also, I didn't want it to end this way. Even if we weren't going to ride off into the sunset together on a white stallion, I didn't want us to end things over a misunderstanding. That's all it was, right? A misunderstanding?

Lila's words flitted through my mind. *You have nothing to lose, Callie. Leave nothing on the table.*

A quick glance around the bar produced a big dart board in the far corner. Yes, that would do. A friendly game of darts. I put my hand on Emilie's shoulder and leaned in to whisper, "I need to do something."

Her eyes were full of questions, but she just nodded her head.

"Julien, wanna play darts?"

Raising his eyebrows in surprise, he shrugged his shoulders and pushed his stool back from the table.

Encouraged by his response, I hopped down from my stool, gave Emilie a quick hug promising I'd be back soon, grabbed my beer, and walked over to the back of the room. Most of the tables were empty, so we had the corner to ourselves.

Choosing the table closest to the big electronic dart board, I took a swig of my beer before setting the mug on the table and walking to the board. The machine stood tall, with a black plastic board with red and yellow plastic lines marking the areas of the board. A door on a latch swung open to reveal a chalk scoreboard. I grabbed the eraser, cleared the board, and wrote a giant J on one side, a C on the other, and put a line down the middle. Then I replaced the chalk and removed the darts from the board. Julien's eyes followed my every move.

Darts in hand, I walked back and stood next to him, catching a whiff of his tantalizing cologne.

"I hope you're ready to be wowed," I said playfully, trying my best to defuse the tension between us. Picking up the darts, I squared my hips, stared at the board with one eye closed like I was boss, and lined up my dart. I was painfully aware of his presence so close to me. I launched the first dart confidently. It not only missed the board completely, the dang thing ricocheted off the wall and shot back at me.

Julien snickered. "Wow is right."

I shot him a playful glare. "I just needed a warm-up throw."

Julien's shoulders relaxed and he offered me a slight smile. "If you say so."

My second launch was not much better, but at least the dart hit the frame of the dart board.

"You're really good at this, Callie. Can you give me some pointers?" Gentle sarcasm oozed in his voice as he relaxed onto a stool at our table and sipped his beer, licking some froth from his upper lip. I tried not to let that distract me.

"Smart ass." I inched a little closer to the board, hoping he wouldn't notice, and lined up again. One eye squinted shut, I released the dart.

"I hit the board! And it stuck!" I squealed, hopping as if I'd just won an Olympic medal, rather than landing a dart on the far-right edge of the circle. Moving to the table, I threw my arms around Julien in excitement and then quickly let go before he had a chance to hug back.

"You do realize it's supposed to be inside any of those sections, preferably the center, right?" he leaned in close to me, his voice husky, breath warm on my neck.

It took great restraint not to turn to him, place both hands on his face, and kiss him. Instead, I moved over to my beer, grabbed it, and took a sip. Then I looked at my handiwork. It was on the farthest edge of the perimeter possible.

"At least I hit the board!" I shrugged.

Shaking his head back and forth, a smirk on his lips, he walked over to the board to collect the darts. I watched his bum, appreciating the way his jeans fit. Racking my brain, I tried to come up with anything flirty to say, finding nothing. Instead, I walked up closer to him, leaned in, and whispered, "Good luck."

Turning to me, his eyes squinted. "Don't try to distract me." His tone was playful. He took his position and I'll be damned if he didn't hit the bullseye on the first try.

Julien shrugged, in a cocky yet adorable way. The ice was melting. Should I just let it go, move past it? Terrified to reopen the conversation just as we were gaining ground, I kept all my questions silent and let the game continue.

He threw the second dart. Bullseye. I squealed. And third, just outside of the bullseye to the right. Whistling, I teased, "You should have warned me you're an expert."

"Where's the fun in that?" He returned to the board to retrieve the darts and returned to me. Julien grabbed my hand and placed the darts in them, letting his fingers linger for a moment on my wrist. I didn't blink. I didn't breathe. I just stood there frozen in place. Neither of us moved for a moment, and I willed him to lean in and kiss me.

Finally, he broke the silence. "I shouldn't have responded that way. Let me tell you about Céline."

Taken aback by his unexpected suggestion, my immediate response was to her name. Céline. I instantly hated that name. It was so *French*. Unsure if I really wanted to know about her, the girl he spent five years with, I licked my lips. Yes, I had questions, but what if he said he wasn't over her yet? My heart pounded so hard I was sure he saw it beating through my sweater. Sweat broke out on my back and I stepped back. Carefully pulling off my sweater, holding my t-shirt underneath it in place, I waited for Julien to say he was still in love with someone else.

With nothing immediately forthcoming from Julien, I pulled myself up on the stool at the table and wrapped my clammy hands around my beer. The shock of the cool class was a relief. He followed me and sat down.

"Okay," I said, staring into my beer. "Tell me."

After a moment of reflection, another sip of his beer, and a long glance at me, he began. He held his beer mug tightly as he spoke.

"Céline and I started dating when we were really young. We dated through high school and when I went to Uni we stayed together even though she was still in high school. I thought that we were going to get married."

Oh no. Now I regretted wanting to know more. I looked frantically over toward Emilie, hoping she would wave me back over, extricating me from this, but they were all involved in a conversation, paying no attention to the two of us.

"I was madly in love with her and would have done anything for her." He paused, searching my eyes for understanding. I forced myself to nod, encouraging him to continue, even though every word out of his mouth felt like a thousand tiny shards of glass in my heart. I took another gulp of beer.

"She was really sweet and naive, and made everything exciting and fun. I thought she would be the perfect wife. Second year of Uni we got an apartment together," Julien said. "My mother adores her and pressured us to plan our future together at an inappropriately young age."

Red flag alert. His mother loves her. He had not put that in the past tense. Oh crap, I really didn't want to hear any more of this. Bile rose slightly in my throat, so I drank more beer to push it back down.

"But then she cheated on me," he said.

I put down the beer mug and looked directly at him, my full attention on him. "I'm sorry," I said compassionately, my heart aching for him, as I moved one hand to cover his.

"I'm not even sure what happened, but I came home from classes early one day and she was with another guy. In our shower."

I sucked in a deep breath. The ultimate betrayal. "Oh Julien. That really sucks." *Way to state the obvious, Callie.*

He pulled his hand away, stepped away from the table, and rolled a dart between his fingers, glaring at the dartboard.

"When did this happen?" I asked, softly.

"September," he said.

Not long after my heart had been crushed.

"I'm sorry." Racking my brain for something more meaningful to say, I had nothing. Why do we struggle so hard to share words of comfort? And why do we always say we're *sorry?* A therapist I'd seen for a bit had tried to help me work on my habit of over-apologizing.

"Saying you're sorry indicates blame," she'd told me. She'd coached me to say, "I'm sorry this happened *to you,*" but I always forgot to add that last bit. Not this time.

I was clearly not to blame for this pain.

"To you!" I shouted.

He jumped, jerking his head in my direction.

"I'm sorry this happened *to you,*" I said, more softly.

He said nothing. Shrugging his shoulders, he focused intently and launched a dart, missing the board completely. He turned and smiled sheepishly. "I guess you're wearing off on me."

Something about the way he said this, his vulnerability

shining through even his attempt to tease me, fueled my courage. I left the table and walked to his side, placing my hand on his arm. "You didn't deserve that, Julien." And then I wrapped my arms around his neck and hugged him tightly. At first, his arms hung limply by his sides, but after a moment, he wrapped his arms around me, nuzzling his nose into my neck. We fit well together physically, and I didn't want to break the embrace, but I pulled back, staring into his eyes.

"Thank you for telling me all of that. If anybody understands heartbreak like that, it's me." But I wondered if he was emotionally ready to be with anyone else. They had grown up together, knew each other's families, and had even lived together. And she was still calling him. Five months was not a lot of time to disentangle from a relationship that serious and move on, especially if he was still stuck in the pain.

Julien kissed me softly on my cheek and opened his mouth, but instead of speaking, turned and retrieved his rogue dart. He returned slowly, his lips pursed.

He approached the table and took a swig of his beer before turning in my direction. His voice broke slightly as he said, "Thank you, Callie. It's been wonderful spending these last couple of days with you. It's really taken my mind off things."

The air seemed to take physical form and then shatter around me, clinking to the floor. I struggled to breathe as I realized the simple truth: I'd merely been a distraction. Unable to ignore the stinging sensation coursing through my body, I dropped his hands, grabbed the darts, and did what I do best. Avoided the conflict entirely.

I lifted the dart to eye level, licking my lips in concentration, and threw it at the board with such intensity that it hit, ricocheted off, and came back straight toward my head. Squealing, I dropped to the floor as the dart whizzed past, crashing into the empty chair behind me.

Standing up slowly, I wiped my hands on my pants and confidently said, "It looks like I'm clearly the stronger player here."

Once his astonishment had passed, Julien doubled over laughing, slapping his hand on his leg. Gasping for breath, he coughed out, "Yeah, absolutely no room for improvement there."

While I collected the darts, Julien moved back to the table, sipping his beer in silence. I joined him at the table. Turning to me, he quietly said, "Until I met you, I convinced myself I'd never fall in love with someone else again."

I squeezed the darts so hard I expected blood to seep from my hand. Slowly releasing my death grip on the small weapons in my palm, I blinked.

Did I hear that right? Does that mean he's falling in love with me now? Oh my gosh oh my gosh oh my gosh. Simmer down, Callie girl. Keep your cool.

He ran his hand through his hair, avoiding eye contact.

"This is a big part of the reason Philippe and Fred are so excited to see me with you." He turned, those blue eyes nearly melting me into a giant puddle of goo again as he gazed into my eyes. I grasped the edge of the table to steady myself. *Breathe, Callie.*

"I haven't been with anybody since her, but it really hasn't been a super long time, and I wasn't sure if I was ready to be with anyone else."

"*Are* you ready?" I asked, still frozen in the same spot, alarm bells ringing in my ears. Before he answered, I placed both my hands on the tabletop and nearly growled, "*Are* you still in love with her?" I wasn't sure if I wanted to know the answer, but I needed to ask it. The room whirled around me as I waited for his reply. I desperately wanted him to tell me he wasn't and was falling in love with me. I wanted him to pull me into his arms, kiss me passionately, and tell me I was so much better than her.

But if he wasn't—the whole situation was nuts, but if he was still in love with her, that would certainly make it easier for me to detangle my feelings and cut ties. *You've known him for two days. He had years with Céline.*

He took a deep breath and blinked his eyes a few times. Staring down at his hands, he shrugged.

That was not the answer I wanted.

20

Rooted in place, my legs wobbled as I struggled to keep bile from rising in my throat. My beer mug was empty. The darts rolled off my hand and onto the table, and I grabbed the mug.

"Want another?" I asked, my voice squeaky.

"Wait, Callie," he grabbed my arm, "I didn't mean..."

Shaking free from his grasp, I stepped away. "It's okay," I called back over my shoulder, beelining for the bar. The bartender approached, smiling, and took my order for another round for our group and I returned to the table with Emilie, Philippe, and Fred.

"You want to join us to play darts?" I asked the rest of our group.

Fred nodded eagerly. Philippe looked at me and shrugged, still a little grumpy from the sex shop escapade, and Emilie turned to face me. "Is everything okay?"

Shaking my head yes, I quickly replied, "I ordered another round."

We made our way to the table as the bartender delivered the drinks and our cheeseburgers, and Fred grabbed the darts.

He explained the rules to his version of the game and gave us our game order. Julien and I were last in the lineup. Sipping my beer on the tall barstool, I swung my feet back and forth and hoped the smile plastered on my face looked genuine. Julien stood behind me and placed his hands on my shoulders, causing me to stiffen. Then I dropped my shoulders, relaxing under his gentle touch, and the breath slowly escaped my lungs as I leaned back into him. No decisions were necessary right at this moment.

Philippe's phone started ringing. He gave it a perplexed look and then ignored the call. It started ringing again. He ignored it once more. The third time it rang, he looked at me, then at Julien, back at me. "Dude, you've got to stop ignoring her. Now she's calling me."

A sick feeling spread through my abdomen at the realization that it was Céline calling, again. The phone stopped ringing, and then started again.

"Céline will never let him go," Fred said to no one in particular, through a mouthful of cheeseburger. The grease dripped off the bottom of the burger onto his plate, and my stomach churned at the sight. "He should just recognize that and marry her."

My jaw dropped to the floor as a small squeak escaped. Emilie looked at me, a stunned look on her face, then back at Fred with disbelief, who was completely oblivious to the impact of his comment as he continued to chomp away at his cheeseburger.

Philippe shot a death look at Fred and smacked him on the head. "Ignore him! He speaks without thinking."

"Fred!" Julien said sharply, shooting him a look that clearly implied, *Not cool dude, knock it off.* Julien grabbed my hands, his face, filled with concern, suddenly very close to mine. "He's wrong. It's over."

Julien squeezed my hands, but I froze in place. Was Fred right? Had I been wrong about these feelings? Maybe the best thing for Julien would be to stay with Céline. I should end this now and forget about spending tomorrow with him.

"Callie?" Emilie asked softly.

My gaze shifted to her, but I had no words. And then the damn phone started ringing again, the sound sending ice up and down my back.

Julien snapped at Philippe, "Give me your phone."

Philippe handed it over and Julien powered it off, before handing it back. He looked around and asked, "Who's up next?"

Clearly, he wanted to move beyond this conversation and ignore the big ole elephant named Céline in the room, but the mood was soured for me.

"Actually, I think I'm done." I looked at Emilie, who visibly released a big tension breath. "What do you say we head out as planned?"

Julien swiveled in my direction, frowning, brows knitted together. Surprise also registered across Emilie's face as she inquired, "Are you sure you want to do that?" Her eyes searched mine and although she didn't seem to be a fan of this entire development, she likely wanted to make sure any decisions made were intentional.

Fred wiped his hands and mouth on the napkin, and stood, moving to me, avoiding eye contact with Julien and Philippe. "Don't go yet!" he insisted. "I'm sorry I'm an idiot. I've had a lot of beer," he justified.

Eyes cast downward, I twisted my finger, needing to escape this situation. My mind and heart were at complete odds, and time was running out for me in Paris.

"Don't go. Please," Julien said as he touched my arm, those gorgeous blue eyes silently pleading with my mind to trust my heart. "These two," he pointed at Fred and Philippe, "will be leaving to get their bags and catch their plane in about an hour." He looked to Emilie, then back to me. "Am I still staying at your place tonight? What about tomorrow?"

Suddenly feeling panicky and short of breath, the thought of leaving Julien behind was too much to bear, but I knew it would only get worse with the compounded feelings of another day together, only to leave without him. The bar and everyone in it spun around me in slow motion. Like an out-of-body experience, I saw our group. Everyone else in the bar was laughing and having a good time while we stood in stunned silence, listening to "Wonderwall" blare across the bar.

"I need a minute," I said, and grabbed my coat.

"I'll come with you." Emilie reached for her coat, but I put my hand on her arm.

"Alone," I said.

She nodded, and I quickly exited the bar and onto the street. My head spun, thoughts attacking from all directions. Julien's world was here. Mine was five thousand miles away. This whole scenario was a crapshoot.

The world bustled all around me as I lit a cigarette. People raced to get in from the cold, tourists wandered from pub to pub, studying menus in search of the right place to eat. Cars rushed by, with their horns honking, swerving around buses that stopped along their route. This wasn't my world anymore.

I needed to exit this picture. They would continue without me, as if I'd never been there at all.

I stubbed out my cigarette and reentered the bar, firm in my new decision.

Four sets of eyes watched me walk toward the table, but before I had a chance to utter a word, Emilie piped up.

"We came up with a plan." She looked expectantly at me.

"Ohhhhkay," I said slowly, eyebrows knitted together,

perplexed as to why Emilie wouldn't be ready to just hightail it out of here with me.

Emilie offered a small smile, eyes twinkling. "Julien's staying with me tonight. Fred and Philippe are going to take the train as planned in a couple of hours. Don't forget I'm working all day tomorrow. It would be such a shame to spend your last day in Paris alone, right? Julien can help you clean your place!"

She waggled her eyebrows at me. It was a little disconcerting how she'd gone from being completely against this situation to now trying to help us work it out.

Cocking my head to the side, my tongue thickened in my mouth.

"Wait, what? You didn't tell me that was part of the plan!" Julien joked.

Indecision paralyzed me as I looked back and forth between the two of them. Despite my resolution to walk away from it all just moments before, spending every moment possible with Julien is what my heart cried out for.

No one spoke, all eyes on me, waiting for me to respond.

Impatient, Fred broke the silence. "Come on Callie! It will be more fun than being alone."

Philippe swatted him on the back of the head. Julien stared at the ground.

Slowly, my mouth started moving. "No, it wouldn't be fun to be alone on my last day, for sure. And yes, it requires manual labor."

Emilie put her hand gently on my arm. "We can still spend some time together this evening. Julien's got to get his stuff from the hotel, and he'll go back to my place. You two can meet up tomorrow?"

That sounded okay to me. This would give me time to process everything, take a step back, and still have some time with Emilie. "Okay, I agree with your plan."

Fred whooped, and Julien looked up and smiled. Philippe patted him on the back. *What a weird moment,* I thought.

"Girls' night?"

Emilie nodded, wrapping her scarf around her neck tightly.

"Ah, come on girls, don't ruin the fun, we're leaving in just a bit anyway," Fred slurred, his head resting in his hands, elbows propped on the table. "Can't you stay just a little longer?"

"As much fun as that sounds, this is my last chance to hang out with Emilie." Leaning in, my lips brushed Fred's cheeks, then Philippe's. "It's been lovely, I hope to see you guys again one day." Placing my hand on Philippe's arm, I continued. "Visit me if you're ever in the States."

"Can I walk you out?" Julien asked.

Pinching my lips together tightly, I agreed. Emilie hung back a moment, while Julien placed his hand on the small of my back and ushered me toward the door. Tiny shivers exploded up and down my back, despite the heavy jacket and my determination to not allow myself to fall any deeper.

Julien followed closely behind me out of the bar and onto the street. Turning me toward him, his hand firmly on my shoulders, his eyes moved to my lips. I licked them instinctively, and Julien pulled me in, planting his lips on mine, first gently, then with more urgency. A tiny pinprick in my heart burst into an expansive flow of warmth, rushing through my entire body and drowning the urge to push him away. Greedily, my hands pulled him into me, kissing him back.

No. Stop. Iceberg ahead! Warning bells sounded in my head, causing me to pull back.

He released me, panting a little. "So, I'll see you tomorrow?"

"If that's what you want." Kicking at the ground, irritation coursed through me for giving in so easily and for being so passive. *If that's what he wants? What about what I want?* Who was I kidding? The pull was too strong to resist. So many questions still lingered—mostly about my ability to spend another day with him and then be able to let him go without a thermal meltdown.

He furrowed his eyebrows, shooting me a look of disbelief, mouth turned down in a frown. Leaning in for a hug, he planted a kiss on my forehead before his arms released me and he turned back toward the door. Looking over his shoulder one last time, blue eyes piercing through me like a laser beam, he shook his head one more time. "I'll see you tomorrow."

The wind rushed out of me as Julien reentered the bar. I placed my hand on the side of the building to steady myself.

Emilie burst out of the bar. "Shall we?"

Head down, hands shoved in my pockets, I nodded.

She pulled me into a hug and whispered, "I'm sorry."

I fought back tears.

21

WITH NO CLEAR plan for the evening, Emilie chose a direction and we started walking. Silently, she laced her arm through mine, and I followed her lead as we headed down Boulevard de Clichy. Walking toward the eight-lane intersection, the Moulin Rouge came into view, lit up in bright colors as the daylight began to fade. The large red windmill on the roof of the building was a global icon for cabaret and cancan dancers. Wide red planters with small shrubs lined the street in front of the Moulin Rouge, creating a little buffer zone around the front of the building. This area was filling quickly with patrons dressed in their evening attire, queued to watch the next show, something I'd never done. The tickets were outside of my budget. Maybe next time I was in Paris I could go.

Turning left on Rue Pierre la Fontaine, we headed in the direction of the river. Emilie and I knew this city well now, after months of walking, busing, and metroing through all the streets. How could it have only been two days since I met Julien? Our first night replayed in my mind. His finger, tracing a line from my neck, lingering on my collarbone. His hands rubbing my neck, or running down my back, the sensation I had of a lock and key when his fingers interlaced mine, fitting so perfectly together. The way he shivered when I ran my hand across his tight abdomen. His Hugo Boss smell. I released a loud sigh.

Eyes wide, Emilie turned to me. "You okay?"

"I screwed this all up."

Emilie pursed her lips. "You've really developed feelings for him, haven't you?"

"It was supposed to be light, fun. But now I feel like I'm on the express train to heartbreak," I admitted.

No reply. Emilie kept walking, staring straight ahead. Her body language was shouting, "I told you this would happen." If she was irritated with either of us, she certainly was not in the wrong. Yet she said nothing. We turned down Rue Blanche, making our way back in the direction toward Avenue de l'Opéra.

Beer and anxiety mixed in my belly, burning unpleasantly. Please let food be in our near future. "So, where are we heading?"

With a lightness that surprised me, Emilie replied, "You'll know when we get there!"

"I love the mystery, but I'm starving and my legs are so tired."

Emilie stopped and quickly consulted her pocket map, the same one I carried. We'd bought ours together when we first arrived. "Let's hop on the next bus. Otherwise, we'll be walking a long way."

Nodding in relief, I had a renewed sense of energy as I now knew I only needed to make it to the next bus stop, which wasn't far from us.

Drifting into my own thoughts, the hard realization hit me

that not only had I had developed strong feelings for Julien, I'd completely fallen for him.

And then screwed it up.

At least if I just ended it now, there wouldn't be any sad feelings at the airport, no false promises of how we'd make this work—if he even wanted any of that. Maybe I'd just tell Emilie to tell him not to come see me tomorrow.

But there was no use in making that decision right now. *Focus on what's in front of you, Callie.*

In a stroke of good fortune, the bus appeared quickly. Climbing on board, Emilie showed her pass and I time-stamped my ticket before we shoved our way to the middle of the bus. As usual, it was standing room only. I clung to the shiny metal pole close to the middle door, turning my back to Emilie to stare out the window.

Difficult as it was to pull myself out of my thoughts, and despite having seen these sights a thousand times, I drank in everything on the bus ride, committing everything to memory. Beautiful white marble buildings, small shops, the mopeds zigging in and out of traffic, stands with fresh fruit, vegetables, and flowers. The tourists, wandering around, looking up, nearly crashing into other pedestrians. Hustle and bustle everywhere. A lump added itself to the burning in my stomach. In two days, this would no longer be my home. Emilie also homed in on the scenery beyond the bus windows. At some point, we'd need to exchange words, or this would be a long evening. But not here.

The bus stopped frequently, winding through several streets, down to the Avenue de l'Opéra, past the Louvre, and across the Seine River.

Placing my hand on Emilie's arm, I smiled when she turned to face me. She returned the gesture and leaned into me. At least if I had mucked things up with her brother, we still seemed good.

Sisters before misters, right?

"What's on your mind?" I asked Emilie.

"Mostly the yummy food we're about to eat." Emilie waggled her eyebrows, licking her lips devilishly.

Giggling, relief flooded through me. She wasn't obsessing over my stupid situation. "I am so hungry. I'm so glad we're in sync on this!"

She chuckled. "If I had a dollar for every time you've said that over the past six months..."

"You'd be a very wealthy woman! I have to get this stuff while I can!" Patting my stomach, I demonstrated exactly where all the good treats needed to wind up.

The bus lurched forward, honking at a car that darted in front of it. Emilie and I giggled as we righted ourselves after nearly being launched into the laps of the people sitting to our right.

"Let's get off here," Emilie directed at the next bus stop. We were near the Sorbonne. I immediately knew what she had in mind for food.

"Paninis!" It might have seemed like an ordinary item to choose as our final meal together, but one, I couldn't find these at home, and two, we had a ton of good memories associated with this panini stand. My office was closed Wednesday afternoons, and Emilie had a long break between classes, so I'd often walked here to meet her for lunch. We'd grab food and walk to the Luxembourg Garden, as I hoped we'd do this evening, and chat about our lives and plans while people-watching.

They were more than just paninis.

"Is this okay for you tonight?" Emilie's brow creased. "If you want something fancier, we can totally go somewhere else."

"I can't think of anything better for our final meal together!"

Her face lit up and we hurried to the food truck, placed in its usual position, tucked off the street.

As hard as I tried to stay in the moment, my thoughts drifted back to Julien. He'd be saying goodbye to his friends and heading to Emilie's apartment soon. What was going through his mind? His heart? Would he change his mind about seeing me tomorrow? Did I still want to spend the day with him? We'd be alone in my room. Would I be able to resist him? Did I even want to?

"Callie?" I moved forward, realizing it was our turn to order, mentally smacking myself for sliding so easily back into Julien la-la land.

"Just thinking about my long to-do list," I said, a bit sheepishly.

"Uh-huh." Emilie turned toward the food truck, greeted enthusiastically by the large man grinning at us from behind the silver counter.

"Mesdemoiselles! How can I help you?" Multitasking, he turned to pull a panini, steaming and glorious, out of the machine, wrapped it in paper and a napkin, grabbed a small bag of fries from behind him, and presented it to the gentleman waiting beside us, who snatched it eagerly.

"How many times do you suppose we've eaten here?" I asked.

"Enough that I know your order by heart." Emilie winked.

Emilie addressed the portly man in the stand. "I'll take a ham and cheese panini with fries and a Coke."

"Good choice! And I'll have…"

Emilie cut me off. "Mozzarella and tomatoes, fries, and a Coke!" We giggled. Emilie's smile lit up her dark brown eyes.

Balancing sandwiches, fries, and beverages in our hands, we moved quickly in the direction of the Luxembourg Gardens. I paused.

"Hold this please," I demanded, handing her my fries. I shoved the unopened Coke can in my coat pocket and unwrapped the panini, biting off a huge chunk.

"Sweet jumping beans, this is delicious," I mumbled, my mouth full.

Emilie, hands full of all her food and mine, laughed loudly.

"I'm sorry, I was so hungry, and this," I waved the panini in front of her, "is going to be cold by the time we get to the gardens. That would be a waste of that poor man's efforts!"

Rolling her eyes, Emilie passed the fries back, also handing me hers and repeating my actions, releasing a loud "Mmmm" as she bit into the sandwich. We ate in silence as we walked, a lightness between us that hadn't been there since before I met Julien on New Year's Eve.

Everything caught my attention along our route. The noise of Paris that had become almost invisible to me now seemed to scream at me. Cafés and bars hopped with activity, filled with friends or lovers meeting for an end of day or perhaps a beginning of the evening beverage. Cute shops with their adorable window displays seemed to call out to me, *Don't leave.* Horns honked and trucks that looked far too large for this city rumbled down the streets.

What if I stayed?

The thought caught me off guard. Until three days ago, I'd been perfectly ready to go home, find a job, and get on with my life. But as I took in my surroundings, munching on the fries now that my panini was long gone, I tried to imagine living here. And dammit if the thought of living here in a little apartment with Julien didn't pop into my mind. His plans were to move here after graduation. Could we have found a cute studio? Maybe a one or two bedroom in case we had visitors? Would we meet up for lunch breaks? Get married?

Stop it right now.

The idea of living here permanently seemed out of reach now. I had been fully prepared to start a life here with Vic, but as much as I adored living in Paris, working as a bilingual secretary and living this dream life as an American in Paris, I missed my home, my family, and my life thousands of miles and an ocean away. And Julien was likely nothing more than a fling, despite our deepening connection. I was coming to accept this fact. No matter what happened tomorrow, his life was here, mine was not.

Forcing myself from these daydreams, I turned to Emilie. "You have cheese on your chin."

She laughed and wiped her glove on her face as we finally entered the magnificent Luxembourg Gardens. Even in the winter, it took my breath away, so fairy-tale-like with the moderate "castle" and the massive gardens. You could easily lose yourself and imagine yourself hundreds of years ago in this setting—assuming you ignored the loud street noises. On one of our lunch meetings here, Emilie and I had concocted an entire story about a girl who was visiting this castle and somehow accidentally time traveled back to the eighteenth century, waking up as a princess in a foreign land and time.

"We should write that book together."

"Huh?" Emilie looked at me as if I'd lost my mind. We walked toward the pond, searching for a free bench.

"Remember the story about the American girl who gets lost and wakes up as a princess?"

"Ooooh." The lights went on for Emilie. "Yes, that was a fun story. I'm not sure I'm up for writing a book. But go for it!"

Shrugging my shoulders, I pointed to a free bench in front of us. "I'll add it to my list..."

We sat down, though our food was long gone. I pulled the Coke from my pocket and cracked it open. "Remember our first week in Paris together? You got here just a couple of days after

Vic dumped me, and I was holed up in a hotel, not expecting to be on my own."

"No, you've got the details wrong." Emilie turned to face me. She took a swig of her Coke. "I got here the same day Vic dumped you."

"No, that can't be right."

"Yes, I swear. Remember my dad and I picked you up? We went to that Japanese restaurant and you drank allll the saké."

Red spread across my face. "There's a reason I don't remember that night." We both laughed.

"Well, my dad remembers, and he won't stop talking about it." Emilie turned back toward the pond.

"Apartment shopping sucked." I giggled and she nodded her head smiling as well.

"Dead chickens!" Emilie exclaimed, both of us laughing hysterically as we recalled a particular neighborhood we had visited while checking out available places, where there had been a dead chicken in the road.

"You screamed 'Voodoo!' and took off running!" Emilie and I bent over in hysterics, remembering some of the wild things we had seen in the depths of Paris, in the places that tourists never see.

"That was so terrifying!" I chimed in. We'd found ourselves in a sketchy neighborhood with a lot of strange things happening. Let's just say, girls of our upbringing were not used to seeing things like drug deals, and certainly not random dead animals that were not roadkill in the middle of the street. We'd hightailed it back to the metro, crossing that neighborhood off the list.

Emilie, still smiling at the memory, turned to face me. "We've come a long way for sure. Look at us now, like we freaking own the place."

I sighed. "Full circle. While we have learned our way

around this big city, I started off heartbroken, and it looks like that's the way I'll leave it." I stared across the pond. It was getting dark, and my view was mostly limited to what was lit by the park lights.

"Your heart healed before, and you..." Emilie stopped as tears filled up her eyes. She struggled to get out the next words. "Callie, I'm really proud of you."

"You are?"

"I think if it had been me, I would have gone running home, tail between my legs. But not you." Emilie grabbed my hand in hers, squeezing it. "Despite being completely knocked on your ass, you got back up, you made a life for yourself. You showed everyone how strong you are."

I didn't really know how to respond to that, and just focused on holding back the tears that wanted to flow. Despite my best efforts, some escaped.

"Thank you," I finally managed. "I didn't feel strong. You and Lila, you held me up."

Emilie squeezed my hand tightly. I knew that no matter what happened in my love life, I would always have these two girls.

She nodded. "I'm sorry that I tried to stop this from happening."

Turning to face her, eyebrows knitted together, I pursed my lips, trying to understand what she was saying. "Did you try to stop this? Cause Julien has done his fair share all on his own with this whole Céline thing."

"I didn't do anything to sabotage you two, but I wasn't exactly supportive. And I may have been a little jealous."

"Jealous?" That admonition shocked me.

"I didn't want to give up our last few days together."

"You did warn me. I just assumed you were ticked that I ignored you and chose time with your brother over you."

She shrugged. "Probably some of that. But mostly I was worried that you were trying to squeeze in a happy ending, the one you didn't get with Vic, and that you and Julien would just end up suffering."

"Well, looks like I totally avoided that!" I snickered. Humor was always my first line of defense.

Her lips turned up in a small smile. She reached for my hand again and for a few minutes, we sat in silence on the bench, holding hands, doing nothing other than watching the world pass us by.

Polishing off most of the rest of my Coke, I turned toward her and looked her directly in the eyes. "I understand why you would think that. And you were right to worry. Because Emilie, I'm falling in love with him. And it's not going to end well."

Her shoulders slumped, brown eyes cast downward, and took in one heck of a deep breath. "I know," she said.

"But it doesn't really matter anymore." My shoulders slumped. "I just don't see any way that this can work."

Emilie rubbed my arm gently. "I love you, Callie, but you fall so fast. Are you even sure you've had the time to properly heal from the loss that you had with Vic? Maybe this, whatever this was, was what you needed to give your heart some closure and to know you can meet someone else and find happiness again?"

"I can tell you, without a doubt, I am over Vic. I hadn't thought about him in months until a few days ago, and that, I'm sure, is only because I'm rehashing everything as I prepare to go home." I nodded my head emphatically. "I'm over him."

"Okay," Emilie turned back in my direction. "So, let's say that you are indeed over Vic, ready to fall fully in love with someone else."

I nodded, waiting for her to continue.

"I'm not sure Julien is over his ex." She turned her body

back toward the pond, staring out into the distance, avoiding eye contact.

Oof. All the air left my lungs. While I wasn't surprised by this, it hurt to hear someone else say it. "That's my impression too." I squeaked out. "All the phone calls."

Emilie looked off in the distance, continuing slowly. "They've been together since high school. They've broken up many times, yet Céline always seems to find a way to get him back."

I stared down at my hands. My worst fears confirmed.

"I'm just not sure it's over for good," Emilie continued, still avoiding eye contact. "And I don't want you to get more invested than you should at this point." With these words, she reached out for my hand again. I knew it was hard for her to be so honest with me, even if the words hurt.

My mind replayed the events of the last few days. While Julien had told me the big picture, we hadn't spoken that much about Céline and his thoughts about her, about them and their future. He'd told me that it was over, but apparently that had happened a few times. Without even realizing it, Julien might have used me to test the waters of his own feelings. Ross and Rachel popped into my mind. Sometimes you explore other options when you're angry, right?

"We were on a break!" I yelled, throwing my hands up in the air in exasperation.

Emilie tilted her head and squinted her eyes. "What?"

"We were on a break! You know, the line from *Friends* after Ross hooks up with someone else after he and Rachel had their big fight."

Her expression was blank.

"Oh, come on! *Friends*! Ross and Rachel! The epic love story! Ross has been in love with Rachel for decades. But she's never been into him. He lives his life, then the stars align,

Rachel falls for him, and after they *finally* get together, they get in a fight, and Ross mucks it all up."

Her eyes showed absolutely no sign of recognition at this story. I don't know who was more surprised. Emilie, that I was telling such a random story, or me, that with all the *Friends* obsession in France, she didn't know what I was referring to.

"I don't have a TV," she reminded me.

Huffing, I continued. "Okay, so it's this epic story. Ross has been in love with Rachel forever, and when they finally get together, it's like the planets have aligned, until they have this huge stupid fight, and Ross goes off and sleeps with someone else."

"After one little fight?"

"Well, it was a big fight! Rachel naturally finds out, confronts him, and there's this famous scene when Ross gets all wild, yelling, 'We were on a break!'"

Emilie squinted her eyes. "So, how does this apply to any current situation you're in?"

The full realization hit me like a truck. I didn't want to be the break girl. I wanted to be the whole deal.

"Julien and Céline. Love story, breakup. Maybe I am just a 'break' for Julien?" Using air quotes when I said the word break, I chuckled again, thinking of another *Friends* reference— Joey and his air quotes.

"What's funny about that?" Emilie asked.

"Doesn't matter." There was no way I was going to try to explain that episode.

"You Americans and your TV shows." Emilie snickered. "For what it's worth, I don't think you were just a bounce-back girl," Emilie said, sincerely.

"You mean a rebound?" We both giggled. Another chink in her almost-perfect English!

Watching the pigeons flock as a passerby threw chunks of

bread, neither of us spoke. I slowly put my thoughts together while I swirled the remaining few sips of Coke around in my can. "I'm just wondering if you're right, though. Maybe I'm not a 'bounce back' but still, I created a fairytale ending to what is simply a fun fling and certainly stands no chance of happily ever after."

Emilie leaned over, setting her empty Coke can at her feet. She met my gaze with love and concern in her eyes, causing more rogue tears to run down my cheeks. I clamped my eyelids shut tightly to hold back the flood.

Pulling me in for a hug, Emilie rubbed her hands across my back. "I don't know if this is just a little fling or if it's more. But I know the whole situation, not just this weekend. And since you've arrived, well, it's a lot to process, Callie. In a very short period of time, you've had your story rewritten several times. And you're about to completely uproot yourself again."

I cuddled into her, and Emilie pet my head gently. "Truthfully, I'm glad Julien decided to stay in town tonight."

"You are?" Even though they'd worked up this plan together, I had my doubts about whether she really approved of it.

"I think you deserve the chance to see how it plays out."

Looking up, I searched her eyes to see if she was sincere. "Really?"

She pulled in a long breath, and I pulled back out of her embrace. Her eyes held mine as she carefully selected the right words.

"Now that he's told you about Céline, you have more facts. But not all the facts. You can proceed more *cautiously*."

I nodded as she took a breath. "I don't want you to end this if something magical might happen. Because right now, neither of us know if he feels the same way you do," she said.

"Good point," I agreed.

Emilie reached out, wiping a tear from my face. "But I can tell you this, Callie."

Squirming impatiently while I waited for her to continue, I tucked my hair behind my ear.

Emilie proceeded cautiously, as though she were about to share with me the secret of life. Leaning in, eyes big, she said, "I've never seen him look as sad as he did when you walked away from him tonight at the bar."

Staring across at the bare trees, trying to process it all, I hoped she was right.

"Maybe I was wrong," Emilie finally admitted.

I turned back to her. "Wrong about which part?" Was she wrong about us potentially being a thing, or wrong about her assessment of his earlier sadness. I needed to know.

"Wrong about you two being a bad idea together." Emilie looked down at her hands, suddenly very interested in the cuticle on her index finger. "He's still here. You have a day to figure things out. If you're both on the same page about what you want, a little distance isn't going to end that."

"What did you do with my friend Emilie?" I asked, sarcastically. "You must be an impostor!"

I knew admitting to being wrong was hard for her and I didn't know how to respond seriously, so humor won. I'd spent the last few hours building a wall around my heart. And now, the one person least likely to support this mission was telling me not to give up hope? It was a lot to take in.

"I love you, Callie. And I want nothing but your happiness. You're always telling me to live life with no regrets. It's time to take your own medicine."

Snuggling in closer to her on the bench, I rested my head on her shoulder again. As I thought through everything, there were only two choices. Option A, back way off, spend the day with him as a friend, and look for nothing more. It would sting, cause great sadness, and, knowing me, I'd go the rest of my life wondering if I'd screwed up the best thing that ever happened to me. Option B, tell him how I felt and make him tell me the truth about his feelings. We could have an honest conversation about what he wanted and felt. I might still get hurt, but at least I'd have closure. That was something I'd never had with Vic. And it had eaten me alive.

"Okay. You're right. I don't want to go home wondering 'what if?'"

Suddenly, panic clutched at my heart. I pulled back, turning to face Emilie, and whispered, "But Em, what if I'm wrong? What if he wants nothing more than just a fling this weekend?"

"Like I told you New Year's Eve, Julien's not the fling type."

22

THE SUN FILLED MY ROOM, and my eyes opened slowly. Sitting up, I crawled over to my window and stared at the Eiffel Tower.

"What do I do?" I asked aloud. Not surprisingly, she didn't answer.

My conversation with Emilie had left me fueled with bravado to tell Julien everything. Get it all on the table. But now, butterflies danced through my belly. The thought of seeing him soon, hugging him, hopefully kissing him, thrilled me but also terrified me. What would I say and how would he react?

Maybe I say nothing at all, I thought, throwing the covers off, stretching my whole body and yawning. Let the pieces fall where they may. Better than opening up my heart to be hammered.

Have a fun day, get on the plane tomorrow, and start the rest of my life, leaving all of this behind me? Easy-peasy, right? How many months of therapy would this take to get over? Especially without Lila and Emilie to help me.

Sighing loudly, I slid my feet into my fuzzy slippers and pulling on my robe, walked the three steps to my hot plate, filled the kettle with water, and willed the water to boil faster.

My phone rang, startling me.

"Did I wake you?" Julien's sultry voice pulled me right out of my sleepy haze.

"Nope, somehow you timed it perfectly. I just woke up."

"Great. When can I see you?"

Shivers spread up my arms at the thought. My landlord was coming to inspect the room and collect the key in about three hours. There was little time and much to do. The cord of my phone did not stretch far, so I pulled out the chair and sat down. "That depends on if you feel like helping me pack?"

"That sounds like an incredibly thrilling activity!" Julien's tone was playful, which I took as a good sign.

"You've clearly never had the joy of packing with Callie!" I teased. "If you're not up for that, no worries, I can meet you out in a few hours?"

"I'm totally up for packing!"

Laughing at his feigned enthusiasm, I gave him directions and hung up. He'd arrive in about twenty minutes. I had just enough time to take a combat shower and pull on a pair of jeans and a t-shirt. A new cup of tea in hand, I started organizing before the phone rang again.

"I'm downstairs."

"Ok, I'm coming down." My nerves rattling, I flew down the eight flights of steps and burst through the door into the corridor. My instinct was to throw myself into his arms, but I held back. He approached me cautiously as well, maybe even shyly, removing his beanie and brushing his shaggy, sexy hair away from his face. He wore the same shirt he'd worn on New Year's Eve, which hugged him so well in all the right places.

"Good morning," he said, with his voice low. He tucked some stray hair behind my ear and, hands on my shoulders, searched my eyes. When I thought I might pass out from not breathing, he bent down, bringing his lips softly to mine. His mouth lingered on mine for just a moment, his hands running down my arm and grabbing my hands with his.

"Is that okay?" he whispered.

"Mm-hmm." My stomach flipped as he smiled. He didn't let go of me immediately and instead ran his hands up and down my arms with his ocean-blue eyes locked on mine, causing goosebumps to break out everywhere on my body.

Biting my lower lip, I cocked my head toward the door. "My place is this way." Dropping his hands, I turned to the entryway, unlocked and pushed open another door, and led him up the narrow set of stairs. Plain, straight stairs, nothing grandiose like Lila's building had. Eight butt-burning flights. Was he checking out my derriere as we climbed?

"How far up are you anyway?" he asked after four flights.

"This wearing you down, buddy? I thought you were a soccer star?" I teased.

He snorted. "This? I'm fine."

Yet by the time we got to the top he was huffing as heavily as I was. He reached out, putting his hands on my waist.

"You do this every single day?"

I grabbed his hand and feigned pulling him up the last few stairs. "Sometimes more than once."

"Wow, no wonder you can eat the way you can and drink the way you do!"

"Did you really just say that?"

He winked at me and popped my butt. "Am I wrong? You did put down more beer than I did last night."

Flirty. I liked it. Playful was safest right now. "True statement," I replied. "But I'm not sure that's entirely due to these stairs. I walked halfway across Paris to get to work every day."

He just nodded.

Reaching my door, my hands trembled a bit as I tried to put the keys in the lock and they fell out of my shaky fingers, hitting the ground. Turning around to face him, our eyes met, vibrations slamming between our bodies. Keeping his eyes locked on mine, he bent down and picked up the keys. He stood slowly, running his hand all the way up my leg, my hip, and tracing my arm before placing the keys back in my hand. My breathing quickened, as I arched my back against the door, pressing my body toward him. Julien kept his hand around mine, wrapping his other arm around me and turning me to face the door. Then he pressed up against me, guiding the key into the lock, his breath warm on the back of my neck. His warm lips found the back of my neck, peppering my neck with kisses, running his free hand up and down my other arm. I pressed my forehead against the door, moaning.

Somehow my fingers managed to turn the key in the lock, and the door sprung open. We tumbled into my tiny little room, our moment of passion momentarily broken as we laughed. Relief at having a moment to cool off and reset the moment flooded through me, competing only with the burning desire spreading through my lower body.

"So, this is what a *chambre de bonne* looks like!" Julien glanced around the small space.

"Yep, this space is alllll mine," I said, sarcasm oozing in my voice. I had explained to him the other night that my tiny little room was actually a converted maid's room from a period when the people living in the grandiose apartments below housed their hired help here. Now it was a hallway with eight small rooms rented out, mostly to foreigners.

"Yeah, it's uhh... so small! My dorm room is bigger."

True statement. This room was half the size of my last dorm room. "You can see now why I spent so much time at Lila's and Emilie's."

Julien turned in a half circle, observing the small space. "Well, I guess you have everything that you need here. Cute little table, two chairs, a dresser, a shower. And of course, a bed." He talked as he walked, and sat down on the bed.

Knees nearly giving out, I giggled nervously as he took inventory. Trying to think about anything other than the fact that he was sitting on my bed, I blurted out some random facts. "But would you believe that I am the only person on this floor that has my own shower!"

My eyes landed on his full, tempting lips, remembering the moment we'd just shared outside the room, insides churning as I watched him chew on his bottom lip.

"No," he said in disbelief. "What do the others do?"

Pulling myself back in from the full-on fantasy developing in my mind, it took me a moment to realize he was still talking about the showerless residents.

I filled him in on the other tenants, painfully aware of how close he was standing to me. "We're a group of ragtag immigrants, and I'm pretty sure I'm the only one that's here legally. My neighbor Lucy showers at the sports center a few blocks from here."

"I can't even imagine not having access to a shower." His face contorted and I burst into a fit of giggles.

Both of us stopped laughing, staring intently at each other. Moving toward him, my eyes locked onto his hungry eyes, glazed over in desire. I fingered the zipper on his coat.

"You must be hot." My fingers slowly unzipped his jacket, and I ran my hands up his shoulders to help him take his arms out. His eyes never left mine and one arm came out of the sleeve, and then the next. I admired how his t-shirt clung to his pecs. I tossed his jacket to the side and stepped one step closer. His arms wrapped around my waist, and he leaned his head in, hugging me tightly, head on my chest, hands on my butt. My breath erratic, I rubbed my hands up and down his back, peppering his soft hair and forehead with kisses.

Raising his head, he cupped my face in his hands, his thumb tracing my lips. My lips parted slightly, and I leaned into him. Our lips met, slowly, gently, and then hunger kicked in. His tongue parted my lips, exploring, pulling me closer and tighter into him. He leaned back, pulling me on top of him on the bed, and I let loose a moan as he kissed my neck and moved his hand under my shirt, caressing my back. Heat flowed down my body, and I wrapped my arms around his neck, running my fingers through his hair. Panting, my legs tightened around his body, pulling him in closer, tighter. I wanted nothing more than to give everything to him, to lose myself in him, to completely surrender to the desire that pulsed through my body.

My head turned to the left as he kissed down the side of my neck, and I saw the Eiffel Tower in the distance. Stunned, I lay still. This felt too big. Too fast. My hands and legs released him, and I rolled off him. He lay on the bed, questions in his eyes.

Leaning in, I kissed him softly one more time. "You came to work, remember?"

He released a huge sigh, face full of disappointment, and pulled me into him, bringing his lips to my neck once again. "Do we have to?" he whispered against my throat.

"'Fraid so, mister. I'm running out of time." Although it was the last thing I wanted to do, I untangled myself from his arms and slid off the bed, pulling down my shirt and readjusting my bra straps. Turning back to him, I shrugged, playing it cool when in fact I wanted more than to hop right back where I'd been, and then stepped over to my bag, throwing it up on the bed. He sat up, moved his legs out of the way, and sighed as he ran his hands through his hair. Smiling sweetly in his direction, I opened the bag and started tossing clothes in, trying not to get too lost in a completely ridiculous overanalysis of what was happening between the two of us. I had to assume that no matter how hot and heavy things got, for him, this was something fun to do while he was away in Paris. But tomorrow, I'd be headed to the United States, and he'd be on his way back to figure things out with Céline. That was just what happened. I'd seen it too many times.

Sighing, he hopped off the bed, bending over to kiss me once more on the head. "What can I do?"

I patted his arm in consolation. "Okay, so first on the agenda. I need to pack up the items I'm giving to Emilie, so I can enlist your help to take them to her later."

"That sounds fun," he deadpanned.

"Don't worry, nothing too difficult. Then I'm just going to cram the rest of my clothes into these three bags." I pointed at the bag on the bed and the two others on the floor next to the bed. "I've got to take all of these photos off the wall." I pointed to my collage of memories that covered the entire wall between the bed and the table next to the door. "And I've got to scrub the sink and the shower."

As I ticked off each item, he nodded his head and moved over to grab the stack of CDs I'd pointed at.

"Then we just need to move everything into the hall and wait for the landlady to come get the key."

"You're quite the taskmaster," he said, as I handed him a box.

"Ok, I need the CD player, pretty much all electronics, the robe... what else?" I surveyed my tiny room. "Oh, yes, this pan is Emilie's. All in here, please." I gave him a peck on the lips with this order and grabbed one of the CDs from his hands. "On second thought, we need this."

Julien grabbed my wrist. "Hey, how am I ever going to make progress if you keep unpacking what I've packed?" His voice was gruff, and our faces were inches apart. Before giving into the pull toward his face, I turned quickly.

"We need music, babe!" I selected the Chili Peppers. "Ooh, I love this one. Lila and I saw them play at Bercy in November."

Californication. It seemed wildly inappropriate, but it was a good CD nonetheless. The bass intro to "Around the World" pumped into the room and I danced around playfully.

"Life *is* beautiful around the world," Julien said, admiring my moves.

"Get to work!" I teased, swatting his hands off as he tried to pull me in.

Julien stuck his bottom lip out, then returned to placing items in the box, filling it quickly. "What next?" He skillfully air guitared along with the song.

"I need all of these to come down," I said, nodding in the direction of the pictures stuck to my walls. "Carefully," I added, showing him how to remove the pictures and gently pull the putty from the backs, placing them in a folder.

The music slowed down as "Scar Tissue" came on, and I swayed to the beat. Working on the same wall, removing one picture at a time, we periodically exchanged glances. Julien asked me about the people and I told him about my family, my sisters, my parents, my friends, my cats. He laughed at the pictures of me, Emilie, and Lila, clearly having a good time out on the town, and the trips that Lila and I had taken to Normandy to visit the World War II memorials and the beaches, and our adventure to Mont St. Michel.

"You've clearly made good use of your time while you've been here."

"Yeah, I'm glad I chose to stay, even though I wondered, when Vic and I first broke up, if I should just go home." I paused, holding a picture of Lila and me at one of the bunkers in Normandy. "If I'd gone home then, I would have missed out on so much. Life here, adventures, friendship." Placing the picture in the box, I turned to him. "You," I whispered.

Closing the distance between us, Julien placed his hands on the wall on either side of me. Licking his lips, he gruffly said, "That would have been unfortunate," before leaning in and kissing me. My arms wrapped tightly around him, and I closed my eyes. "You're special, Callie," he whispered into my ear.

With my insides completely melting, I turned quickly to hide the emotions on my face, wiggling free from his grasp and grabbing my large suitcase from the floor. Throwing it on the bed, I emptied my drawers into it with little organization.

Tears pricked my eyes as I leaned over my bag. Julien approached and wrapped his arms around me from behind. We stood together, listening to the music as a tear slid down my face. I turned and looked up into his face, eyes searching each other's for solutions, bodies pressed closely. I melted into him as he peppered my face with kisses, moving to my chin and finally reaching my lips. His breath was hot, his tongue hungry. I was not sure that I'd be able to stop.

Desire ripped through me, while my brain kept trying to intercede. I recognized this feeling. This, *I don't want to go a minute without being next to you* feeling. I kissed him almost angrily, nipping gently at his bottom lip, fighting the full-on battle that was happening right now between my heart, my brain, and my physical body. This would not end well for me. I had to stop.

I broke the embrace and nuzzled into his chest, letting the tears flow.

Julien said nothing, but held me tightly. He planted soft kisses on the top of my head, caressing my back.

Is this my moment? Should I tell him now? I wanted nothing more than to whisper, "I love you," in his ear. What if he didn't say it back? What if he laughed? What if he just left?

Turning toward the clock, I rolled my eyes, placing my hand on his chest as I stepped back. He cocked his head and I pointed.

"My landlord will be here in thirty minutes!" Now scrambling, I grabbed every loose item and shoved it in a bag. My landlord scared me. She was an unkind woman who had insulted me at every opportunity.

Julien sighed deeply. His expression was unreadable. Gesturing at the remaining items, he asked, "What are we going to do with all of this?"

Our tender moment was officially over. I'd have to tell him my feelings later. My clothes and most precious souvenirs were mostly packed. A box loaded with Emilie's stuff sat next to the door. Pointing at the bulging bags propped up on the wall, I said, "That's garbage. It needs to go down to the bin."

Julien heaved up two of the bags of trash, arms flexing, and headed to the door, his soft lips grazing my cheek quickly on his way past. "Be right back."

I fought the urge to pull him into my arms, turning to the sink for distraction. While imagining fun scenarios, I quickly wiped down the sink and then dragged my bags into the hall. A quick sweeping of the tiny space and I declared it good enough. I scanned my small, tidy room, with all signs of my life and memories here packed or thrown out, then darted over and hopped onto the bed, pressing against the window.

"This will be the last time I talk to you from here," I whispered in the tower's direction, thankful that I'd had a moment alone to say goodbye to her from here.

The door opened.

"Is this everything?" Julien asked.

Hopping off the bed, I nodded, shoulders slumped as the realization hit me that this was it. Grabbing the one remaining bag of garbage, I stepped into the hallway where Julien waited, and closed the door.

23

Surprisingly, the interaction with the landlord went quickly. She made sure nothing was broken or missing, took the keys, and handed me my deposit before she turned to scrub the sink down again, mumbling about dirty Americans.

We hailed a cab, loaded my items, and crawled into the back seat. The taxi whirred by all the sites, unnoticed due to the, er, heavy petting and kissing. The driver announced our arrival at the hotel I'd chosen to stay at for that night, and I sheepishly retrieved my bags, avoiding eye contact with him. While Emilie had offered to let me stay at her place, this was one of my final remaining Paris bucket list items—stay in a nice Parisian hotel near the Eiffel Tower.

Julien and I lugged my overstuffed bags into the quiet lobby. The attendant informed me that the room was not ready, so we left the bags in the storage room and made our way to Emilie's apartment with the box of her items. I waited as Julien darted into the building with the box, blowing me a kiss and waggling his eyebrows mischievously as he went. *That boy is going to be the death of me.*

After what seemed like seconds, he exited her building, huffing. "Where to now?"

"This feels so freeing!" I lifted my hands toward the sky. "My list of official tasks is almost done."

"Almost done?" Julien asked apprehensively.

"The last task is not bad. I want to get a couple of CDs before I leave."

"I can handle that," he replied, visibly relieved. "Music stores are fun." Placing his hand on his abdomen, he gave me a pathetic pouty look. "Then can we grab some food? I'm starving after all that physical exertion."

"If you behave in the store," I teased him, chuckling.

Julien reached for my hand and we walked quickly, a far different experience than our leisurely stroll a few nights before. There was so little time left. I pushed the thought from my mind, imagining it was just a normal trip to a music store in our normal lives together without a giant deadline looming in our near future.

Hand in hand, we wandered the aisles of the music store, like a couple who'd been together for ages. Julien recommended some good artists, if I was looking to take home French music. A few of them I had already, but most of the artists were new to me. Like me, Julien had an eclectic taste in music.

"Oh, no, put that down!" Julien insisted, as I picked up a Patrick Bruel CD. "Overrated." He shook his head and I giggled.

He bit his upper lip as he concentrated, thumbing through the stack of CDs. Glancing up at me, he smirked, his blue eyes full of mischief. "I know just the artist for you. I'm just trying to find the right album."

The buzzing in his pocket interrupted the search. With an apologetic look, he pulled out his phone and frowned at the screen. He mouthed, "*Ma mere,*" his mother, and answered.

I wandered a few steps away, giving him some privacy, but my ears pricked up when I heard the words, "I'm just hanging out with Emilie, I'll be home tomorrow."

The air vanished from the room, leaving nothing but a hot, heavy space. Had I heard that right? Had he just said he was hanging out with Emilie? My heart raced, acid swirled in my stomach, and heat rushed through my body. Was the building on fire? Frantically, I tugged at my coat, pulling it off to cool down. Was I not even worthy of being mentioned? *Calm down, Callie. Maybe you misunderstood.* He said he was staying with Emilie, which was not a lie.

Or perhaps I wasn't important enough to him to mention.

Frozen in place, I made my mouth form some sort of appropriate response when Julien turned back toward me and winked. He raised his hand, gesturing the quacking symbol, indicating his mother was chattering away. I nodded. Mothers could be invasive. I could understand why he wouldn't want to open up Pandora's box at this moment to face a multitude of uncomfortable questions. I got that. I'd probably do the same if I was talking to my mother.

As the conversation continued, Julien put more space between us. Did he not want me to hear? Unable to control my curiosity, I snuck in his direction. The music seemed to grow louder. What did this store have against me? Mentally willing the store to turn down the volume a few notches, I crept closer. As if on cue, "Creep" by Radiohead started playing.

I strained to hear Julien's side of the conversation, nearly drowned out by the music. He talked faster to his mother than he did to me, and I couldn't pick up all the French words. Flipping through CD racks, I followed slowly, edging around to the other side of the display he was standing next to, and leaned forward. Did he just tell his mother it was *no big deal?* Warmth spread across my cheeks as I pushed down the panicky sensation that I'd perhaps fallen for a guy who was just having a fun weekend away. Pretending to focus on the CD selection in front of me, I hummed along to the words about being a creep and a weirdo. As the next line played across the speaker, I froze.

"I don't belong here..."

I rolled my eyes. Now the *music* was sending me subliminal messages as well?

"I want you to notice when I'm not around..." crooned Radiohead. Would Julien notice and miss me when I was gone?

Prickles of doubt rose in the form of goosebumps. Maybe he had no intention of ever telling his mother about me. Leaning in further, I heard, "No, I'm not going to see her." Followed by, "No, do not invite her to dinner." Huh? What was this all about?

"Mother, is she there now?" Julien threw his arms up, clearly irritated.

Oh no. They were talking about Céline.

Blood pounded through my head, and the air felt trapped in my lungs. There was no way he was over her. Clearly, his mother was team Céline all the way. Inching just a little closer, I pretended to peruse the display of Britney Spears CDs.

"Fine, I'll talk to her when I get home tomorrow." Making a judgment error in distance, I tilted too far forward. I watched in horror as the entire display of CDs came crashing to the floor.

Julien spun around, mouth gaping in surprise.

Frozen in place, I sheepishly shrugged my shoulders. "Oops."

Despite his surprise, Julien burst into laughter. As two store employees came our way, he grabbed my hand and dragged me out of the store, me yelling apologies over my shoulder.

"I'll call you back, *Maman!*" he said, through an uncontrollable fit of laughter.

"What did you just do?" he asked me. He bent over laughing, and I, although completely embarrassed, hurt, and a little angry, burst into laughter too.

But the laughter ceased when I remembered his last few words. He was planning on seeing her. Tomorrow.

Julien smiled, extended his hand palm up, and said, "Sorry about all of that. My mom's a little irritated that I didn't come home yesterday as promised, but she'll be okay."

Unsure of what to say next, I ignored his outstretched hand, busied myself adjusting my scarf and hat, and then shoved my hands in my pockets.

"I'm freezing," I squeaked, and started walking forward at a very brisk pace. This guy I was falling in love with was withholding information from me. I wouldn't be blindsided twice.

"Callie, wait for me... What's wrong?" He ran up beside me, grabbing my arm.

"Don't worry, it's not important." I desperately tried to convince myself that none of this was a big deal.

Confusion clouded his face. "I'm not sure what just happened."

I wasn't sure I was sure either. But I did know, despite the loving caresses and the fiery chemistry between us, despite the deep conversations and the strong connection I'd been so stupid to imagine between us, he was going back to see Céline tomorrow. And he'd not found it important enough to mention anything about me.

"Are you hungry? I'm starving."

He reached for my hand again and this time I let him take it.

Julien tugged me toward him, stopping me in the middle of the sidewalk. "Tell me."

"It's nothing, Julien. Really." I smiled and pecked him on his lips. I had no intention of causing a scene in the middle of the street. Besides, he'd just made it a lot easier on me. I no longer had to have the dreaded conversation. "Let's just find some sandwiches."

A few drops of rain hit my face, giving me a great excuse for walking quickly, in silence. Disappointment raged through me as I mentally rehashed everything he'd said during his phone conversation. He'd never mentioned me. Torn between trying to understand his position on this subject and wanting to demand answers to my many questions, especially as they related to his feelings for me, I kept my head down and concentrated on finding food.

WE ENTERED the next sandwich shop. I ordered a ham and cheese baguette, and Julien ordered an American. Of course he did.

As we found our way to a small table in the back, I said, perhaps a little coldly, "You know, we don't actually put french fries IN our sandwiches in the US?" I'd always found it amusing that they topped the "American" with french fries.

"I didn't know that. Regardless, this sandwich is amazing." He crammed a giant bite in his mouth, grinning.

"What kind of sandwiches do you usually eat? I'll have to come visit soon to see for myself."

"Not if your mother has anything to do with it," I quipped, feeling slightly guilty that he was making an effort to have a light conversation while I took every opportunity to add snark. *You can still have a nice afternoon with a nice guy, Callie, even if it's not forever.* Despite my efforts to convince myself this was a possibility, I no longer believed this.

Setting his sandwich down, he looked directly at me. "What does that mean?"

"Nevermind. Nothing." I reached for my bottle of water and promptly knocked it over.

Julien jumped up quickly as water pooled in his lap.

"Oh no!" Hopping up, I darted over to the counter to grab a stack of napkins.

He snatched them from me, blotting the water on his pants and wiping the chair down.

"You're on a roll today, Callie. The CDs, the water. Are you okay?"

"I guess it's just predeparture nerves," I said quietly, sitting back in my seat. Thankfully the water had missed the American sandwich, and we continued to eat.

After a few minutes, Julien spoke. "One thing is certain. I am going to miss you."

Stewing about his impending visit with his ex the next day, I found that hard to believe. The weight of what I'd overheard him say to his mother continued to pull at me, making it difficult to return to the lightness of our earlier interactions. Clearly, we were in different emotional spaces about what was developing, or not developing, between the two of us. Instead of telling his mother to send Céline away because he was falling in love with someone else, he sounded like he was doing his best to hide the fact that he was with me. The giant lump in my belly grew heavier.

Scratch *romantic outing together to the Eiffel Tower* off the list. My only goal for the moment was to survive this lunch without saying something regrettable. That, and finding a good excuse for cutting our afternoon short.

"Since it's wet outside, do you want to just hang out at Emilie's?" he asked. "We can make tea, listen to music, whatever."

Like maybe "Creep," on repeat? Shrugging my shoulders in halfhearted assent, I stood, threw away my trash, and put my coat back on. My hotel room wasn't going to be ready for a few more hours anyway. So I might as well stay warm and dry at Emilie's. And deep inside, my heart still rooted for Julien.

Faking happiness did not come easily to me, but I put on an Oscar-worthy performance. I held his hand, smiled, and responded politely to his questions as we made our way to Emilie's.

Once we got to the apartment, I immediately turned on the kettle to make some tea.

Julien stood on the other side of the room, staring outside. How had we gone from wanting to rip each other's clothes off to barely making eye contact in such a short time? Teacups in hand, I walked to the couch.

Julien turned. "What's on your mind, Callie? You've been different since we left the music store."

"I am just sad about leaving," I said. I hoped he'd believe that was it. I placed our teacups on the table and waved for him to join me.

He looked at the floor. "I know. I'm sad to see you go too."

Please offer more, I begged silently. *Ask me if we can stay in touch or keep things going.*

He moved over to me and gently tucked my hair behind my ear before sitting on the couch and picking up his cup, but said nothing. I sat down on the couch, leaving plenty of space between us.

He turned as if to say something, but the ringing of his phone interrupted him. He looked at his phone and declined the call. It rang again. I knew exactly who was calling.

"Take it," I said, resigned. "She clearly really needs you." This girl was bound and determined to ruin any shot at having a normal day together. Even though I'd given him permission, it still hurt when he answered the phone and ducked out of the apartment to talk to her in private.

I flopped back on the couch, throwing my arms over my head. After a moment I hopped up. Unable to sit still, I paced back and forth, drinking my tea. I picked out a Bob Marley CD to lighten the mood, and after two songs and no sign of Julien, I added more water to the kettle and turned it on, before crossing the apartment to step out onto the balcony. I saw him down below, but couldn't make out any of his words. He threw his arms in the air, face contorted. So that was what angry Julien looked like.

Passion equals feelings, right?

Maybe these two were meant for each other, and I was the one blocking his future. Or could he be telling her about me? Seemed unlikely. I lit a cigarette and stood watching as Julien walked back and forth and gesticulated beneath me.

He was still talking animatedly when I finally crushed the cigarette butt in the ashtray and returned inside to make another cup of tea. Swirling the tea bag around in the teacup, my insides also swirled. I made a cup for Julien, too, hoping it wouldn't be cold by the time he came back in.

Finishing my second cup of tea, I turned to face Emily's refrigerator and stared at the pictures she'd stuck to the front. They were all memories of our time here together. A picture of Emilie, Lila, and me caught my attention. We'd been out at a bar celebrating Lila's birthday. We held our champagne glasses high in the air, huge smiles plastered on our faces. My free arm was around Emilie, and Lila leaned her head into me. We'd been deliriously happy that night. Removing the picture from the fridge, a piece of paper that was pinned behind the picture fell to the floor.

The list. Oh my gosh. Emilie, Lila, and I had written this one night when I'd been rehashing my breakup with Vic. We'd stayed in at Emilie's and drunk an extreme quantity of wine, and Lila had shared her idea to help me move beyond my heartbreak.

"We're going to need to write two lists," Lila had instructed.

"Two?" Emilie had demanded, incredulously.

Lila bobbed her head up and down. "The first list is all the qualities to avoid at all costs. We'll burn that list before moving forward to tell the universe what you're not looking for."

Chuckling, I remember how disgruntled Emilie had been at the idea. "That's the stupidest thing I've ever heard!" she'd complained. Lila's face fell, so Emilie had backtracked, softening her tone. "But if you truly believe this is the magic to finding a perfect mate, what can it hurt?" She'd dug a piece of paper and pen out of her drawer, and we started with the burn list before continuing with the wish list of attributes for what I'd like in my perfect guy.

It was short and simple, because no one is perfect, right?

A nice smile.
Kind.
Honorable.
Interested in world events.
GRAND GESTURES.

Clenching the piece of paper tightly against my chest, I returned to the living room and fell

back on the couch, remembering what I'd said to Emilie. "I want a guy who's willing to show me, without a doubt, I am the most important person in the world to him. Vic never did that."

Emilie wrote that down, and then, in a very non-Emilie gesture, made me kiss the paper before sticking the piece of paper on her fridge. For accountability.

I knew Julien wasn't Vic. Julien had many of those qualities, but he hadn't been willing to tell his mother about me, or ignore phone calls from his ex. How hard was it to tell your ex-girlfriend to stop calling you and your friends and your mom? He'd failed the grand gestures test. Shoot, he'd failed the "make me feel important" test too. Ignoring these and allowing myself to be a second choice or "good enough for now" with the guy I was crazy about was no longer an option for me.

It was time for me to end this.

24

THE LONGER JULIEN WAS GONE, the more certain I became in my decision. I mean there still had to be something between the two of them, right? Fidgeting on the couch, I worked on perfecting the speech I would deliver upon his return.

To occupy myself, I returned to the kitchen and made yet another cup of tea for myself before returning to the couch. Time dragged. This was not what I'd had in mind when I'd asked the greater powers to slow down time for my last few days.

The door finally flew open, startling me. Jumping to my feet, ready to make my case for why this needed to end now, I froze as soon as I saw him. He pulled off his hood and shook his hair. His blue eyes shone brightly, reminding me of the first time I'd seen him at Lila's. His face lit up with a smile when he saw me, those dimples melting my heart once again. My resolution instantly wavered, and I had to fight the urge to run across the room and throw myself into his arms. What kind of voodoo was this guy working?

My heart beat harder as he took his time taking off his shoes and coat, finally approaching where I still stood in front of the couch waiting to hear his explanation. Neither of us said anything for a moment and I shifted my weight from my left leg to my right. His face drawn, he rubbed his hands up and down my arms. He kissed me on my forehead and my nose, and finally landed on my mouth. I froze like a statue, not responding with any warmth.

Oh no. Here it came. He was going to break the hard news to me before I had the chance to end it. I'd seen this before— this sweet gesture before telling me to piss off. My legs shaking, I dropped onto the couch, preparing for the blow, my head berating me for not ending things earlier.

He sat down next to me, leaning forward with his elbows propped on his knees, staring down at his feet.

Not knowing what else to do, I leaned forward and grabbed the second cup of tea I'd made for him, which was probably frigid by now.

"I made this for you." He took the cup, smiling a little.

Turning to me, he set the cup of tea on the table and placed his hand on my leg, giving me a little squeeze. "I'm sorry, Callie, Céline is having a really rough time, and I didn't want to just hang up on her. Even if we aren't together, we have a long history."

I didn't give a crap about their history right now. What I cared about was the fact that he had left me to go talk to her for over twenty-five minutes. On two different occasions. "Please stop," I demanded, somewhat sharply.

"Stop what?" Julien asked.

"Stop talking about her while touching me." I shifted, putting a little space between us, and Julien withdrew his hand from my knee as if he'd been stung.

"I, uh, I'm sorry. I thought you would want to know what was going on," he added defensively.

I placed my hands on my hips. "What I want to know is why you answered her call today. When you're with me. And we only have today together. She certainly still seems to be a part of your *now*."

"First of all," he said, crossing his arms across his chest, "you told me to answer that."

He wasn't wrong.

"But you didn't have to talk to her for over twenty-five minutes! If my ex were to call me right now, there's no way I would walk off to talk to him instead of spending time with you."

"I'm sorry Callie, it's complicated." He threw his arms up and then cradled his face in his hands, elbows propped on his knees.

I stood quickly. "It's really not, Julien. It's quite simple. I'm the idiot here, for allowing myself to develop such strong feelings so fast. I should have known this," my arms waved wildly, pointing between him and me, "this was nothing to you."

Julien also stood, meeting my eyes, and reached out. I stepped back, so he jammed his hands in his pockets. "I thought you of all people would understand."

"Me? Of all people?" Again, my hands flew into the air.

"Yes. I thought you were a caring and considerate person. The type who would understand why I can't just ignore my ex's calls when her mother is dying!"

My face fell, and I blurted, "Obviously I had no idea her mother was dying." I tried to process this new information. The caring Callie sympathized with Céline. It must be so terribly difficult to lose your mother at such a young age. Then, catching myself, I pushed my sympathy aside and advocated for my own needs. I poked my finger into Julien's chest.

"You'll be going home soon and can talk to her any time. We have practically no time left. And you're prioritizing her!" My voice got louder and squeakier with each word.

Eyes cast downward, Julie said softly, "I thought you would understand. Maybe we don't really know each other."

Julien's words stung. I stood there for a moment. Unable to move, unable to breathe. Regrouping, not thinking about the words that came next, I shot back, "I have been nothing but real with you. An open book. And I wasn't hiding a relationship from you."

"I'm not hiding any relationship from you! We have a lot of history. Romantically, it's over, but..."

"Well, you haven't been exactly forthcoming. Clearly, you don't feel as strongly about me as I do about you, and it seems you aren't over her, Julien, so I'll just make this easy on you. Thanks for a lovely couple of days. I wish you nothing but the best." I stood and moved toward the door.

His face froze in a weirdly contorted look, a blend of sadness, anger, and surprise.

"Callie! Don't go!" He approached quickly, reaching for me, but I grabbed my coat and purse, shoving off his arm, and marched to the door. Not looking over my shoulder, I stormed out, slamming the door for good measure. I stood there for a moment in the hallway, feeling stunned.

Julien ran out of the apartment, no shoes on, no coat. "Wait, Callie! Please don't leave. Just wait for me to get my shoes." He ran back into the apartment and I bolted toward the stairs.

I hadn't made it three steps before sobs began to wreck me. I forced myself to keep moving forward, down the stairs and away. Away from him and from the pain. As I exited the building, I bent over and tried desperately to catch my breath.

Thankfully the rain had stopped. Part of me wished I had never flirted with him, never kissed him, never gotten myself to this point, but the thought of missing out on the last few days caused searing pain in my heart.

No matter how hard I had tried to keep this light and play-ful, I had fallen. Hard.

Gulping in deep breaths, I tried to keep the sobs from racking my entire body. With my vision blurred by tears, I turned left instead of right, in the opposite direction from the way we would normally go, hoping that would keep him from finding me. If he even followed me, that is. Practically jogging for several blocks to get as much space as possible between us in case he somehow figured out I'd gone the other way, my anger began to mix in with the tears that flowed. Anger at myself for developing such strong feelings in such a ridiculously short amount of time, at Emilie for giving me hope last night, when I'd almost had the courage to walk away, angry at Julien for answering the call from Céline. And raging mad at Vic for dumping me, which had ultimately led to this entire situation.

Finally, I stopped and looked around for a familiar land-mark, and realized I was lost. Just great. Pulling out my handy map, I found the closest metro station and made my way down to take a train toward the hotel, wondering the entire time if I had just made the biggest mistake of my life.

WARM AIR HIT me in the face as I entered the hotel and approached the counter. This was the nicest place I'd ever stayed, with a grand high ceiling, beautiful artwork, and chan-deliers. A small bar area to the right of the foyer was already packed, even in the middle of the afternoon.

Sniffling, I approached the counter. "I'm Callie Sparks. I checked in earlier and dropped my bags, but the room wasn't ready yet."

The attendant, an older, stuffy-looking gentleman with a uniform that encased his body so tightly I wondered how he moved, shuffled through some papers and a file box before pulling out a room key. "Yes, we have your room ready now. I already had your bags sent up."

I guess that was the advantage of a swanky hotel, right? Well, let's be real. It was probably a three-star hotel at best. I wasn't living the celebrity life here. But it was nice enough to deliver my bags to my room.

Smiling politely, I half listened to his directions for getting to the room, took the key, and made my way to the stairs. The room was on the third floor, not far from the stairs.

Pushing the door open, I stopped, stunned. "Wow." The room was gorgeous. It was filled with antique-style furniture, a large bathroom occupied one corner, and I could see through the double French doors to a big balcony. I'd used the entire refund of my apartment deposit to pay for this room, which was ironic because it was at least twice the size of the room I'd lived in the past few months.

I'd specifically requested a room with a view of the Eiffel Tower, and I'd gotten my wish. Through the doors to the balcony, I could see her standing majestically in front of me. Opening the French doors, I stepped out and approached the rail, wet from the rain. I placed my hands on the rails, leaning forward to take in the surroundings. The view was everything I'd hoped for.

I stared out at the tower standing majestically in front of me.

"It's just you and me. Now what do I do?"

Well, finish your bucket list at least, Callie girl. You can't leave without climbing the tower.

Grabbing my jacket and my bag, I stopped in the bathroom quickly to wipe my face, exited the room, and bounded down the stairs to exit the hotel.

25

Sniffling, I approached the ticket window. Thanks to the crappy weather, the line was nonexistent for the stairs. Most of the queue was for the elevator.

"One ticket for the stairs, please," I asked, shoving my collection of remaining French francs forward.

The older woman smiled politely, pushing her glasses up on her nose. "Would you like a ticket to the top? Elevator only for that part. But I don't know how much you'll see today, with the weather."

I nodded. I didn't care about the view as much as accomplishing this goal, romantic ending or not. Staring up at the stairs in front of me, my quads quivered at the idea of the number of stairs to my destination.

"Game on, Tower. It's only three hundred-something stairs to the first level. I can do this. My apartment has trained me for this moment." In response, she groaned. But maybe that was my imagination.

Head down, I started ascending the metal stairs, ignoring the irritating whirring sound of the elevator that taunted me for my decision to climb instead of ride. My thighs burned. I stopped to breathe and admire the view. *Halfway there, you can do this.* I trudged on.

When I finally reached the top, I pumped my arms in triumph, like Rocky Balboa reaching the top of the stairs of the Philadelphia Museum of Art, and headed straight over to the edge. My breath caught as I took in the view of the Seine River and the Champs de Mars expanding down to the École Militaire. None of it was any less magnificent with the cloudy backdrop.

"Wow," I said. Only the tower was in listening range, and she already knew.

Making a quick tour of the first level, noting some of the cool facts about the construction of the tower, I stopped on the side facing Trocadero Square. The Musée de l'Homme stared back at me, reminding me of the encounter with Lila just a few short days before. It seemed like years ago that we'd demolished those crêpes, rehashing my anger at Vic.

Nope. No Vic today. Instead, I imagined what it would have been like if Julien and I had visited here together today. Would he have complained about climbing the stairs? Based on his complaints at my apartment, not likely. He probably would have sprinted up, laughing at me for huffing and puffing, and then once I'd made it, he might have draped his arm around me, quietly admiring the view, occasionally leaning in for a quick kiss.

It no longer really mattered. He wasn't with me, and I was here. Alone. I stepped back, turning to complete my walk around the first level, passing a family that seemed quite distressed. The mother yelled at her son, who looked about six.

"If you don't stop complaining, we're going back down and no ice cream for you!" she said. This caused me to snicker under my breath. And also yearn for a time in my life when I would yell at my children for, well, being children.

Fixating on the many bridges along the Seine, I wondered on which bridge Julien had embraced me so passionately, but there were so many of them I couldn't pick out the one we'd stood on. As the cold wind picked up, a few raindrops pelted my face. Most people were making their way back to the elevator. Not me.

Okay, Callie, let's do this. I stared up at the staircase to the next level, faltering for a moment. My enthusiasm for conquering the whole tower flickered. Did I really want to do this? My leaden legs were making a strong case against climbing the stairs. And this was not the romantic moment I envisioned. With a heavy heart, I turned toward the stairs that would take me back to the ground level instead of continuing up.

The tower creaked.

No, Callie, you're not going to go home with regrets. Climb to the second level.

"Why are you doing this to me?" I asked out loud.

Climb.

Two heartbreaks in Paris had turned me certifiable. What would Lila think if I told her I was now having two-way conversations with the Tower?

Even if it *was* all in my head.

I climbed. Now all the parts of my body were talking to me. My thighs screamed. A few minutes later, my calves joined the chorus. An elevator whirred loudly by, making me regret anew the decision to take the stairs. This was a badge of honor I'd be able to brag about later, right? That one time I painstakingly climbed 674 slippery stairs to prove something to myself?

With each miserable step I thought about the events that

had led me here. Had I grown? Had I changed? Or was I going home the same Callie I'd been when I arrived?

Heaving myself up the last few steps, I emerged onto the covered platform of the second level. Descending a few steps before reaching the perimeter platform, I immediately faced a couple snuggling tightly together as they took in the view. His arm wrapped tightly around her, and her head rested on his shoulder. He kissed her on the top of the head and then gently on the lips.

Throwing my hands in the air, I turned around and stared up to the top of the tower. "Seriously?" I yelled, frustrated.

Startled, the couple looked toward me and moved in the opposite direction. My chin quivered as I gasped to catch my breath, fighting the sobs.

"Why did it have to end this way?" This time, I definitely heard a groan in response.

Rain pelted my face. But the rain didn't bother me nearly as much as the increasing pain in my heart did. The ache in my glutes wasn't enough to diminish the pain of my heart breaking into a million tiny pieces. Tears blended with the rain on my cheeks. This was not how this day was supposed to end. How this week, this whole trip should have ended.

My hand dragged along the chain-link fence as I slowly toured the perimeter, stopping when I faced toward Montmartre, barely visible through the low-hanging clouds. Sacré-Cœur stood magnificently on the hilltop. Memories of laughter and hugs, kisses and tender moments as we watched the world wander around us in the Artist's Square next to Sacré-Cœur flashed through my mind. A lifetime had passed since that artist had chased us, insisting on capturing our love. That apparently had not been love after all.

Now what? I was virtually alone on the second level—most other visitors were smart enough to leave by this point—but I caught up with the couple who'd evaded me earlier. Now playfully fiddling around with a telescope, he stood behind her, arms wrapped around her as she looked and then motioned for him to look. Before he took his turn, he kissed her gently.

This time there was no stopping the tears. Turning away, I walked slowly in the opposite direction until I found a bench and sat down, facing Trocadero and the Seine. Heaving sobs racked my body.

Now that I was sitting, I realized I was soaking wet, and my body shuddered with chills. Taking in a few deep breaths, I stood slowly. It was time to say my goodbyes to Paris, make my peace with this ending, and go.

I walked slowly to the stairs. Descending was obviously easier but still took a little longer than the advertised ten minutes as I clung to the railing, determined not to fall. A woman in front of me slipped and landed hard on her behind, something I did not care to copy.

Still not ready to go all the way down to the ground yet, I exited onto the first level. Very few people milled around. Most chairs and benches were open. Selecting one facing the river, I hugged my legs up to my chest, resting my chin on my knees. I buried my face into my knees, allowing the last of my tears to escape before digging in my pocket to find some Kleenex. A piece of paper fell out on the bench. The list. Sighing, I shoved it back in my pocket and blew my nose. So much for grand gestures or any of that fairy-tale muckety-muck.

You'll be fine. You'll be better than fine. That might have been me or the Tower, I wasn't sure anymore. But I believed it. The tears stopped, and I stared down the river.

A hand gently squeezed my shoulder, surprising me. They must be kicking everyone off the tower due to the weather. Lowering my legs, I reached down for my bag, and turned slowly. But rather than facing an employee of the tower, sky-blue eyes met my gaze. I froze.

"I hoped I'd find you here."

I blinked a few times, wondering if I'd gone straight-up crazy. Talking towers, imagining people.

Julien walked around to the front of the bench, stopping directly in front of me, rain droplets dripping from his square jawline. His face, obscured by the hood of his coat, was framed by a few wisps of brown hair that lay matted to his forehead.

"Julien?" I squeaked. Which was a stupid question, because of course it was Julien. But how?

He said nothing, gently pulling me up off the bench. Stunned, my legs wobbled like limp spaghetti as his arms wrapped around me and his lips found my face, peppering it with kisses. "I've been looking everywhere for you."

I squeezed my eyes shut and then opened them slowly. Yep, he was still standing in front of me. "What are you doing here?"

Cupping my face in his hands, he leaned in. His gaze intensified, eyes misted over, holding me captive. "You. I'm here for you."

"How... how?" So many questions. How was Julien standing in front of me now? How had he found me?

His hands moved down my body, grabbing my hands in his.

"I called Emilie. Well, first I went to your hotel, but they said you hadn't come in yet." That made sense because I'd gotten lost and wandered half of Paris before getting back there. We must have just missed each other. "Emilie reminded me of your last bucket list item."

"Climbing the Eiffel Tower," I said, smiling, realizing that Emilie had swooped in to save the day.

"Yes. I came here and climbed all those stupid stairs.

Searched both levels. I've been wandering around here for at least an hour." His breath was hot on my neck.

I said nothing, staring at him in shocked disbelief. The grand gesture!

"I ran up and down these stairs at least three times. Circling both the first and second level. I even rode the elevator to the very top. Let me tell you, today is NOT a nice day for the top," he said, his tone very serious, clearly pained from the effort.

My laughter started as a small giggle and evolved into a belly laugh. Doubling over, I imagined him running all around, up and down those horrific stairs, while I was wandering around scaring cute couples.

He smiled, cocking his head slightly. He looked confused and perhaps hurt, which sobered me. Regaining my composure, I placed my hands on his chest. "You've been up here in this terribly cold wind for me?" I practically squeaked out the last two words.

He nodded his head.

"Are you nuts? Why didn't you call me?" I playfully thumped him on the chest.

He grabbed my hands and brought them to his lips. "My battery died a long time ago. And let's be real, would you have answered?"

I shrugged, "Probably not."

"I'm sorry, Callie. I should never have put her needs before yours. I should have told you everything and trusted you'd understand."

I took a deep breath. "Thank you, Julien. I'm sorry I reacted the way I did." I leaned in closely, blinking back a few tears, and whispered in his ear. "I'm glad you came for me. I was so scared I'd never see you again."

He wrapped his arms tightly around me, brushing the top of my head with his lips. "I was scared of that too."

I pulled back to look directly into his eyes. Now was the time to say what I'd been planning to say earlier. "I know it may seem so soon and so crazy, but I love you."

He beamed. "I love you, too. I think I've loved you from the moment you needed a boost onto the top of the bus stop."

I smiled, and then laughed again.

"What's so funny?" he asked.

"I'm so sorry. Just imagining it. I came down those stairs like a granny because I was terrified of slipping and falling. Not to mention, I thought I would die climbing the steps, and you've run them multiple times? Are you going to be able to walk tomorrow?"

His face lit up in a grin, eyes sparkling. Rain ran down his face, but none of this seemed to bother him at all. "I don't care if tomorrow I'm with you."

I grabbed his head and pulled him in, kissing him first very softly, then diving deeper, hands running through his hair. As his tongue danced with mine, I didn't care about the details. I only wanted to be with him.

Julien broke the embrace. "Listen, I could do this with you forever, but I'm freezing and my legs are shaking from the stair workout. Let's go somewhere warm. And dry."

I grabbed his hand and pulled him toward the stairs. "Let's go to my hotel."

We descended the stairs as rapidly as possible, being careful not to break our necks in the process, and then darted through the rain toward the nearest metro entrance. The trip zipped by as we kissed, murmuring words of affection.

The concierge shot us a look of disapproval as we burst into the hotel looking like drowned squirrels, giggling loudly. I flashed my room key on our way to the elevator. The doors had barely closed when Julien pressed me up against the wall of the elevator, peppering kisses up and down my neck. "I can't believe it's only been four days since I met you."

"I guess anything is possible in four days in Paris." I wrapped my arms around him and clung tight until the elevator reached the third floor, anxiously awaiting the door to open and sprinting to my room.

"After you." Julien swept his arms, motioning me inward. He closed the door behind him, unzipped his coat, and gave me the most intense look. He moved in closely, pushing my hair off my forehead. "I love you, Callie."

"I love you too, Julien." I had never been so certain.

26

UNRULY. That was the best description for the line at the ticket counter where I waited patiently for my turn to check-in.

Sighing deeply, I checked and triple-checked that I had my passport and wallet. It was time to return home. I was no longer a resident of Paris, though it pained me to think of myself as simply a tourist.

Someone shoved my back and I lurched forward a bit. One thing Americans *did* do better than Europeans was form a reasonable queue. We make lines and for the most part, stay in them, but here, it's everyone for themselves and screw any rules. Pushing my bags forward, I crept up as close as possible to the person in front of me, lest I be taken out by an anxious traveler behind me. Consumed by giddy joy, lost in the memories of the night before, the impatient people didn't bother me.

Julien and I had ordered room service and talked, okay, mostly talked, almost all night. Falling asleep in his arms, albeit for only a short rest before my alarm blasted, had been sublime. We'd shared our secrets, hopes, and dreams, and planned out how to make this international relationship work. Stealing kisses in between all of it, naturally. My cheeks grew hot at the memory of our night together. Pushing my bags forward, I inched another few steps toward the person in front of me as my thoughts lingered on how we had gently touched and explored each other. I pulled my scarf off and unzipped my jacket, fanning myself, suddenly very hot after remembering the kisses and caresses.

After our night together, the only thing keeping me awake was the adrenaline coursing through me and the hope of getting some caffeine soon. My eyes closed for a few moments as I reveled in how this trip had ended with the most perfect night.

"Madame?" the ticket agent repeated, not politely. I hadn't even realized I'd made my way to the front of the line. I got my new boarding pass, waited patiently while they weighed my bags (letting out a huge sigh of relief as I skated in just at the weight limit) then wandered over to the window. It was another gray day, and I just hoped the plane would not be delayed.

"Well, were they able to change your seat?"

I turned and threw my arms around Julien, nearly knocking the two cups he held out of his hands as he raised them out of the danger zone. Laughing as I kissed him all over his face, I said, "Yes! I am now in the seat next to you!"

He kissed me back. "Wonderful."

Hands on my hips, I stood squarely in front of him. "I'd like you to know just what a sacrifice this is. I gave up an aisle seat at the front of the plane for a middle seat in the back of the plane, just to be with you."

He tilted his head down in a playful bow. "I can only hope you'll accept this as a meager token of my gratitude," he said as he lifted one of the cups toward me.

"Oh, you darling man!" I gratefully accepted the espresso.

"I forgot the milk," he said, sheepishly.

"Don't you worry. I can handle a straight shot of espresso

from time to time." The taste of straight bitter coffee assaulted my tastebuds. At least he'd put a little sugar in. The things we do for love.

"As for your seating situation, at least you'll be able to cuddle with your seatmate," Julien teased.

"Yeah, I sure hope he's cute!" I winked and Julien snorted. "Touché."

Finishing my coffee, I turned to him. "Is this crazy?"

Julien nodded. "Yes. It's absolutely insane. And it's also the most wonderful thing I've ever done."

I smiled over my cup. "I love you, Julien."

"I love you too, Callie."

They were the most beautiful words I'd ever heard.

"We should go." I grabbed one of my carry-on bags. Julien reached for my other bag and the backpack he'd brought for his weekend in Paris, and we made our way to the passport check and security.

"Why did you have your passport with you this weekend? That seems random to take for a trip within your own country?" I asked once we'd cleared the control.

"Because when I fly home, I fly into Switzerland. They don't always check it, but I heard with all the extra security because of terrorist threats for the New Year, they were more likely to. I wanted to be certain."

"Destiny," I sighed. That was amazing luck. Otherwise, this plan could have never gone through.

Julien squeezed my hand, rubbing his thumb along mine as I bit the inside of my cheek, trying to wake myself up if this was a dream. *Please don't let this be a dream.*

The boarding announcement for our flight blared across the loudspeaker. If it was a dream, it was weirdly detailed. I snuggled up to Julien, tilting my head up for a kiss. At some point in the middle of the night, we'd cooked up this crazy plan.

He didn't have to be back for classes until the last week of January, so he bought a ticket to spend those weeks with me. We weren't sure what we'd do after that point, but we knew we were not ready to say goodbye.

"My mother may never talk to me again, but I guess that's a risk worth taking."

His mother. *My parents!* I grabbed his arm.

"Julien! I never called my parents! They are going to freak out!" With no pay phone in sight, and no international plan on our cell phones, there was no way to reach them now.

Julien grazed his hand across my face, leaning down to scoop up my bags. "One day at a time, babe."

I sure hoped he was right.

Once we were settled in our seats, I wove my arm through Julien's and stared out the window. I imagined the Eiffel Tower, strong, bright, and shimmering, standing grandly before me. Under my breath, I said, "See you later. And thank you."

Epilogue - Twenty-Two Months Later

Lila burst through the restaurant door and moved quickly in our direction, waving excitedly. Julien, Philippe, and I all stood as Lila reached the table.

"I'm so sorry I'm late! Matt was supposed to meet me, but he's not going to make it." Her face contorted briefly as she said the words.

I wrapped my arms tightly around Lila. "Is everything okay?" I had hoped to spend some time with Matt before he was occupied with wedding guests and activities, and disappointment filled me.

"Everything's great!" Lila cooed. "And you? You look amazing!" She stepped back to fully assess me. "Married life suits you."

"Well thank you! Nonprofit life suits you!"

Lila glowed. She'd cut her long hair to shoulder length and looked relaxed, still sporting her hippy look. Now that she worked for a global aid nonprofit, she wore what she wanted. They had no specific dress code, especially since a large part of her job required trips to South America, Africa, and the Far East.

Julien leaned in, pecking Lila on each cheek, before stepping aside for Philippe to greet her. I poked Julien and tilted my head in Philippe's direction. Certainly I wasn't the only one to notice the beet-purple color of Philippe's cheeks as he leaned in to kiss Lila. He stepped back, staring down at the ground, growing even darker purple if that was possible, as Lila gushed over seeing him.

"I'm so excited that your trip coincided with Matt's and my wedding," Lila said, placing her hand on Philippe's arm. Julien and I shared a knowing glance. Had it been a coincidence?

"Yes, I didn't get to see enough when I made the short trip for Callie and Julien's wedding," Philippe said.

We sat down and a server took our orders. Lila turned to me. "So, tell me everything! Have your parents finally forgiven you?"

I rolled my eyes. My parents had been less than pleased when I'd shown up with Julien. But despite their initial shock, by the time he had returned to Strasbourg two weeks later, he'd had my parents wrapped around his finger. Knowing he would have to face his mother and make sure Céline knew it was over for good, I had opted to stay behind so that my first time meeting his family would hopefully be smoother.

Placing my hand on Julien's and giving it a squeeze, I smiled at him, grateful that he'd kept all his promises. We'd agreed to see each other every quarter while he finished school, and I worked odd jobs to save money so that I could move back to Paris when he moved there in the spring. In the most romantic of gestures, he'd proposed in the Christmas market in Strasbourg. Julien and I had a June wedding in my hometown and moved to Paris over the summer. Now in October, we had returned for Lila's wedding in Virginia.

"It took them some time to get used to the idea. But Julien charmed them." I glowed. "Julien's mother on the other hand..."

"Oof," Philippe said. We all laughed.

"Oof is right," I agreed.

"Oh, come on. She loves you, in her own special way," Julien said.

"It's special, alright," I agreed. I twisted my wedding band around my finger. It hurt deeply that his mother still hadn't accepted me. Julien assured me she just needed more time. She was never cruel to me. No, she was just polite the way you'd be polite to a complete stranger. A bit dismissive sometimes. Julien's mom and stepdad had not attended the wedding, which hurt both of us deeply. Claiming they were too scared to fly, they had promised to throw us a reception at home in Strasbourg, which still hadn't happened. But Emilie, their dad, Fred, and Philippe had made the trip for the wedding, joining Lila, Matt, and my family and friends from home. It was a small but wonderful event, despite our sadness about Julien's mother's absence.

Julien placed his hand on my thigh, squeezing it. He leaned in to kiss my cheek. "You're the most important person to me and she knows that. She's just not good at showing her affection."

Lila frowned. "I'm sure she'll come around. You're hard not to love, Callie."

I smiled back, basking in the outpouring of love from Julien and Lila.

"And the job situation? What's new there?" Lila asked, changing the subject.

I perked up. "Really well! I had my second interview at the Embassy and basically we're just waiting on paperwork. You remember the bureaucracy the French have. Julien's got to be vetted as well. Fingers crossed, I'll be working by January."

"That's great news! No skeletons in your closet we should be worried about?" Lila winked at Julien, who crossed his fingers in the air and we laughed.

Lila turned to Philippe. "And you? Are you in Paris now?"

Philippe blushed, arranging his napkin just so. "Yes, I landed the job with the human rights group I told you about at their wedding." He lifted his beer mug quickly and took a sip.

"That is wonderful! All of our dreams are coming to fruition." Lila raised her glass. "To happiness!"

"To happiness," we repeated, clinking glasses. I reserved Julien for the last, and held his gaze, mouthing, *I love you*. He leaned forward and kissed me lightly. "I love you more," he whispered.

Lila leaned in, whispering. "Remember that day we stood in front of the Eiffel Tower and you were convinced you'd never find love again?"

I flushed, bobbing my head up and down slowly. My heart swelled as I turned my gaze to Julien. My friend, the tower, had in fact fully delivered on her promise.

THE END.

Dear Reader

This book is a love story, but not just between Callie and Julien. I hope you also felt the strong bond of the friendships with Lila and Emilie, and the love for Paris and all things French throughout this story. While this is a fictional story, it *is* based on real life events from my time in Paris. This time in France impacted me so heavily that I wanted to be able to tell some of my favorite stories, while also writing a love letter to my closest girlfriends.

If you're curious, here's what is real. Callie resembles me quite closely. I did actually work as a bilingual secretary in Paris through the fall of 1999 and returned home early 2000. Lila and Emilie are based heavily on two of my real-life friends and there are so many details that are very similar to my friends Lisa and Tia. I also enhanced their characters with some elements of my other close friends, from my time in France since I couldn't include all of them in this particular story. And naturally, there are many pieces that are truly just fiction. I absolutely lived in what was formerly a servant's quarter on the 8th floor of a big building, that was barely big enough to move around in. Lila and Emilie's apartments are described from as many details of what my memory could recall of their places.

And yes, I did actually meet a guy on New Year's Eve and spend the night walking around the city with him. While we did not fall in love and end up married like Callie and Julien, we did stay friends.

I originally began writing this story as part of a healing journey, trying to reconnect with a part of my life that was, hands down, the glory days. But Callie took over at some point, making it her own story. And I loved every minute of allowing her to create her own identity.

Be sure to visit my website to learn more about the next book, which is Lila's story, find pictures from our adventures in France in 1999, and follow my adventures as I continue to write stories of friendship, travel, and love. I'm also available to meet with Book Clubs, virtually and in person! Reach out at hello@lexihaddock.com.

Acknowledgments

It takes a village! There are so many people to thank for helping me bring this book into the world, and so many people who have encouraged me and cheered me on during the process. I have an incredible support system!

I would have never had this story to tell if it hadn't been for my parents supporting my desire to study abroad and helping me return to France to live after I graduated college. My parents' love of travel and enthusiasm for other cultures lit a fire under me to learn and explore as well. Thank you for dragging us through every single cathedral and museum you could find in Europe while we were stationed in Germany. I wish my dad was still here to see this day.

This story would also have never come to be if it weren't for the incredible friendships I developed while I was coming of age in France. I met the most wonderful people, who shared their lives and culture, took me on grand adventures, danced with me in night clubs, cooked for me, laughed with me, fed me snails and frog legs! To the whole crew from Mulhouse... you changed my life. But especially Kerry, Tia, Charlotte, Smail, Seb, and Ludo.

Brooke Warner, my first writing coach and mentor, showed me how much I needed to learn about writing a good story and provided the tools and resources to get me started. Kirsten Oliphant, your friendship and guidance made the difference in lighting the fire for me to get this book written, amidst a life of many moving pieces. Thank you for meeting with me weekly for almost a year to hold me accountable! Jen Milius and Dakota Nyght, my editors. Ladies, your guidance and expertise allowed me to transform this book from a good story to a book I am so proud of and excited about. Thank you, thank you! Pamela Sheppard—thanks so much for all the encouragement, guidance, and professional help on the description!

My beta readers! The feedback you gave me really helped shape the final book and see things I'd completely missed. You're amazing. Special shout out to the Pickles—Kate, Jess, Amy, Michelle, Carol, and Eileen—I'm so glad to have found such a wonderfully supportive group of fellow authors!

My situation is a little different than many authors, as a publisher and established publishing professional, I am lucky enough to come into this with a team of publishing professionals at my side. I can't express enough thanks to my team. For their support through the writing, publishing, marketing, which they would have done anyway, but truly for the love, encouragement, support, and friendship that makes this journey as an author so much sweeter. Nancy, Raewyn, Sarah, Cayce, Lauren, Pam, Mandi, and Maddi... you are the best team and some of the greatest friends ever. I'm so grateful for you.

To the entire community of the Women in Publishing Summit—you all are so encouraging and uplifting, so full of light and love. It's an honor and a joy to be a part of your ranks.

Andrea, Robin, and Gayle—thank you for supporting me through this journey, loving me, and helping with my kids when writer life took over! I don't know how I'd do this life without my sisters.

And finally, to my children. Though you demanded my

attention when I wanted to be writing (just kidding, maybe!?) I want you to know that you are the biggest loves of my life. Everything I do is to build a better life for you. May your lives be full of laugher, love, and adventure. I'm doing my best to show you how. I love you to the moon and back.

About the Author

Lexi Haddock writes stories about travel, romance, and Paris - France, not Texas! While she resides permanently in Columbia, SC, with her 3 kids, you'll find her in France whenever time and budget allow. Her debut novel, 4 Days in Paris, is set in Paris in 1999 and is sure to appeal to those who love anything about Paris, romance, or are nostalgic for their own European adventures.

Follow her on Instagram @LexiHaddock_author or visit the website https://lexihaddock.com. And stay tuned for book 2 in this series.

CPSIA information can be obtained
at www.ICGtesting.com
Printed in the USA
BVHW042217041222
653455BV00001B/10